COLLECTED TALES FROM THE RIO GRANDE

Valley Byliners

iUniverse, Inc.
New York   Bloomington

COLLECTED TALES FROM THE RIO GRANDE

This is a work of fiction. All of the characters, names, incidents, organizations, and dialogue in this novel are either the products of the author's imagination or are used fictitiously.

iUniverse books may be ordered through booksellers or by contacting:

iUniverse
1663 Liberty Drive
Bloomington, IN 47403
www.iuniverse.com
1-800-Authors (1-800-288-4677)

Because of the dynamic nature of the Internet, any Web addresses or links contained in this book may have changed since publication and may no longer be valid. The views expressed in this work are solely those of the author and do not necessarily reflect the views of the publisher, and the publisher hereby disclaims any responsibility for them.

ISBN: 978-1-4502-1976-1 (sc)
ISBN: 978-1-4502-1977-8 (ebook)

Printed in the United States of America

iUniverse rev. date: 4/02/2010

Contents

About the Valley Byliners

Valley Byliners was established in 1943 by a group of writers who wanted to improve their skills and enjoy fellowship with other writers. Throughout the years, the group has sponsored many writers' workshops, conferences, and writing contests.

In the 1970's and early 1980's, they published a trilogy of books on Valley history that received wide acclaim. In *Gift of the Rio*, the first in the trilogy published in 1976, the authors sought to answer the questions about the place, the ecology, the soil—all gifts of the Rio Grande. *Roots by the River*, published in 1978, told about some of the area's pioneers, as did *Rio Grande Roundup*, which followed in 1980. Strong threads interwoven through the three books reflect the merging cultures of the peoples on both sides of the Rio Grande.

A new generation of Byliners delved into the culture of legends and tales of the supernatural spun by the people to create *Tales Told at Midnight along the Rio Grande* in 2006. Old ghosts were resurrected and new ones created for a memorable reading experience.

In *Collected Tales from the Rio Grande*, the writers' group presents a collection of stories and poems by authors from the Rio Grande Valley with subject matter as diverse as the countryside one would see while floating down the Rio Grande from its headwaters to where it empties into the Gulf of Mexico. We hope you will enjoy reading it as much as the authors enjoyed writing it.

Current Byliners include published and unpublished writers who love to write and are interested in learning how to improve and market their writing. Members meet monthly on the second Saturday at 1:30 p.m., usually at the Harlingen Public Library. They enjoy diverse monthly programs, inspiring workshops, and the fellowship of other writers. New members and visitors are always welcome.

Marjorie Johnson
Member since 1960

ACKNOWLEDGEMENTS

When the Valley Byliners decided to produce another book in the wake of their successful *Tales Told At Midnight Along The Rio Grande*, the membership was enthusiastic but could not decide on a theme. The history of the area, personalities, roots, legends and myths were explored in the four books published previously. After much unsuccessful tossing about for a suitable theme, the members decided why have a theme at all? Why not let the writers produce an anthology of whatever fun stuff comes to mind? The result is the book you hold in your hand.

In here you will find mystery, humor, suspense, poignancy, spookiness, science fiction, local culture and reminiscences, all of which reflect the various interests of the writers who submitted the stories and poems for publication.

We thank all the authors who allowed our editors Jack King and Yours Truly to pore over and nit pick the submitted manuscripts. Also, a special thanks goes to members of the Writers Forum who accepted our invitation to participate.

Most of all, we thank you, the reader, for spending your hard earned money for this new collection of stories from South Texas writers. We hope you find them interesting and enjoyable.

Don Clifford
President, 2009-2010

A NECESSARY EVIL
By Hernán Moreno-Hinojosa

PROLOGUE

The Hog's Breath Saloon North Harris County, TX:

"Craziest thang I ever did see Floy, in all my years of policin'." Deputy Ernie Smith took another swallow from his mug of Shiner beer to lubricate his parched throat. He'd been talking nearly nonstop for half an hour.

"That little sports car was jest a-setting on its top, pretty as you please, not hardly a mark on it nowhere. Yes sir, it was near pristine. Like you could just upright it and the driver'd take off agin. 'Cept that driver, he wasn't goin' no-where, no-how. No siree."

The jukebox wailed another hurting song about someone doing someone wrong. Deputy Smith wiped his mouth on his khaki uniform shirtsleeve and ordered another round.

"No sir, that driver wasn't goin' nowhere 'cept to ah funeral home 'cause he was deader than a doornail inside that little red car. Darned fool wasn't wearin' his seatbelt."

"Ernie," Floy replied with contempt, "what the hell do you know 'bout investigating accidents?"

"Just fill in the blank, Floy. Besides, just to cover my ass, I called the city boys and talked to one of them badass accidint reconstructionists. Ah…fellow with a funny last name," Ernie's eyebrows pinched together in concentration, "last name sounded something like…*Gentleman*. He told me it sounded to him like a major one-car rollover feytallity accident. He couldn't come out though, on a-count of the accidint bein' way out of his jurisdiction, but he'd try to have a look see at the crashed car when the wrecker brung it on in to the city."

1

PART I
BLACK MAGIC WOMAN

My name is unimportant although you should know that the Gentry Family has always been fascinated by the written word. Perhaps I should say 'Gentry-Rodriguez' since I am of mixed heritage, bi-racial or whatever politically correct term is currently in vogue for children of White and Mexican pedigree. Father was obsessed with Genesis and mother possessed a certain fervor for the New Testament. My sisters all dabble in poetry and my brothers and I are avid readers. Perhaps it is this inherent fondness for letters that explains the perversity, which necessitates documentation of the following events. Or is it simply that everyone has a story to tell? From his garbled mind the idiot can spin quite a yarn, if only he can find his voice and a willing ear to hear. The twenty thousand denizens who call the streets of Houston home could tell of their fall from grace and subsequent descent into hell, but who would listen? In my case, anonymity is necessary, even as necessary as the evil that men do.

Evil has been with Man since the Fall. Demons and devils, some hold, are mere devices that allow Man to masquerade beneath a façade of civilization or a veneer of religiosity. I do not know the truth of devils and demons but I do know that we live in a nation of myth information. We grow up believing in the Tooth Fairy, Sleeping Beauty and the Lone Ranger. Pain, once endured, is rewarded. Prince Charming rescues the fair maiden. Justice prevails. No wonder we are conditioned to believe yet another fallacy, that no one can commit the perfect murder.

Death came like the proverbial thief in the night for Mr. Henderson, self-made man, entrepreneur, multi-millionaire and philanthropist. After a minor fender-bender both motorists stopped, in accordance with State law, to exchange information. A karate blow deftly delivered to the left side of the cranium snapped Henderson's neck like a dried twig. Propped behind the steering wheel sans his restraining harness, a rapid push sent his bright-red Porsche sailing over the bank at the apex of a curve on a deserted country road. Like an upside down turtle his Porsche came to rest on its top, all four wheels flailing wildly. *Requiescat in Pace*, Mr. Henderson, and may the Lord be merciful….

If the big-bellied deputy-sheriff who responded to a woman's frantic 911 call—about a little red car overturned in an open field—suspected any foul play he failed to so articulate in his official report. Even the long arm of the law can serve some nefarious purpose when ignorance is bliss—a fatal one-car rollover, nothing more. And so today the headlines read:

J. V. HENDERSON KILLED

In smaller print it says *one car rollover* and that the driver was not wearing his seatbelt. The particulars add that he is survived by his young widow, Ashley Lamar Henderson.

"Ashley," I said, invoking her name in the solitude of my tiny apartment. "You always did look good in black." I crumpled the front page with both hands and chucked the bunched up wad of paper into the nearest trashcan.

I didn't know the late, great Mr. Henderson but I did *know* the grieving widow, at least in the Biblical sense. If I may be perfectly candid, I rue the day I ever laid eyes on Ashley. Not that I didn't know better, I did. Nor was I blind-sided. Eliazer did warn me. He called her a black magic woman.

"When you touch," he asked, carefully wiping his chrome-framed bifocals with a red bandana, "like when you shake hands, do you feel an odd tingling sensation?"

"Absolutely!" I answered with all the enthusiasm of a sixteen-year old talking about his first love to his closest confidant. "A jolt of electricity runs from my fingertips to my elbow."

Eliazer arched an eyebrow and said, "That means she's negative, or you are negative and she is positive. Opposites do attract but that doesn't mean you are necessarily compatible."

Eliazer took another drink from his sixteen ounce Miller beer and looked thoughtfully at a squirrel that chattered noisily from atop a rusting lawn tractor. The brash, grayish-brown creature with the dark bushy tail scrambled down the tractor, raced across the neatly manicured carpet grass and clambered up the nearest pecan tree. Eliazer casually added, "Be careful little brother, of that black magic woman."

My big brother the philosopher. It was good to see him dressed up in his nice Wrangler™ jeans, cowboy shirt and eel skin boots rather than his usual oil-smudged work overalls. We didn't go anywhere. We sat beneath the lush-green paper shell pecan trees that dotted his backyard, drinking

COLLECTED TALES FROM THE RIO GRANDE

beer and trading stories until the afternoon forfeited its warmth to the evening shadows bidding us goodnight.

During simpler times before liability became such an issue, my brother left the doublewide, chain link gates open to his spacious backyard. This way college kids from the nearby campus could come to gather pecans. They filled grocery sacks full of fresh pecans, which they sold in the park to keep them in beer and pot money. Once, when I chided my brother about his contribution to higher education, he paused and a dark expression crossed his face. Then he threw back his head and said, "Pot? I don't know what that's good for." Smiling incorrigibly, he added, "but a little beer does wonders for the soul!"

I returned his smile thinking that by his reckoning my own soul must be spotless, long ago bleached lily-white by that demon-spirit in the twelve ounce red, white and blue can who, rather than St. Peter, held the keys to the Kingdom of Heaven. Ah, if only it were so!

With his flair for the dramatic Eliazer should be telling this story. Maybe he will one day if he finds my notes after I'm gone, when he can no longer be implicated in my little *faux pas*. For now, Eliazer devoted his life to raising a large family, repairing small motors and drinking beer, in no particular order.

By a strange quirk of fate, I became a career policeman. Policemen deal in truth, not fiction and so this account is put forth as I see it, through jaded eyes that have perhaps seen too much. Policemen are also lousy husbands and so I never married. Nor have I stayed with any one department long enough to rise above the rank of patrol officer, but I do love my work.

A special assignment put me at the right place and time to meet Ashley. Ordinarily, we didn't move in the same circles. Late for roll call, as usual, one fine Wednesday, the sergeant sent me straight upstairs to see the assistant chief of police. This could only mean bad news. When I wheeled around exiting the roll call room, someone murmured *he's always late!*

Upstairs, Eden, the assistant chief's lovely secretary gave me a worried, puzzled look. "The deputy chief can't see you right away." Then she leaned across her desk and with gorgeous green eyes opened wide she asked in a hushed tone, "Why are *you* here?"

Eden broke everyone's heart by marrying her high school sweetheart, but before then, we dated a couple of times and we have remained friends. If she knew anything, she would tell me.

"Eden," I tried to appear nonchalant. "I haven't a clue."

The damned mule, I thought. The night before, I found an old mule wandering along the roadside on my beat. Animal control is never available after five and not having a lariat to lasso the ornery animal, I shooed it into the nearest pasture. That was it, I was sure; the beast got back out and caused a traffic accident. Someone is surely suing!

It was forty-five minutes before the assistant chief could see me. I know I dozed off because my mind had started to wander back in time to her. *Don't leave me*, she cried. Her long soft fingers slipped like sand from my grasp as I reluctantly returned to the wakened world.

Deputy Chief Cunningham, a big Black gentleman, barked an order to Eden over the intercom. Eden paled, stared at me with wide green eyes and meekly said, "He'll see you now."

"Sit down." He commanded as soon as I breezed through his door. "Department gossip holds that when an officer is called into my office he is automatically in trouble."

"I've heard as much Deputy Chief, but tell me, why am I here?" I hoped my tone was confident.

The Deputy Chief appraised me for a moment, then, with a ghost of a smile, he said, "Someone sent Mayor Hank a love letter."

"A love letter, sir?"

"Yes. It was pasted to a piece of recycled paper from a child's Big Chief notebook. The letters were clipped from different magazines and stuck to the page with white children's paste. The lab identified one of the magazines as a popular woman's fashion magazine."

"Rather infantile."

"Infantile or not," Chief Cunningham snapped. He slammed his fist on his mahogany desktop, "Mayor Hank is the most popular mayor we've had in years. Any threat to his life must be taken seriously."

Oh! That kind of love letter.

"Absolutely!" I was quick to agree. "Now where do I come in?"

Deputy Chief Cunningham leaned way back in his swivel chair and gave me a long stare. "The lieutenant highly recommended you for this assignment."

I shrugged. The lieutenant was easily impressed.

The Deputy Chief straightened, took a folder from his desk and thumbed through it. He casually asked, "You are our number one Spanish-English translator?"

My straight back chair was not made for comfort. Still I tried to appear relaxed and at ease. "I speak, read and write and can translate either language."

"Castilian Spanish?"

"*Si Jefe, yo hablo castellano y diversos dialectos de español. ¿Porque?*"

The Chief finally smiled, "You are saying that you speak Castilian and diverse dialects of Spanish, am I correct?"

"I am impressed Chief."

Looking down as if to stay a blush he added, "I grew up in San Antonio and I picked up a bit of conversational Spanish on the streets, mostly from the lovely *señoritas.*"

"Best way to learn a new language Chief but why does my quaint ability to speak both languages interest you?"

Deputy Chief Cunningham looked up suddenly, "Oh, I forgot to tell you, the letter—it is written in perfect Castilian Spanish. Go home. Report to City Hall first thing in the morning in a Class A uniform. You start immediately."

PART II
IT WAS PERFECT...

Bright and early the following morning the blaring alarm jarred me into awareness. After years of working Evening Shift, I had become unaccustomed to relying on an alarm clock to prepare for work. The rude sound interrupted my peaceful slumber and dreams of simpler times and better days...and of her, The Lobster Lady. If I hurried, I'd still have time for a quick breakfast at Vera's Taqueria.

Taquerias, the Mexican restaurant version of fast food, have really become popular in Houston within the last ten years or so. Vera's is my very favorite taqueria. A few years ago Noah Webster finally incorporated the word "taqueria" into his famous dictionary as a new English word.

On the new assignment, the days quickly melded into weeks. My dreams of her continued just before waking. *I don't love you,* she said, *I never did. Before, when I said I loved you, I lied.* Her words plopped all around me like big wet drops of freezing rain, *I lied, I lied, I lied....*

One fine day I wandered into the lobby of City Hall looking for likely suspects, or at least suspicious activity. What then should my wandering eyes behold but a vision, absolutely the most beautiful woman I have ever seen. Petit, perhaps five-five with jet-black hair that descended in lazy, shy tangles to her flawless shoulders. She wore a *little black dress* that clung to her every curve. Ashley. A lot of women dress that way and only manage to look like they are on the make. Ashley made this look natural. I guess that is what *class* means. She flowed gracefully toward me in high heels that really accentuated her long, firm shapely legs. She wore a smile that said we have always known each other even though we have yet to meet.

Just like that, I ceased to be the experienced, professional police officer guarding the mayor. She walked up to me smiling. Her face, mouth, eyes, and those twin dimples really disarmed me. Her eyes, Gypsy eyes, complimented with luscious, curly eyelashes so dark brown they looked black. If I live to be a hundred I'll never forget those eyes - so bright and full of life.

"I'm Ashley Henderson," she announced, "and you must be the mayor's right-hand-man!" but I flushed just the same. "No Miss," I blustered. "I'm not as important as all that. I'm only here on a special assignment."

She flashed a smile that said, I love a man in uniform. "Oh well, perhaps we can have coffee sometime."

Just then, Mayor Hank, a white-haired man whose persona reminds one of a favorite uncle came up and ushered Ashley into his office. He glared back over his shoulder at me with that special look reserved for kids caught leafing through girlie magazines at the corner convenience store. Now I understand how one might want to murder this personable town boss.

Without a doubt, Mayor Hank lords over his fiefdom. His word is law, his decisions are unimpeachable and even my job exists at his very whim. Yet, in the scheme of things, higher powers remain in charge because Ashley returned when I got off-duty at five.

She quickened her pace and called out, "Officer, would you walk me to my car?"

I halted in my tracks, smiled broadly and said, "I am a public servant, my lady. I will walk you anywhere you like."

On the elevator, between the lobby and the underground parking garage I managed to drop my keys three times. She simply smiled, knowing she had that effect on me. In the dank basement parking lot where our voices echoed and the air, permeated with the musty odor of ozone and ancient dust, my heart sank to the pit of my stomach. There I ordered it to remain until I have the time to drown it in a lake of booze. Reality check. I am entirely out of her league. My yearly salary won't pay to wash and wax her car, a milk-white Mercedes Benz 600. She dutifully thanked me as I opened the driver's side door for her. Then she dropped her window and earnestly asked me if she can give me a lift some place. Like the village idiot, I stood there shaking my head.

"Is there…someone?" She purred.

I continued shaking my head. She smiled coyly, gave me a dainty wave and drove off. That night I dreamt of simpler times and better days and… of her, the Lobster Lady. Someone once said, time heals all wounds. What the hell did that fool know?

With Ashley's committees, fund-raisers and who knows what else, she is around City Hall nearly every day. Male ego, fragile thing that it is, I try hard to convince myself that she really isn't coming by to see me. She isn't, but she always manages to stop and chat for at least twenty minutes.

She has to be married but I just can't bring myself to ask her. I suppose I really don't want to know.

Ashley asked me if there was someone and I simply shook my head. Truth is I still dream of her and God is in His Heaven and all is right with the world. Perhaps Ashley is the one who can make me forget her once and for all.

On a Friday after the Sunday I related my story to Eliazer, Ashley walked up to me and said in perfect Spanish that her husband will be out of town. "Perhaps," she suggests, "we should have that drink we talked about."

Never expecting her to speak to me in Spanish I didn't understand her at first. The words barely registered. "Coffee?" I lamely asked.

Really invading my space, she smiled and said, "If that's what you want. I prefer something stronger. You do drink, don't you?"

"When I'm off-duty."

"You're off this weekend?"

I nodded.

"Are you familiar with the lower Rio Grande Valley?"

"Of course," my eyes must have opened wide, "why that's my old stomping grounds."

Smiling sweetly she hands me a key, "Then you know where the Echo Motor Hotel is?"

"Edinburg, Texas on South Closner Boulevard?"

"The very same one!"

Wow! A leisurely jaunt southeast along the beautiful Coastal Bend on Highway 77 to Rivera. Then 285 to Falfurrias and 281 south all the way to Edinburg.

As she walked away, she glanced over her shoulder coquettishly mouthing, *Saturday, sevenish!*

Waiting on Ashley, nervous as a one-eyed feral cat with a broken tail hiding from a pack of dire wolves, I envisioned the worse. What if this is only a bad joke? A knock on the door... Laughter... My entire platoon barging in...you didn't really expect Ashley, did you! I kept feeling for my off-duty, Walther PPK/s .380 Auto that I carry in an SOB holster. SOB is a marketing acronym for small-of-the-back. "On the street," the advertisements read, "you need an SOB behind you." Yeah, I knew a lot of those and probably they were all lurking outside just waiting to pounce on me!

Ashley finally did walk in closer to eight than seven. Without a word she sauntered right up to me taking my face between her lovely hands. My own clumsy hands settled gently on her shapely hips as she pulled me down and gave me the best kiss of my life, twice! Another kiss like that and she would own me. My lips tingled and my mouth savored the spicy lingering after-taste of cinnamon. Just as abruptly she pulled away leaving me in quite a stupor.

"Fix me a whiskey on-the-rocks," she requested matter-of-factly, walking toward the bathroom, "while I slip into something more…appropriate." The pause before the word 'appropriate' suggested anything but, and filled the room with expectation of a muted promise for mischief.

The sudden hiss of the shower, the wispy tendrils of steam beckoning like a wraith from the open bathroom door made me spill Chivas Regal all over the fancy hardwood counter. Uncouth bastard that I am, I took a deep gulp straight out of the bottle to help me stave off the urge to peek. Moments later my chivalrous conduct was amply rewarded. She materialized leaning lazily on the doorframe, left hand on her hip, right hand elevated carelessly above her head. She wore a sheer black teddy that would make Victoria blush. From the top of her head to the bottom of her feet, from shoulder to shoulder and from hip to hip she was truly a credit to her gender - perfect and gorgeous.

In the light of her beauty, I felt base, oafish almost. Would she notice my uneven teeth or some other imperfection? Would she laugh? Would she turn and leave? I would gladly stare at her forever in total awe of her beauty but now I could appreciate why lovers often prefer to romp in the dark. If we all were as perfect as she there would be no need to hide in the dark.

I held out her drink as she slowly, deliberately walked up to me one hip at a time and relieved my unsteady hand of its burden. She never licked the rim nor did she kiss the glass, yet somehow, she made the simple act of sipping her whiskey seem incredibly erotic. She looked down and, with some measure of determination, set the glass on the table making the ice jingle against the glass tumbler. Then having finalized some decision in the dark recesses of her mind she looked up at me and reached to embrace me. My hands automatically found her perfect behind, which, I was ecstatic to discover, was a delightful double-handful! In fact, she fit into my embrace like the crucial missing piece from an old jigsaw puzzle that someone forgot to throw out. She took my hand and led me helpless as a lost puppy to the bedroom. Fortunately, or perhaps by design, the walls were soundproof.

Sometime after daybreak, I heard her say from afar something about how she wished she weren't a married woman. Slowly returning to the land of the living I managed to mumble something in agreement.

"If something were to happen to JV," Ashley suggested abruptly, "we would inherit all of his money."

"WE?" Immediately I went from stupid drowsy to full alert. I rolled over and faced her.

"We are together." She leaned on a red satin pillow and stared at my spent form from her side of the bed. "We are alone. Do you really need to ask who "we" means?"

I didn't need to ask.

"He is always speeding," she said in a somber tone of voice. "I'm scared to death that some traffic cop is going to shoot at him for refusing to stop, or something."

What was wrong with this picture?

Suddenly she asked, "What kind of gun do you carry?"

Stalling for time to get my head on straight, I asked, "On duty?"

Her perfect face beamed as she nodded.

"A 10mm."

"A real hand cannon." She smiled and primly pulled the red-satin bed sheet over her bosom.

I couldn't help but wonder why women bothered to cover up that way. After last night what was there to be modest about?

"He keeps a .38 in the glove box..." She spoke almost in a whisper. "...a Colt Detective Special and he doesn't even have a concealed carry license." She swung her lovely legs out from under the covers and reached for her clothes.

"Good gun," I said. I pulled on my jeans and looked for my boots. "Lousy caliber."

"Why?"

"In the old days we called the .38 Special the widow-maker, because it was likely to make a widow out of the officer's wife. Bad guys always carried something more substantial. But tell me, how come a man like Henderson doesn't have a concealed carry permit?"

She frowned and looked down, "Something from his miss-spent youth kept him from passing the background check."

Ashley listened, or at least pretended really well. Perhaps it was simply the term "widow-maker" that held her attention. I decided that it was part of her charm, her personal magic, a way of making others believe that she really did listen, that anything you had to say was truly important. A neat trick she managed really well. Where the hell was my shirt?

Hurriedly, she added, "Did I tell you that JV never bothers to pay his speeding tickets? Do you know that he has DPS warrants?"

"Cupidity," I muttered under my breath.

Ashley appeared confused. "What?"

"Never mind." I wondered why people who have everything think they can even get away with...murder?

PART III
ON THE ROAD TO PERDITION–
EDINBURG, TEXAS

Tomorrow will probably be a good day to bond with my brother Eliazer. I'll buy some ribs, beer and we'll barbeque in his backyard, beneath the lush-green pecans, amongst the un-repaired lawn tractors. Today there is much to do and soon I'll leave town, start up some place else. I suppose I can break it to him then. I can already hear him, "Not again bro, the last time you vanished for seven years...."

I've always said that my forte is knowing my weakness and so it is. I just wish I'd been strong enough to stay away from her. I guess I'll go north this time. I've always wanted to see the Northern Lights, and I can't remain in Texas. I know. Ashley knows that I know. That attorney boyfriend of hers knows that I know. Too bad I can't just go to the district attorney with this. They'll try to kill me, of course. I know too much and murder is their forte. Maybe I should just kill the attorney and keep Ashley. Nah, Ashley is a black magic woman. She'll lose the lawyer when she is ready to move on; after all she is the deadlier of the species. Why fool myself, she could never really fall for a common man like me. Too bad. I really did fall for her.

To Mr. Henderson, Ashley was just a trophy wife and perhaps he took her for granted. Still, that doesn't give anyone the right to commit murder. It can all end here, today, now and forever. I can simply leave town and never be found. I've done that and am quite good at it. Perhaps I'll even e-mail Ashley saying that her secret will always be safe with me. I am a man of my word and I will never blackmail her or her boyfriend. Money means nothing to me, only justice. I can even be magnanimous and wish them every happiness. Or possibly I'll be cryptic saying: I know the two of you will be very happy together until...*Death* do you part....

After considerable soul-searching I simply called Ashley on her private line. I offered my condolences and asked her to meet me again at the Echo, sevenish. Really important, I added. Next, I left the key with the number seven neatly written on a cocktail napkin on the windshield of her boyfriend's car. Good thing he has his own covered parking at the Y where once a week he instructs martial arts for under privileged kids. No one will mess with his car and he will find the key when he leaves at three.

People say, dead men tell no tales. That's not true. The truth is, dead men tell no lies. Any forensic scientist can tell you so. Any accident investigator worth his salt can look at a wrecked car and tell you what happened.

It was professional curiosity that made me notice the minor fender damage with bright red paint transferred on his ice blue Lincoln Town Car. He should've buffed it out with rubbing compound. I guess he figured that no one could reconstruct the accident. Or should I say crime? Henderson's Porsche was bright red, the very same shade. The front license plate hanging askew from one bolt on the Lincoln's front bumper told the rest of the story.

Ashley's boyfriend, Mac, a tall handsome dude in an eight hundred dollar suit, showed up without preamble about ten past seven. He strutted into room seven of the Echo Hotel like a bad boy, his jacket slung carelessly over one shoulder, his silk tie undone and a $75 bottle of Champagne in hand.

"The lady likes whiskey," I sat comfortably in the brown easy chair I had moved to the middle of the room. "You did know that, Mac, or did you get your lady friends mixed up?"

Mac froze, "What...what are you doing here?" He looked about the room; then convinced that we were alone, he stared with the most incredulous look on his face.

"Shut the door Mac." I gestured for emphasis with the gun. The gun in my right hand fascinated him. For a moment the thought crossed my mind that Mac could be armed but he made no furtive movements to indicate he might try to pull his own piece.

"Why so glum Mac; surely you knew that the lady and I were... involved."

"INVOLVED?" He glared through hooded eyes. "Don't flatter yourself, bud. Do you know what Ashley called your involvement? She said it was a necessary evil." Mac gloated and did a double take. "And what do you think you're going to do now? Arrange a *ménage a trios?*"

I have to admit that it took grit to say all that, with me holding the pistol, but I recognized his tactics. He was trying to talk down to me, to browbeat me by using French!

All I could do was flash a sarcastic smile. "Not to worry Mac. I'm not into threesomes, but you and I are going to play a little game."

By now, Mac really looked worried.

"We can play the waiting game, Mac, or we can play the snitching game."

Something like hope flashed briefly in his eyes; my cue to continue. "Some hold that confession is good for the soul. What do you think, Mac, is that true?"

He glared at me, "You are a very sick man."

"Me?" With my finest De Niro 'are you talking to me' impersonation, "I'm not sick Mac. I'm not the one who let my girlfriend fool around with another man. I didn't suggest a *ménage a trios*. No Mac, I'm not sick at all. I'm just...crazy!"

Mac raised his eyebrows that said, are you serious?

"That's right Mac. I'm crazy...positively certifiable. You see, Mac, I entertain delusions of immortality. Imagine that...I think I'm gonna live forever. Now is that crazy or what?"

I just sat there smiling, letting reality take hold. "How good are your martial arts skills, Mac?" I held my pistol loosely, tauntingly, daring Mac to do something. Before he could act I said, "I would say *mon ami*, Mac, but I don't like to lie. We both know we're not friends so let me just ask you one thing."

"What?"

My eyeballs drilled his as I said as remorsefully as I could, "You're not entertaining any notions of immortality yourself, are you Mac?"

Mac's gray eyes widened and he blanched.

"That would never do. You see Mac, I get real nervous when I have to play the waiting game." Shaking my head slowly from side to side I added, "My trigger finger tends to...twitch."

"Ah, okay, okay—it was all Ashley's idea, you know...."

I just smiled a thin smile and nodded pleasantly at Mac as if we were two old friends reminiscing old times.

"She's the one who sent that...that note to Mayor Hank. Did you know that she's fluent in Spanish?"

More pleasant nodding. Finally in control, I felt positively giddy.

"We went through the office files and found your name. You're kind of a los—LONER, not married, moved around quite a bit... You even dated Eden de la Garza a few times—"

"Mac, it was hardly dating. We did lunch. That can't be in the file."

"Grapevine...grapevine anyway, you had to like Ashley," Mac gestured helplessly with his hands, "I mean, you dated Eden."

"I can see the connection but why threaten the Mayor?"

"Well...ah...you are the *numero uno* translator. That was the only way we could get you that special assignment guarding the May—now don't get mad!"

I got a two-handed grip on my pistol. It never ceases to amaze me how people at gunpoint will hold their hands out as if they could ward the bullet off with their hands.

"Look," he continued, sweating bullets, "you can come out of this smelling like a rose. Think of your career, you're—I mean, none of us are getting any younger. Women like Ashley are a dime-a-dozen. With a man of my influence and affluence to back you, why in a year's time you can be sitting behind Cunningham's desk. The Police Chief is retiring this year and Cunningham is a shoo-in to succeed him. City Council owes me a lot of favors—I'll make you the new deputy chief with Eden as your personal secretary! That's a pretty sweet deal, huh? What do you say?"

"I like Eden just fine. In fact you can say I love Eden, but she's a married woman. Now Ashley, she's a widow. What if I like Ashley better?"

Mac scowled, "Ashley's not available." Then his eyes opened really wide, "Look, she's got to go to prison. I mean, justice must prevail in an urbane and genteel society. Why you and I, we are on the same side, crusaders for law and order aren't we? Ashley must go to prison for the murder of her husband."

"Prison?" I said the word with a bad taste in my mouth, "I don't think she would like that...." Before I could finish, the door opened and Ashley slipped in.

Mac looked at Ashley. Then he looked at me all bad boy again, "That's a mighty big gun for such a little girl."

The man was slick: Negotiating his own blameless posture, making me the next deputy chief of police and setting up his girlfriend for murder all in one easy step. I could just picture this petty politician running for the office of governor and that would never do.

On the outside chance that Ashley really did love Mac I didn't want to distress her by killing him in her presence, but how to separate the two? I may be uncouth but I'm not a heartless bastard.

Mac, tried to take command of the situation. He shouted, "OFFICER, as County District Attorney I ORDER you to arrest that woman for the murder of her husband Jesse Vernon Henderson." Mac pointed an accusing finger at Ashley as if there were more than one woman in the room.

Ashley and I stared blankly at Mac. I looked at Ashley. Could petite, proper Ashley deliver the powerful karate blow that had snapped her husband's neck? Would any jury believe that she had the upper body strength to wrestle 200 pounds of dead-meat into the death-Porsche? How did Mac plan to get a conviction?

Mac continued staring at Ashley, mouth slightly open, breathing asthmatically. Suddenly he turned to me glaring, blue-spit dribbling out of the corner of his mouth and he demanded, "Officer, DO YOUR DUTY—"

A .380 is a wonderful equalizer. It treats the affluent and the destitute, the beautiful and the ugly with the same impunity. One shot through the heart with the untraceable .380 automatic I picked up at a pawnshop long before the ban on high capacity magazines for handguns.

The first bullet was a high shock slug. Ashley let out the slightest gasp. Mac the DA uttered a common expletive just before I introduced him to eleven 95 grain, full metal jacket .380 slugs. Only eleven, I had to save one. The .380 out of a full-length four-inch barrel is not as loud as you would imagine. Certainly not loud enough to be heard through the sound proof walls of the Echo Hotel. Still, I had to hurry with this unpleasantness.

After removing the District Attorney from office I took Ashley's still limber hand in mine for the last time and made it fire the last bullet harmlessly into the carpet. With the slide locked back on empty I laid the nickel-plated Browning pistol with the double-stack pre-ban magazine on the carpet near Ashley. I knew that the local police would take the path of least resistance: Ashley, distraught over the death of her husband and perhaps wishing to atone for her infidelity riddled her boyfriend with bullets and then killed herself. No powder burns but then women wish to remain beautiful even in death, which is why they seldom shoot themselves in the head. Ashley just naturally held the gun as far from her body as she could. Unable to determine in what order the bullets were fired they will assume that the last one killed Ashley Henderson. Eleven shots went into her boyfriend and one went wild, striking the floor. No one will ever guess that they have three unsolved murders rather than a murder-suicide. All the better. Three unsolved murders would send ripples of panic through the very fabric of society.

It is a real pity that it all ended this way. Ashley and Mac didn't know that now and then I took the Law into my own hands. But how could they know? Some information is not to be found in any file. Had they known I don't think they would have ever involved me in their murderous intent. But then, how could anybody know? Anyone I could tell would automatically become an accessory. In Mac and Ashley's genteel and urbane society no one should have to be an accessory to anything as vile as murder.

So you may wonder, what is my role in all of this? Am I simply the self-appointed avenger of poor little rich boys murdered by their money-grubbing wives and boyfriends? Am I perhaps truly mad? Or am I more like the holy assassin of the Old Testament who so deftly dealt with that evil enchantress Jezebel? For my part I believe that Ashley had it right all along. I am simply...a necessary evil. May the Lord have mercy...on my soul! *Requiescat in Pace*, sweet Ashley.

EPILOGUE

The road from Texas to Alaska is long and lonely, nearly as long as the road to perdition. Eliazer understood. He always does. He knows we'll see each other again. Someday. Deputy Chief Cunningham just shrugged when he read my letter of resignation.

"I just need a change, Chief. Too many memories here, too many... ghosts." Besides, I couldn't tell him that I did my job and saved Mayor Hank from a lot of grief.

"Will you be back?" he asked.

"*¡Quien sabe!* Who knows, Chief, who knows...."

Ashley is not on the road to perdition anymore. She is a soul in Purgatory and can one day hope to see Heaven. I should be as lucky!

I still dream of her. Not Ashley...the Lobster Lady, my one true love. Strange sobriquet for her. One would never imagine such a gorgeous woman being called the Lobster Lady. She earned that epithet the day she left me.

"I don't love you," she said, "I never did. You'll never be more than just a cop. You can't afford me. I have caviar taste. I want steak and lobster for dinner every night...."

I hope she's happy, wherever she is. No. I lie. What I really hope is that one day she'll call to say that, she is sorry, that she was wrong and that she wants things to be like before....

Dream on!

A CUP OF HUMILITY
By Judy Stevens

I almost turned away from the door to McFastfood when I noticed more people than usual inside, and the line they had formed was strangely spread-out. Then I shrugged and chalked it up to human nature. We all know people can be weird before their morning cup of coffee.

Although people crowded the little brightly colored room, each person seemed lost in his or her own thoughts. That was just fine with me—all I wanted was coffee before I faced work.

As I stood there pondering whether to add a McSomething to my order of plain coffee, a curiously heavy thought intruded on my fine, crisp October day. Restaurants, like libraries, malls, movie theaters and airports, just might be the true classless gathering spots in our otherwise segregated and isolated modern world—the modern equivalent of the well where everyone comes to get water. People who otherwise might never cross paths mingle in these neutral spaces to get what they need, discarding friendly banter along with the trash at the door.

But in this place, the line to the counter was spread out, as if someone important stood in its midst, with fans giving wide berth. At that thought, my heart skipped a beat. Celebrities did manage to find our quiet little corner of the world from time to time, though it was hard to spot some, for they seldom matched their images when seen in person. I strained to see who it was, then gave up. I was born too short.

Abruptly the line broke apart. Some people left without placing their order, wearing an expression of disgust. As the line thinned, I saw why, and it seemed my thoughts mirrored the collective thoughts of others in this supposedly neutral, classless place.

This man was no celebrity.

My thoughts turned darker... he didn't belong here.

The line had become sparse. Now he stood right in front of me. Though his back was turned, I thought I knew exactly what he was. The faded brown suit he wore had not seen a closet—or a dry-cleaner—in a long time, nor had it been fashionably distressed to look "poor," which was the fad this year. I told myself it could be worse: though he was shabby, the man was not dirty in the way street people get—no telltale odor or filth. He seemed in fact, the embodiment of the old-fashioned vagabond, that "jumper-of-trains" straight out of the Great Depression. As I stood there, I realized that he reminded me of those poor hobos that showed up at my parent's back door when I was a kid. I felt a tinge of sympathy.

I wondered why my decision to stay and get my coffee had felt so noble. I began to feel a little shabby myself.

The line moved; the man shuffled forward and I saw that he was thin but not gaunt; nether was he bent with age, though silver hairs peeked out from beneath his billed cap. Dressed otherwise, he might have been mistaken for a professor at one of our local colleges—or a retired businessman. He was obviously homeless, and weren't the homeless almost like fixtures on the streets of the city, pushing their lives before them in shopping carts "on permanent loan" from local grocery stores? And this man...wasn't this man just a part of the socially invisible, anonymous class, kept safely distant from the rest of us by charity and tolerated whenever they used public spaces—or so I'd been taught through public opinion?

Then he turned and I saw the dignity of the man. Our eyes met ever so briefly, yet in his was ageless humanity that refused to be dulled by the rigors of living—an undiscovered treasure in a plain brown wrapper. His faded blue eyes twinkled as he glanced around, his brows raised slightly as if by a private joke.

Then he turned and I saw again only his back, but it was different this time: he had lost his anonymity.

He placed his order and took the change. Then with a faint smile, he reached into his pocket, added a few more coins and dropped the lot into the kid's fund box on the counter—the box all the rest of us had ignored. That simple gesture spoke volumes of the man's character. It was as if I watched a Saint Nicholas impoverishing himself to bring happiness to others, or perhaps it was the modern-day equivalent of the "widow's mite."

It humbled me. Yet, it appeared no one else in that brightly colored place noticed.

The gentle man took his coffee and sat down all alone among people who still gave him wide berth simply because they all thought he didn't belong among them.

As for me— I left there carrying a large cup of humility.

A TEJANO COUNTRY CHRISTMAS
A Remembrance By Edgar Clinton, Jr.

Hewing wood, fetching tamales mid December, getting drunk by the garage fire with the in-laws as the Norther rages at all that was and is warm. The women cook, and talk and watch TV inside. Men by common agreement and innate concordance converge apart from the split tails free of female censoriousness and disapprobation.

And now, it's time for perhaps the Season highlight! Just as the Jews in the time of Jesus would ritually slit the throat of a lamb, so, too, the *Tejanos* had a tradition of *La Matanza del Marrano*. First, it involved the selection and run down of the prize porker by mostly the younger *primos*. Then the selection of the largest caliber handgun. Then the obvious choice of the *Matador de Puercos*, i.e.the guy that was most drunk. The *varoncitos* were called to watch the ritual sacrifice.

The women with brains would try to herd the young ones off in another direction with some promise or distraction. It was none too safe. The pig would be shot at point blank range between the ears, but more often than not the great matador would miss. Bam!! There goes an ear. Pow!! Part of a snout. Kaboom!! That pig will never walk straight again. Bang!! There goes a *primo* to meet the *Virgin of Guadalupe*...A wise woman would get her kids out of Dodge, *prontisimo*.

Family histories oozed out as *viejos* left the warmth of the fire flames for the solace of their blankets and the dreams of what might have been. Fronts and face and façades and family dignity drain into the black cold of the night. All that remains is the tale itself, told so that in its expression something may be understood— as if a thing lacking even one fundament of reason could make sense in some way—that some one may care, if for no more than for the time it takes to hear. At the least, there is a release in the expression. Few ask for more.

Many fled Mexico, fleeing for their lives. There was no right side to be on. All sides were in the killing business and *dios sabe* who was going to come out on top. Crossing the Rio Bravo when the moon gave the least of her light. The *patrón*, the patriarch, ruthless more than cruel. Cruel as well when cruelty must be called upon. The great Ranchos of Texas, their Mexican cowboys. The *braceros*, the *mojados*, the opportunities, the theft.

The bachelors, the old maids, those crippled before their prime. *Los niños*, like little gods and goddesses, the adoration of the innocent. The twisting of little minds. The church and the *padres*. The sisters of withered breast and bone, set loose upon the youth. Deprivation does not kill desire, it engenders a mutant strain. The peoples veneration, adoration, on the other hand, how they were despised.

Lusts and desires and romance and jealousy, tenderness and revenge, *devoción y tradición* and all the while Santa Claus was on his way. And tomorrow was another day. There would be tamales soon. And fishing in the *desague*, if the front blew through and out…making no distinctions, reserving all reservations. Life here was not to be questioned but to be lived.

Both can be done, but not at once.

ABORTION LULLABY
By Milo Kearney

Of course, Dolores knew that the Dean Porter Park Resaca was supposed to be haunted. Who in Brownsville had not heard the stories about how *la llorona* appeared there from time to time, or how sometimes she was heard, sobbing inconsolably? Everyone knew how the weeping woman drowned herself in the *resaca* after the father of her child abandoned both of them. Even more horrible, how she took that abandoned child with her to her watery grave.

When Dolores herself was a child, buying a house on this haunted *resaca* was the last thing she imagined herself doing. When she walked to and from Sharp Elementary School along Palm Boulevard, she hurried as fast as she could past the Resaca, half-hidden by the row of houses.

Children are easily spooked, but now, Dolores was a proud graduate of the University of Texas at Brownsville and a certified teacher at Sharp Elementary School. She had learned how to distinguish folklore from reality. So, when the beautiful little house on the other side of the *resaca* across from Dean Porter Park went up for sale, *la llorona* was not uppermost in her mind. The back yard was idyllic – with a tiled porch where she could watch the ducks swimming in the *resaca,* followed by rows of paddling ducklings, and listen to the children's happy voices in the park on the other side.

The house was also close to her job at Sharp School, and—when the workday was over—she could walk around the resaca and relax in the park. Furthermore, the bank offered mortgage loans for far more money than she thought she could ever afford, and she did not have to document the amount of her income. This gave her an unexpected chance to move into such a wonderful and convenient house, even though she barely made it from paycheck to paycheck. In the first weeks after she moved in, everything worked out like a charm in her perfect dream home.

Then came Halloween. Dolores prepared for the little nocturnal visitors with packages of candy, which she bought from Lopez Supermarket and made ready to hand out. She also had Christian stickers and tracts, obtained from her church. Fun was fun, but Dolores knew that the holiday traced back to a Celtic celebration of the evil forces that took over with the start of the dark half of the year. So it was best to counteract any Satanic influence over the innocent children's minds by this subtle witnessing to God's goodness.

For a couple of hours, children thronged to the door—diminutive witches and skeletons, ogres and vampires, all eager for candies to be dropped into their outstretched jack-o-lanterns or paper bags. Some of the children were pupils in Dolores's second-grade class at school. Many more were from Matamoros—brought across the river from Mexico by the carloads and even truckloads. Gradually, the front doorbell rang less and less. Dolores settled down with a book on techniques of teaching second graders, when—after some time—the doorbell rang again. Surprised, Dolores made her drowsy way back to the door, to find three more children waiting. There stood two girls, about ten years old, and a little boy, about eight. These kids were all dressed as ghosts, with muddy shoes sticking out from the bottom of their white sheets, and—to Dolores's astonishment—they spoke a little rhyme in unison. The gist of their rhyme took her aback even more:

We've come to your door for trick or treat.
Do unwanted pregnancies need help quick?
Abortion's handy and discrete.
But is it treat or is it trick?

We are the ghosts who really haunt –
The ghosts of babies killed in the womb.
We won't disappear, despite your taunt.
You cannot keep us in the tomb.

We're found on your block and throughout this town,
Our numbers grow day-by-day.
Nobody wants us. Go ahead and frown.
Even as ghosts, we're in the way.

We appear with staring, accusing eyes,
Especially where toys are found.
You'll see us, too (it's no surprise),
When you pass a park or school playground.

We grimly wait for our moms and dads,
Our doctors, and all who might find it right
To cross to our realm of the living dead
And explain themselves in this dark night.

Dolores stood speechless for a moment after their recitation, and then, mechanically, gave each one a candy, a Christian sticker, and a Bible tract. The little ghosts turned and ran away. Dolores shut the door and sat down, her head filled with racing thoughts. Was this the work of an innovative church group? If so, was this method too confrontational? Were the children reciting these lines, which they apparently took some pains to memorize, at other houses, too? Or did somebody know?

Memories came flooding back. Memories of that night, nine years ago, when she had asked Rick to meet her after work in Dean Porter Park. He seemed a little nervous as she came up, and immediately asked her what was the urgent message that she wanted to tell him. Putting on her most cheerful voice, she had announced, "I've got wonderful news. I'm pregnant."

Rick's response was not what she had hoped, but what she had greatly feared: "Oh, yeah? You're not saying I'm to blame, I hope."

Dolores tried to reassure him: "Yes, you're the father alright. There's no one else. Aren't you happy? We're going to have a baby."

But Rick was not happy, nor did he believe her. He sneered. "Don't give me that! Not after the way you've been hanging around with that rich boyfriend of yours!"

Dolores knew who Rick meant. Before Rick had started dating her seriously, Dolores was flattered when asked out by a wealthy local man. But he was older, not as good looking, and not inclined to propose marriage.

Dolores had disengaged herself from him as much as seemed polite after she and Rick had started sleeping together.

Dolores stated flatly, "It was not him."

Rick spit out, "You expect me to believe that?"

The charge was really unfair Dolores argued. "Come on! He's an ugly sourpuss and old enough to be my father."

Rick was in no way pacified and shot back, "Like that would stop you! I know how proud you've been to be seen on dates with him. And you can't stop talking about his mansion on Palm Boulevard."

Dolores escalated her tone, insisting, "I don't fancy being a nursemaid to that fool when he gets old. I'm telling you, you are the father."

At that point, Rick had paused—a pause that raised Dolores's hopes a tiny bit. But then Rick blurted out, "I get it. He turned you down. He won't accept responsibility for the baby, and so you're trying to stick the blame on me."

Almost hysterical, Dolores cried, "Oh, please! Please! Don't be like that. This should be a very happy moment for both of us."

She reached out to hug him, but he just shouted, "What sort of a sucker do you take me for? I'm not going to spend my life paying for the rearing of another man's brat."

In a final bid to reassure Rick, Dolores pleaded, "Oh, please! I swear the baby is yours. It's <u>you</u> I love."

She tried to embrace him, but he pushed her away and jumped up. When she tried to hug him again, he slapped her. "Stop it! Stop it! I'm getting out of here."

Dolores held on to him, pleading, "No, no! Please! I love you. It will be alright."

Rick made himself clear once and for all. He threw her to the ground and screamed, "I said no! No! And from now on stay away from me!" He rushed away.

She picked herself up from the ground and through her tears, shouted after him. "O.K. then. I'll go to an abortion clinic. And it will be <u>your</u> fault." Louder, she yelled, "It will be <u>your</u> fault."

As Dolores rehashed this painful scene, she asked herself, "What else could I have done?" If she had become an unwed mother, her reputation for high values would have been as muddied as if it had sunk to the bottom of *la llorona's resaca*. She would have received support from her little church, the center of her social life, but would also have become a source of gossip.

And, on her own, she lacked both the time and the money to rear a child. What else could she have done?

President Obama spoke recently of how people in her predicament were demonized. She kept a copy of the President's speech in her desk, and now she got it out to read again. She had underlined certain lines in red: "I come....asking you to look, with open hearts, open minds, and fair-minded words....I have prayed that I might myself extend a presumption of good faith to others, because, when we do that, that's when we discover, at least, the possibility of common ground."

Confused and haunted, Dolores lay awake, debating with herself most of that Saturday night. Thoughts of drowning herself in the Resaca kept gurgling up to the surface of her thoughts, only to be repeatedly pushed back down to the murky depths of her consciousness. When the light of dawn at last kissed her face, like a loving child who has risen before his mother, she got dressed and walked around the *resaca* to the park. There, she planned to collect her thoughts in the soberness of day, before heading to church.

She sat, as she so often did, in the children's playground section, where she had always enjoyed watching the little folk speed down the slippery slides, climb through the tunnel, heave high on the swings, and balance walking along the low wall. This morning, however, only three children sat quietly on the bench next to her. At first, Dolores was unaware of them, but then she noticed that there were two older girls with a younger boy between them. The girls' dark brown locks contrasted with the boy's red hair, the same shade as Dolores' own, and they all had muddy shoes.

The little boy began to speak. A chill came over her as she realized that, like the ghost trick-or-treaters of the previous night, he spoke in verse with adult wording. He chanted mournfully:

"I sit and look out into space.
Why am I here? Where is my place?
My mother hates that I was born.
The sight of me brings shame and scorn.
My father wishes I were dead.
Or am I his? (I hear what's said.)
I was not meant to be.

So, is abortion always wrong?
What if the child will not belong?
Is heartache right to recommend,
Or mercy killing on demand?

Dolores's thoughts bumped into each other. She wondered, "Is this really happening or have my troubles driven me insane? I must be seeing and hearing things that are not there."

What happened next froze Dolores to her seat and filled her eyes with tears of regret. For the two older girls put comforting arms around the little boy and, as they spoke their final rhyme to him, walked with him toward the edge of the *resaca*. This is what they said, there by the water, before all three gradually faded into thin air.

"Little baby, go to sleep
In eternal night.
Your cradle is a garbage can.
Do not take fright.

Best sleep, my baby, evermore.
The pain will soon be through.
The life that you'd been slated for
Held nothing good for you."

AIN'T NO GUN IN MY POCKET
By Don Clifford

My God! What am I doing here?

Marley Peterson's stomach tightened with the thought that she might be in the wrong place at the wrong time. She stabbed the ivory handled Spanish lace fan at a puff of smelly train smoke that billowed through the open coach window. She flipped the fan to her face and coughed—discreetly, of course, as was proper for anyone who attended Miss Hennepin's Finishing Academy for Proper Young Women of Pittsburg.

How does a lady maintain her composure amidst all these roughneck cowboys? Just look at these men! Armed to the teeth!

Her glance took in the dozen or so male passengers who rested loaded carbines across their laps or fingered heavy pistols strapped to their hips. They swayed in rhythm with the clackety-clack of iron wheels on the steel rails that stretched across the South Texas dry lands. Some stood. Most sat. All scrutinized every clump of cactus and mesquite that rolled by. Such intense interest in the passing scenery made her nervous.

Something wasn't right.

Why all the guns? What are they watching for?

One man who had just boarded the train took a seat in front of Marley and her husband, Abe. He asked his seat companion. "You boys seen any Mexican bandidos up this way?"

"Not yet," the companion said.

"Well, keep your eyes open. That civil war in Mexico is bound to spill over to the U.S. side."

"Already has," a third passenger said. "Them danged bandidos robbed and killed two more farmers over by the pump station just south of here."

"That a fact!" another chimed in.

"Yep. Seems that these so-called bandidos are Pancho Villa revolutionaries turned sour. They's about fifty or sixty of 'em runnin' around loose. They's loyal only to theirselves."

I knew it! I just knew it!

Marley took a deep breath and swallowed the panicky thoughts racing through her mind. She reached up with nervous hands and readjusted her new hat—a bird-like thing perched on a twig, ordered right out of Mr. Sear's 1915 picture book. She fastened the hat to her upswept hair with a thrust of a pearl studded hatpin. When she smoothed the wrinkles of her traveler's dustcoat the brilliant diamond solitaire caught the light and sparkled on her third finger left hand.

The tidying up calmed her and she sat back, lost in thought. *I can't believe I let Abe talk me into this trip. "It'll be a working honeymoon,"* he said. *Some honeymoon! A jillion miles from home in the middle of nowhere. "The last frontier,"* he said. *"Last chance to make it rich."* So, like every other dreamer we invested every penny we have in packs of trade goods and bolts of cloth. *"Gonna peddle up one side of the river and down the other"* he said. *I wanted to go someplace nice with trees and flowers and green grass. Instead, we end up where everything pricks, bites and shrivels in the sun.*

Marley twisted in her seat and peered through the window again at the dreary dusty landscape. *What am I looking for?* The more she thought, the more she wondered. *Is that why all those ragged looking cowboys outside of Weller's Saloon were blasting away at whiskey bottles? "Practice,"* they said. *Practice for what?*

"What are you so fidgety about?" Abe asked.

Marley turned to her husband. "When we were pulling away from Six Shooter Junction, did you see that woman hanging a pistol from her apron pocket?"

"You're letting all this talk about revolution and Mexican bandidos spook you."

"Did you notice her kids? Scared! Where was the husband?"

Abe shrugged. "I don't know, Marley. I reckon these folks have a right to be scared. Some say the bandidos raid cattle ranches and rob country stores on this side of the border in order to feed their armies. Others say they massacre anyone who gets in their way and laugh about it later. They don't-give-a-hoot about the bloodshed and violence one way or another. I sure don't want to meet any of them."

"Is that why these men are so heavily armed?"

"Could be; but the last I heard was that Pancho Villa was more than a hundred miles from here. So there's nuthin' to worry about."

"Oh, no," Marley said. "I'm really wondering do we belong here?" The intensity in her voice edged a note higher. "First, I let you sweet talk me into leaving Miss Hennepin's Academy before I could even finish the course..."

"Well, that—"

"Next, we up and run away to St. Louey and get married without telling our folks!"

"But—"

"Then without so much as a 'bye your leave' we're on a train bound for the end of the world—Texas—Brownsville—the Mexican border... and nobody knows we're headed there!"

"It ain't all that bad, Honey."

"It ain't?" Marley sputtered. The Hennepin veneer vanished. "There's a revolution goin' on and all the men on this train are wearin' pistols! You expect me to raise a decent family in the middle of all these guns?"

Tears welled in Marley's eyes. She threw her arms around Abe's neck. They held each other close as he tried to comfort her. "Oh, Abe. I don't mean to take it out on you. I feel like I'm a character in a dime novel western, only I ain't got a gun in my pocket."

A sudden jolt catapulted both out of their seat. Passenger screams cut through the screech of steel on steel. The coach careened off the track and slammed to a stop. Gunshots exploded all around. Bullets zipped and chipped the woodwork.

Marley sprawled on the floor. She heard shouts outside.

"*Viva la revolución!* Death to all gringos!"

"It's Pancho Villa's bandidos!" a fellow passenger yelled. "They's a whole passel of 'em, and they're packin' guns!"

Marley reared up and saw the man poke his pistol out a window and fire.

Blam! Blam!

He fired four more shots before a brace of bullets crumpled his body in a bloody heap.

Marley popped up like a jack-in-the-box. "My ring!"

"Stay down!" Abe pulled her to the floor as a spray of bullets punctured the window frame above them. "Keep your head low and maybe we'll get out of this alive!"

"My diamond ring slipped off my finger!" Marley protested above the gunfire noise. Abe grumbled. "I thought I told you to notch it down to size before we left St. Louey."

Marley scrambled to her knees. Her hands raked frantically under the seat.

The men in the coach traded gunfire with the bandits until the ammunition ran out. The man seated in front of Marley yelled, "Oh, my God!" His face turned white. He jumped up and dashed to the rear of the coach. "They ain't gettin' me!" The bolt to the lavatory door snapped shut.

The smell of cordite and dust hung in an ominous quiet. Moments passed. Passengers hunkered down between the seats and waited, fearful for what would happen next.

"Aha!" Marley shattered the silence as her fingers gripped the errant ring. "I found it!"

The vestibule door crashed open. Marley snapped upright, still on her knees. She watched two burly men wearing wide-brimmed sombreros and bullet ladened bandoliers storm into the narrow aisle, their pistols aimed at the terrified passengers.

"What's the meaning of this?" one man demanded.

Blam! Blam!

Two pistols smoked in reply. The bullets struck the man's chest and propelled him through an open window.

"Now then, *Señores y Señoritas*! You weel place your money and your jewelry eento thees sack." He gave the sack to his companion who prodded loose various "donations" with the tip of his gun barrel.

"But you can't do this!" one traveler protested.

"I do whatever I want, *gringo*."

Blam!

Marley choked, horrified.

"Hold fast!" Abe hissed.

The wounded man collapsed in the aisle.

One of the bandits said something in Spanish to his partner who moved to the lavatory compartment. He put his ear to the panel, then stood back and fired three shots through the door. A loud thump answered from the other side.

Marley let out an involuntary gasp. The still smoking pistol whirled towards her and Abe.

"What 'ahve we here?" The bandit's chevron shaped mustache twitched. Without taking his eyes off them, he bent and picked up the Spanish lace fan peeking from under the seat. "Perhops thees pretty thing belongs to the *Señorita?*"

"Y-yes," Abe stammered, "My *esposa.*"

"How nice. You espeak Spanish?"

"Yes. Uh—*sí!*"

"An' you are married." A gold tooth flashed in a leering grin of otherwise all white teeth. He examined the fan closer. "Perhaps you are from *España, sí?*"

"*Sí!*" Abe lied. "Very Spanish."

The bandit cocked his pistol and placed it against Abe's head. "Then you would favor Carranza, as *el Presidente de Mexico?*"

"Ulp! - Of course!"

The pistol pressed harder against Abe's head. The bandit's eyes narrowed to glints of steel. "Perhops you weel shout, *'Viva Carranza'?*"

"Indeed. I – I will."

Marley froze with fear. Yet, from somewhere outside her, she heard a calm detached voice say, "Abe, give him some money. Maybe he'll go away."

The gunman whipped his pistol toward her and snarled. "*Sí,* I take your money, an' thees pretty ring, too!"

His hand clamped onto Marley's wrist. She closed her fist so the ring would not shake off her finger and wrestled in a vigorous non-Miss Hennepin manner.

"Abe - unh! Help me!"

Abe leaped to grab the bandit's arm. The pistol swung toward him. Marley deflected the swing, but Abe's head collided with the gun barrel.

Blam!

The gun discharged harmlessly but knocked him out cold.

"*Ey, Paco! Vamanos!*" The shout from outside diverted Paco still struggling with Marley. Without releasing his rough grip, he shoved her to the seat. He leaned through the window and shouted back. "*Què pasa?* What's the matter?"

"*Los Rinches* – the Rangers. They are closer than we thought. They come. We go. *Pronto!*"

Marley took advantage of the distraction and with her free hand reached up and grasped the hatpin. She jammed it into the bandit's buttock.

"Aiyeech!"

Paco recoiled in pain. He grabbed his rear with both hands and thumped his head back against the window frame. With all her might, Marley rammed her body against the bandit. Paco nose-dived out the window.

The outlaws saw Paco somersault head over heels and land on his rump. They laughed. One jeered. "Ah-ha, Paco, you always fall for the pretty ones."

Marley did not feel very pretty just then. Her disarrayed hair tumbled about her face. The hat and the bird-like thing lay crushed on the floor, its severed stiff wing scuffed under the seat.

Paco scowled. He did not feel "very pretty" either. Someone plopped a sombrero on his head and two of his mounted friends laughed so hard they nearly fell off their horses. In between laugh spasms, they managed to reach under his armpits and scoop him up onto a waiting saddle. He shook his fist at her. Then, inexplicably, he grinned, waved, spun his horse around and galloped away, laughing.

"Of all the nerve," Marley said, astonished with Paco's audacity. "Laughing. After all this…this carnage!"

Abe groaned. She knelt and cradled his head in her lap. She had wondered how she would adapt to this raw untamed border frontier. All considered, not too bad. She and Abe were still alive. She still had her diamond wedding ring. She found an intestinal strength she never knew she had.

Most of all, Miss Hennepin would have been proud. *The hatpin!* Her voice echoed in Marley's mind. *A lady of class never leaves home without one…especially, since there ain't no gun in my pocket.*

ALL IN THE FAMILY
By Janice Workman

I knew, as soon as I caught a whiff of the carcass, that it wasn't any animal. It was my Uncle Chago

A deteriorating garden shed in an over-grown yard near the city limits housed a fairly recent burial site, which had town folk in a dither. At least, until our forensic pathologist (and part-time funeral director), Ms. Blackwell, declared the bones to be, "Not human." On weekends, I helped Ms. Blackwell with whatever odd jobs needed being done. She preferred to be called "Doctor", but since I was the one that showed her the advertisement in the back of Mom's Woman magazine about "…getting your diploma for only $25.00 and a genuine gold seal for just $30 more", she never corrected me.

This particular Friday, Ms. Blackwell actually called the house, "Would you start the clean-up tonight? I know it's not a school night, and there will be a little something extra if you can get started right away. Oh, and stop by Jesse's Hardware on your way in. They're having a sale on those ratcheted loppers I like so much. Might as well get two. Put it on the account."

I used to think she really liked gardening until the first time I saw her use those things. Ratchets make cutting through a breastbone so easy a child could do it, but the Fisker's salesman wasn't interested when I suggested an ad campaign featuring alternative uses for their products.

Any way, the moment I opened the door to the autopsy/embalming/store room and employee lounge, I understood her hurry. I also understood her absence. *Chupacabra* give off a particularly foul odor in death, which doesn't dissipate even with the body processed down to the bone. For those with olfactory excellence or familial connections, each whiff carries unique sulfuric undertones as individual as snowflakes. Nuances of Chago were heavy in the air.

I never really thought of my uncle as 'different'; he was just "Chago." Whenever he morphed at a family barbecue after a few too many *Dos Equis*, or licked drippings from the fajita platter waiting for the grill, Mom said, "There's one in every family." She just never defined what that 'one' was. It wasn't until I was in my early teens Mom thought to explain our family tree, warts, skeletons and all. I'd already figured out most of it and Chago even filled in some blanks.

"The moment I saw your Auntie Rosa, I wanted her. As soon as she turned 15, we married. She is my one true love. She is my heart," he would say, with a tenderness reserved for her.

I never heard her say anything bad about him or to him either. Even after barbecue fiascos and weeklong disappearances, she would snuggle up to him, calling him, "My Chupa Rosa," which never failed to bring blushes and giggles from folks in earshot.

Chago was a salesman. I'm still not real sure what he sold. He would travel to far-off lands I only read about in National Geographic at the city library. "South America is perfect for me," he told me one summer after several months worth of postcards with exotic stamps collected in my dresser drawer. I never worried about losing my favorite uncle to his wanderlust. He fell in love with just about every country he visited, but he always came back home to the Rio Grande Valley and his Rosa.

"Why is that, Tío?" I asked.

"The people that live high in the mountains understand about my kind." He paused, accepting a mug of strong coffee Mom brought in, inhaling its fragrance with obvious pleasure before taking a sip. "Not like Russia," he said. "*Pendejos* with crazy ideas about vampires, werewolves and bats. Bah! I think the cold and vodka has gone to their heads."

Mom chuckled. We had heard his rants about being lumped in with creatures of the night for months after he returned from Moscow.

I don't think anyone really knows how *Chupacabra* evolved. Even Chago said he wasn't sure, but stories about shape-shifters, Aztec Indians, a beautiful princess and an eternal curse had been handed down through generations. "I don't know about any curse," he would say, with a wink and a smile toward Rosa. "But I've got a beautiful princess."

The first time he heard the theory of a spaceship crashing to Earth, stranding alien beings whose pets sucked blood from livestock for miles around, I thought we were going to lose him. He laughed so hard, his face turned blue and he couldn't catch his breath. I was struck by the irony of the moment a few years later when I saw a photo of a dead *Chupacabra* discovered outside a ranch in Texas. The beast was about the same color of blue, but it wasn't a *Chupacabra*.

The local newspaper published reports of attacks on various farm animals in the surrounding communities over the years, but Uncle Chago was usually out of the country, so I am sure it was a coyote, wild dog pack, or even bored gangs looking to stir up trouble.

In all my 17 years, I never saw him go after a goat, or any animal for that matter, seeking blood. Sure, he'd join us for *cabrito* at our Easter barbecue, opting for rare over well done. I know Mom would save choice organs and cook up blood pudding for him to take home afterwards, but there was never any of the slashing violence so often portrayed in legends. He would shape-shift when he got real tired, or as a prank to liven up a party, but never to scare anyone.

I looked at the jumbled skeletal remains and sighed, wondering what and how to tell my Aunt Rosa. "Mom," I said, into the phone clenched in my right hand. "Mom, it's Tio Chago. "No…" I said after a moment of confusion, "I'm not Chago. He's here…or at least his bones are." I think Mom must have been expecting this, or else it came from raising two teenagers because she was so calm.

Uncle Chago fit perfectly into an empty cardboard box stamped on all four sides with skull and crossbones, "Formaldehyde" and "Do not ingest." Finishing up, I switched off the light, left the ventilator fan on low and headed out to the car.

Driving up to our house, I saw Mom, Dad, Rosa and my dog Max, sitting on the porch in the yellow glow of the bug light.

"I knew this day would come," Rosa said quietly, as she patted the box next to her on the glider. "He kept taking those trips to Europe. We'd talked about the risks, but he wanted to go, so I didn't try to stop him." She sighed and looked out into the night. "He wasn't so much a *chupacabra* as he was a *chupavaca*. He just loved that beef… Monday night football with the Dallas Cowboys and fajitas…He was a real Texan…."

"But Tia Rosa, what…" I interrupted her musings, only to have Mom shush me with 'the look'.

"Mad cow, that's what." Aunt Rosa said. "He wasn't feeling well after his last trip to Britain. Oh, there'd been talk from some of his brothers about a strange illness that was taking the *chupa* overseas, but we didn't make the connection until…" Her voice trailed off. "When he came home last month, he said he was off red meat for good but it was too late. I guess that's why he left that way." She sighed again and wiped her eyes with a crumpled tissue. "We'll bury him in the back under the mesquite, next to Old Blue and Dixie. They'll keep him company until I join him."

"I've already called the family and they should all be in by tomorrow." Mom said, as she laid a hand on Tia's shoulder.

"Even cousin Leonard?" Dad asked, casting a glance upwards. "With the moon in full?"

"Even cousin Leonard," Mom said. "It's been a while and he wants to pay his respects. Besides, there haven't been any "Big Birdman" sightings in the Valley for a while."

"That'll be nice," Rosa replied, with a sad smile. "My Chupa Rosa would have liked that."

"Big Birdman?" I asked. "What are you…?"

"Never mind, son", Dad said, cutting me off. "That's another story for another day."

"BARBAS DE ORO"
(Goldenbeard)
By Julieta Corpus

He snakes around the Pecan trees
Just waiting to be called.
A whistling tune's the incantation
Which galvanizes into action this God of Latin lore.
A midnight cry awakens him
To ready for quick flight—
And creatures with wings open their eyes,
Frail musical notes weave lullabies
To carry him off with much delight.

GOLDENBEARD! GOLDENBEARD!

The voice comes in waves, reaching his ears,
As he soars above green onion fields
And water so blue it makes him sigh.

BARBAS DE ORO! BARBAS DE ORO!

Delightfully swift he glides along,
Each star lines his path: diamonds so rare.
Old magic's at work, pushing him through—
Forgotten no more, this God of Air.
The summons await; he's now a blur.
The tall grass below shivers, then swoons.
An old being of light who has returned.

He winds through tall buildings—
Shrines to new gods.
Unbidden, an image of how it was:
Ripe fruit and incense, sweet offerings,
Bold dances of praise—he hears his name:

BARBAS DE ORO! BARBAS DE ORO!

He winks at the young moon, who looks back in pity,
And onward he flies to Weslaco City,
Where one girl remembered
To utter the spell
Which brings forth the breezes
That the heat do quell.

BARBAS DE ORO! BARBAS DE ORO!

Goldenbeard feels worshipped.

BARBAS DE ORO! BARBAS DE ORO!

At last the call's answered, a mission accomplished.
He's made the leaves giggle; he can feel adored--
One God resurrected from the ashes of memory
By the strength and power of the spoken word.

BROWNING
By Eugene Novogrodsky

Leave the city green to see the drought,
To the country's brown ....

Three goats bite for stubble.
Six hens scratch for stubble.

A funeral procession,
A hundred or more vehicles, lights on,
To the dry dirt heaped graveside.

Vehicles without lights, restless
To pass the procession, which is
Guided by deputies in air-conditioned cruisers,
Lights flashing.

All the vehicles, AC on, blocking
Heat and dry dust.

"He died in June," she says.
"Then my horse strangled," she adds,
"A week later."

Graves, people, horses, dry,
Dirt above ...wind steady,
Sending dust ....

CARNIVAL WORKER QUITS
By Eugene Novogrodsky

Thin, stringy hair,
Cigarette smoke around
His long skinny arms, jeans,
Backpack…

From desert ranch Nevada
To Deep South Texas,
And carnival work, south to north…

"That's it! After years…
I'm going back home.
I fixed one too many carny rides.
Time to get back."

He looks at Deep South Texas,
Dry and flat and dusty…
All the carnivals far off until Winter.
He's back.
He'd started the year in the Rio Grande Valley,
Quit in Amarillo…

"You know, a circus puts its animals away at night.
But the carnival lets us out…
We're the animals."

Charming Sylvia
By Cynthia Aleman Marx

I had just decided that I was the only "crazy old lady" who walked alone along my new street when I saw her.

She came every day at the same time past my house, gliding briskly under overhanging trees: her long skirt covered a graceful gait. Her chin arched up to honor yellow Mandeville vines as their golden trumpet flowers climbed the aged Rio Grande Ash trees. From under her ladylike straw hat, big dark eyes and fair high cheekbones traveled up and over the wanton vines to the calm of the native velvet green Coyotillo at its base. Wordless, we connected: her eyes and mine, smiling at the gleaming freshness. It had rained last night. In this former delta of the Rio Grande, many rivers used to water the land. Now, a drought. No rain for months. For me, too: my best friend had moved her family to Seattle for her husband's job. Dear Winifred died. Ann moved away. German boyfriend was in Europe. We might as well call our generation the Leavers, not the Baby Boomers.

"I'm Sylvia, from around the corner," her smile, as elegant as her slender walk and soft voice.

"I'm Cynthia," I said. "Good for you, to walk so faithfully, every day. Mind if I join you sometime?"

"Yes, but...." She trailed off, seeming to give up.

I was on my way to work, and could not stop to talk. For weeks, we waved as we passed. Then, one day, a quick compliment and small talk. My dogs conducted the introductions, sniffing, panting smilingly, and wagging their middles politely in her direction, waiting to be stroked. Sylvia lived a few blocks away. It seemed she liked what I liked. Boundaries down, she was soon inside with me, sipping iced tea while the dogs cooled their tongues. I made us all a snack. Exhausted from the hot walk, I asked a few polite, open-ended questions, and was glad to just sit and listen to her hushed voice, telling her story, praising the dogs.

Some people tell their story so well that one almost forgets: there must have been others in that story who took a different perspective. With Sylvia, I slipped out of total gullibility early, when my white wolf picked up her head from the floor and looked over at her. Something funny here: the intensity mounted. Answering her questions, I felt suddenly strained and frightened for her. Clearly she was being abused, and her partner Lawrence, too—financially, emotionally, and physically. How could she still be as calm as she seemed, and not fight it — not fight for her rights, for justice, and safety? I wondered. Clearly, she needed some moral support and legal help. We started with the basics: did she have a plan, an escape plan, a support network? Yes, I would be her friend. I would try to help. Before we knew it, dark had fallen. She said she needed to return to her three dogs and the many cats she had to feed. We walked her to the corner and entrusted her to the quiet dark.

Big protective dogs are such a comfort, especially when we feel uneasy about someone a bit strange, someone who knows where we live, and has spent some time inside our boundaries. Pleasant as my new friend was, she seemed to stress our common passions a bit too intensely to be real. No one is that close, that quick. She dropped by for tea, and eventually became a regular at my Sunday night dinners, for weeks and months. But no invitation to her house ever came.

Driving by the street where she lived, I finally slowed down one day to check out her house, wondering why I hadn't been invited. Probably my dogs: she said hers weren't trained yet, and mine chased all cats except our own. What I saw was so incongruous with this punctual, neat, lovely lady's appearance that I asked her twice again, tactfully, which house was hers, blaming my own memory. Truth began its snakelike emergence: this lovely creature appeared to be at home with two rusty, broken down vans, old car seats outside them, and an old red sports car, along with half open bags of trash, and huge piles of ugly junk needing organizing.

She appeared when I stopped, more curious and in a state of shock than friendly. "Oh no," she said. "You can't help me get it picked up! I'm going to sell it on E-Bay!"

I headed back to clean my hands with disinfectant wipes and blow my nose from laughing at this eBay delusion. I even wiped off the dogs.

I thought, (me, the Perfect Person, too quick to judge others, of course,) Sylvia had an irrational dog and cat fetish, hoarded junk, and was poorer than she could admit, much poorer than her speech, obvious education, and upbringing suggested. She claimed she had "several properties." When she'd be gone for a week or so— suddenly missing from her walks—I presumed she was an independently wealthy eccentric who didn't keep house anymore. Quite a few feminists I'd known had given it up, disowning housework along with their husbands. My own house was far from perfect. Each time Sylvia came over after that, I modeled some housekeeping and casually asked for her help. She made herself quite useful in exchange for the meals I cooked for her, addressing all my Christmas cards from my lists, and generally moving toward what I thought was better emotional health. She even helped me clean a little. Any day now, I'd see her front yard cleaned up.

No such luck: we cannot change others. It's hard enough to keep our own side of the street clean. On my street, things were better: a few of the neighbors actually came out to introduce themselves as I passed. Two other mamas spoke to me although most of our grown children had long lived elsewhere. They were my comrades in arms with saws. After the hurricane in July of 2008, we sawed together to take my Sugar Hackberries off their carports and driveways. These strong single women came to me as a committee. They voiced their approval of a man who sought work in our neighborhood: who piled tree debris three stories high for the City to pick up.

In our labors, one mama from down the street, who had seen me walking with Sylvia, insisted that my new friend was completely insane. "I was friendly with her, too, at first," she said. "But she's crazy...completely loco. You'll see."

I responded calmly, though my heart flip-flopped down to my knees. "I'm sorry to hear that. Thanks for telling me. She seemed to really need a friend, and I doubt she would hurt anyone. Still, I think I know what you mean." She wouldn't give me any advice, adopting the sometimes beneficent Anglo way of non-interference—the way I regret I've lived most of my life...detached. You tell the truth as you see it, don't force it, and go away. I've never seen that neighbor since.

But Sylvia kept coming, every Sunday, and then more often. We sifted through my aging wardrobe, donated to resale shops, organized old photos, talked and had fun, created a Facebook site for her, and joyfully reconnected her with three high school friends. We went to the movies, walked, and had the loveliest time that I remember with more fondness than most times with my special women friends.

She ate ravenously, and eventually trusted me enough to admit that she had no money. "For now!" she said. "But I'm suing them." Her inheritance had disappeared, probably from the dropping stock market. Her view was that her broker, whose Social Security number appeared on some forms, had stolen most of her money.

I explained patiently about the market drop and waited for acknowledgment of the truths I thought I knew. But only my food and tea seemed to win her acceptance. If at first you don't make sense, change the subject. I asked about her chic clothes. We exchanged the best resale shop stories. I enjoyed her lovely Spanish. Though she looked Anglo, or maybe French, it turns out her mother was Mexican and never spoke English. She drilled me gently on a few key Spanish phrases I wanted. I gave up trying to stuff her mind with my logic, and put her trash out of my mind—this lady had too much class to do such work.

But I couldn't let her change the subject again. After a few months of nearly weekly meals, I insisted she clean up her yard. It was a health hazard. She ignored me for a few weeks. When I called her neighbor (she had no phone of her own except an emergency cell phone she could or would not even set the voice mail for) I learned the sad facts. She had no water at her house, due to a mysterious act of vandalism (from her ex-, I wondered), or from non-payment of water bills. What great cruelty in this hot climate would destroy someone's access to water? She had spoken of Lawrence, her older companion, for whom she had cared faithfully for years, whose distant family members came to take him away. When I met Sylvia, they had just taken Lawrence, along with her financial accounts. Only recently were her savings and checking accounts restored to her.

After I persuaded the neighbor that I really cared about Sylvia and wanted to help her, she disclosed that Sylva had spent several weeks in the psych ward and not "visiting our properties out of town." No one was supposed to know. If she had broken her leg, or arm, we'd all know. But a broken heart, and the tumorous logic of paranoid thinking and inaction, or being prevented from acting, landed this lovely creature in the cold, rough seas, and bitter poison, of loneliness, without a paddle, in a poverty she didn't understand.

Her paranoia was so intelligent, gentle and pleading. I began to believe in it and urged her to change lawyers. She did get her money back from Lawrence's two stepchildren, who had never spent more than a few years in his household. She kept coming to visit me, and I wanted to deceive myself into thinking my friendship was therapeutic. She would teach me to speak better Spanish, and I would teach her German. She imagined we would travel to Austria, even to Switzerland. Then she found the letters: long, beautifully written love letters from my German friend, a man I had loved long from afar and in some tender, intense trysts. Sylvia thought herself German and wanted to learn German. When my German lover called, she tried to speak to him with a few German phrases I had taught her. He humored her, flattered by her attention.

I build each of my friends up to each other, wanting to form my own instant community. I fantasize a lot about help with the yard and dogs in our "commune." So, when he came a few weeks later, I teased and bragged that he was so handsome that she would steal him away.

Perhaps it would be good for them both, I thought. Of all the intelligent people I knew, here were the two I wanted to help the most, two who had not worked for years, but had many talents. What abuse or perhaps excessive coddling had made both these people able to work well only "under supervision," who lacked autonomy and maturity to develop their own work? I took them both out to a new restaurant, which featured cuisine from India, with terribly slow service, due to its unanticipated and sudden popularity. Indian in South Texas…magic.

During the long wait before dinner, they talked constantly, right past me, playing my game of "what was your favorite place for a date in Europe?" I suspected that her favorite places were made up. A few "consistency" questions established a truth that I silenced with the lentil bread, the Indian Papadam. Their eye contact began to last longer than the conventionally acceptable three seconds, and I saw the love lights begin to shine. I endured a slight regret at the loss I would soon feel, and the relief of my worries for both, a fantasy of relief, a self-deception, thinking myself immune from attachment and even love…ready to move on with my life, ready to find a different adventure.

Worrying that I was not making much progress in changing either, I wanted to change myself onto a different track. I crossed the line. Acting out a temper tantrum, I threw him out and sent him to her, wounded, needy, and enchanted. I left them alone, and as in many terrifying instances in my life, I got what I had wanted too much and lost what I had. After I learned they had acted on their initial infatuation, ashamed of the truth of my intuitions, too strong to resist, I crashed. In my shock, I took charge of my own desires and threw my German boyfriend out of my heart. I cleaned house and told Sylvia it was all over between us, and with her. He wrote to me a thank you note a few weeks later that "being with her was no pleasure," but from this I had to notice again the basic true premise… they had been together.

Burdened by both, now I needed relief. They would surely help each other, since both had key problems in common. That was good. My sorrow at losing him had a good end. But no such luck. As the cliché says, you can lead a horse to water, but you cannot make him drink. After a brief fling with Sylvia, he returned to the well-watered forests of northern Ohio. Never envious, I adjusted to our South Texas drought. Grateful, I drank lots of water just for myself. No wine. I wanted to remember this. Blissfully free of the burden of bringing sanity to two dear souls without it, I was happy to take out the trash myself. I fed and watered the right number of grateful dogs and my old conscientious cat. I mulched the plants and trees I have planted, and admired the brave flowers that can accept the universe as it is, and bloom where they're planted—sometimes even without companions—in a drought.

Finally, it rains. Then night falls. I sit without having to speak and watch stars through arching palm branches, as the great life-saving pleasure dome of Heaven covers us all.

Her yard is clean now: the vans and car are gone…someone called the Health Department. The memory of Charming Sylvia lives on. I like to keep her there, in the yellow, flowering past, in the cool breezes we breathed together. Surely she has not forgotten, like everyone else, the gourmet meals I fixed—perfect in their uniqueness, and never made again quite like that. What we cook up in our heads might be even stronger than memories. Old fears, dreams, and loves often trump all logic. I worked over all the reasons why I should trust my own reason, and never again open my heart, my checkbook, or refrigerator, to those two overly needy souls. Only my dogs and cat appreciate my gourmet fish and soups, as I sit alone. From the wall in the Family Room, "Grandma Graves" needlepoint motto speaks to my condition each day: *Heat not a furnace for thy foe so hot, that it doth singe thyself!* And, *He who does not take, when once it's offered, shall never find [it] again.*

CHICLE NEGRO
By Irene Caballero

There is a substance known, and this is no assumption,
Petroleum-based in form, not meant for our consumption.

Throughout this cultured region, though, some unknowns are still taboo,
But ask about the black gum, see what comes back to you.

"Chicle Negro," as we called it, washed upon the sandy shore,
Surely, remnants of an oil rig, although I'm not quite sure.

You take it and you rinse it. The sand grit gives it texture.
You take some Crisco shortening, and concoct a tasty mixture.

Your jaws will get a work-out—addicting, some would say,
Though research hasn't proven that it's bad in any way.

Such flavors you have not indulged yourself in until now,
But it's likely that this blackened treat won't wreak havoc on the Dow.

Packaging ideas... went south, of that I'm sure.
Too bad, but thank you, Exxon, for not mining manure.

CORDUROY COVERALLS
By Bidgie Weber

How they came to be here, I'll never know,
These old corduroy coveralls from years ago.

But there they are in a neat little clump,
In the back, on the bottom, of Grammy's old trunk.

These old pants once fit my brother just right.
Then I wore them till they were much too tight.

They had no zipper to get caught in your shirt,
Just buttons you could move as you grew in girth.

Now, why do you think at this particular time
I've found these old pants and remembered they were mine?

Well, I know why and I'll tell you all.
First, let me see what I recall.

See this hole in the knee?
Tore that on a nail I didn't see.

And here, see the cuffs and how they're frayed?
They drug in the dirt when we ran and played.

In those I was Roy Rogers, Gene Autry and Tom Mix.
I rode on a horse made from a stick.

They've been to Dodge City and silver mines,
Explored Tarzan's jungles, been on mountain climbs.

They've stowed away on a space ship to the moon
And played pirates in many a sand dune.

Wait! What's this in the bottom of this pocket?
Why, it's a tarnished old locket.

I remember when it was found,
A treasure buried in the ground.

Precious memories brought through time,
Caught in Corduroy that once was prime.

Now here is what I'm going to do.
These Corduroy Coveralls are a gift to you,

So that, someday when you're all grown,
You can share these memories with a child

CROWDED
By Charlene Moskal

Small groups…a few children, some singles reading, others on laptops, some sleeping, waiting for departure, almost every seat taken…crowded. Three flight attendants looking tired with make-up fading, an old woman with a demanding grandson, a young woman with the requisite i-pod and the young man with wrinkled clothes and a beard.

He is Arabic or Pakistani, maybe Indian. Ascetic looking, thin, he has a backpack and a skateboard. He seems to alternate between nervousness and boredom. I am suspicious; I tuck my Star of David under my collar. I wish I didn't feel this way but the simple fact is, I do. I tell myself I'm being ridiculous; it doesn't help. I tell myself he's been checked through security but it doesn't work. I tell myself it's only paranoia raising its cobra head swaying to my fear. Terrorists have done their job well building cities of mistrust.

The young man gets up and goes to the counter in front of Gate # 17. When he approaches the attendant he doesn't say anything, he looks at her and returns to his seat. He appears jittery. He yawns.

He is wearing a plastic name tag; Eddie something. From where I'm sitting, I can't make out the last name. The picture shows a full faced, clean-shaven Eddie. He, on the other hand, has a thick, dark mustache and goatee. The sides of his cheeks and the under side of his jaw show new growth; the stubble only recently coming in as if his appearance doesn't count. He removes the tag and puts it in his shirt pocket. He leans his head against a pillar, eyes closed, hands locked in front of him. I notice he is wearing a wedding band. I'm waiting for my flight to leave from Gate # 18; I don't like the thought but I hope his Gate is 17.

I really dislike the story I've developed about passenger Eddie. I dislike the circumstances that have pushed me to believe this man is dangerous. I want to create a new story for him. Okay...he's very bright, a computer geek, a brilliant mathematician going home to his wife and children and friends and savory cooking and the mosque. He works for Bill Gates or a university or maybe a think tank or maybe....

He's on the telephone; no accent at all and he's talking to someone telling them what his plans are for tomorrow. Thank God, I'm wrong. I almost feel as if I ought to apologize to this Eddie. Of course, I don't, after all I'm not crazy. I'm just an American in an airport waiting to line up at Gate 18.

DEATH COMES WITH A VIEW
By Don Clifford

Plastic I-V tubes rattled against the bedstead as the emergency room intern restrained the struggling 80-year old retired Air Force officer.

"Gol dang it! Set me up straight!"

"Easy, Colonel. You've been in a bad accident."

"Well, if I'm to die, damned if I'll do it flat on my butt! Now, get me up! That's an order!" The more Colonel Justin McQueen struggled the more his arms flapped uncontrollably, threatening to loosen the bandages around his upper chest.

"Let him sit up," Doctor Mordechai Jones said as he entered the room. "He can't hurt himself any more than he is."

The colonel relaxed and let the intern adjust the brace around his neck and crank the bed to where he sat upright in relative comfort. "Thanks, Doc," McQueen said. "Now what's this all about."

"For someone who survived a horrendous five-car pile up, you are remarkably lucid," Doctor Jones said. He held up to the light an x-ray chart that outlined the colonel's skull. "There's a tiny piece of steel lodged near the pineal gland that needs to come out or at best you will likely be paralyzed for the rest of your life."

"At best? How about at worst?"

The doctor just shook his head. "It's too close to the spinal cord."

"Is that why I can't control my arms?"

Partly," Jones said. "Obviously you can twist your torso about, but I don't recommend it. One more slip of that piece of steel and it's wheel chair forever."

"Aw, c'mon, Doc. I've survived worse than this."

"Your medical records certainly bear that out. According to them, you've led a charmed life." Jones flipped through the thick volume of charts, graphs, and reports that accumulated during the colonel's lifetime. "Ah, here it is," he said. "I thought I recognized your name. I was in the medevac chopper that hauled you out of Khe Sanh."

"Long time ago," the colonel said.

"Yes. You were lucky. I suppose that's why I remember you. When that artillery barrage blew off the tail of your C-130 cargo plane, you crashed into one of the bloodiest battles of the Vietnam War."

"They told me I should have died with the rest of my crew."

The doctor closed the volume and on a fresh order sheet scribbled some notes. "I'll have the neurosurgeon stop by and examine you."

"Can you do something about these four walls? Can I look out a window, or something?"

"I can help with that." A beautiful lady in a nurse's uniform entered the room. An inner glow radiated from her, as she seemed to glide to the colonel's bedside.

Doctor Jones frowned. "Thank you, Nurse. Don't believe I've had the pleasure of working with you...yet, you look familiar."

The nurse smiled as she plumped the pillows behind the colonel's back. "With your doctor's permission, we will wheel out to the veranda. Today's cloud pattern promises a stunning sunset."

McQueen stared, thoroughly captivated by her beauty and comforting manner. "Sounds good to me."

The doctor took one last look at the colonel's chart. It was then that he remembered where he had met the nurse...Khe Sanh. During those bloody days, she tended to the dead and dying with loving care...like an angel. He closed the colonel's medical volume and sighed. "All right. Be careful with him," was all he said as he left the room.

Wobbly wheels whispered clish-clish clish-clish as the nurse and intern rolled McQueen's bed down a corridor painted a bright meadow green. The veranda on the other side of the double French doors was a left over from the days of *genteel noblesse*. When contractors remodeled the old hospital, they left most of the exterior's Southern charm intact.

After the intern left, the colonel said, "Alone at last. I've met you before, haven't I?"

"Our paths crossed often, but only in fleeting moments," she said.

"You're prettier than an angel."

She grinned, enjoying the compliment. "And what do you know about angels?"

"For many years, I searched for you. Why is it that such a beautiful lady like you always disappeared?"

"You're such an old smoothie." She caressed his forehead.

"Yeah, well. Snow on the mountain top doesn't mean the volcano is dead."

With a gentle touch, she pushed back a lock of grey hair. "It's just as well we didn't become involved back then."

"Why?"

"Because we wouldn't be here now."

McQueen was not quite sure what she meant, but he had an inkling. He was quiet for a few moments before he asked, "Is this going to be my last sunset?"

The nurse stroked his cheek. She reached for his hand and held it lovingly against her chest. "Let's enjoy it while we can," she said, and leaned her head on his shoulder.

The view was spectacular. Vivid hues of purple and gold tinged with reds and yellows stained the twilight sky. Neither said a word as they watched in silent communion. When the last ray of sunshine dipped out of sight, she leaned over and kissed the colonel. Her lips lingered on his as the horizon faded to black.

DONALD
By Eugene Novogrodsky

I couldn't help it. I thought of Donald when I saw the woman at 5:00 am poking with a piece of metal into a garbage-filled Dumpster to locate cans – the ping when she found one, and the scraping through the garbage to retrieve the can maybe worth two cents; and when I saw another woman out of a job playing lottery games that cost a dollar…Donald…nearly 40 years ago when he milked his last cow and walked down a dirt road….

Why these thoughts? Because they're so recent. I could go back to men who get off buses at the end of the line, and carry one suitcase into the sunlight, blinking, thinking about cold water, thinking about a bed, thinking about how a government check will reach them now that an address has changed.

But, Donald…?

He milked cows for the Verduns up on the Maine-Quebec border for four years, always with machines – though on other farms on both sides of the border, before World War Two, he milked by hand. That's what he was. Donald, a farmhand. Specialty? Milking machines. But three weeks before he walked down that road – maybe to Bangor and then maybe to Boston – Donald received some bad news, news he knew would come but thought that the Verduns were exempt.

"Donald," said Jack Verdun, a third generation French Canadian farmer who spoke French at home and to the cows, but English to Donald, who despite years around French Canadians, knew only several words. "We sell. Have auction three weeks. Then no more. I go to Connec'cut,

60

build planes with wife brother. All go, wife, kids, me, wife mother, my father. That's it. Sell cows, sell farm, all."

Donald didn't say anything. Jack had walked up to him in the spring's soft twilight, after Donald had moved the cows in from the pasture they enjoyed during the past month, after five months of winter in the barn. Jack had always helped with the morning milking after Donald got the cows in. In the evenings, Donald milked the forty-seven big black and white Holsteins by himself. He also cleaned the barn after he cleaned the milking machines – no breaks, seven days a week – in return for sixty-five dollars, three huge meals, snacks, and a room. That's how it was ever since Donald left a Maine orphanage twenty-five years before. Back then the farmers took him in, and fed him, with no pay. The farmers liked the plan; the State did, too. Most of the orphans didn't, but Donald did.

"Much easier there. Work too much here. Better for kids," Jack said.

"OK, Jack. I got to milk, now."

Jack wasn't surprised that Donald had little to say. He could go days without speaking. But, the other farmers who hired Donald in the past – all French-Canadians – always remarked that he was the best machine-milker on the border…that cows always beat their best production record when Donald worked with them. What's more, the State milk inspectors always gave the farms Donald worked the lowest bacteria counts. Now, I have no idea what will happen to the remaining farms on the border – and there aren't many. Orphanages no longer send teens to farmers. Of those enduring farmers, some employ Mexicans and hope the INS won't deport them. Lately, deportations had risen, and the meager number of farms had reduced some more – no one to work them.

But back to Donald….

He learned to play the fiddle and piano while in the orphanage. With the Verdun family, playing was his only pleasure. During winter nights, Donald would come in from the barn, after cleaning up. His hair was always sleek and brushed. He'd go the kitchen for supper, after the family had eaten; then he'd go into the parlor, where one of the several wood stoves glowed red, and sit at a battered piano and play English and French polkas and waltzes. During the warmer nights, which up on the border lasted from May to September, Donald sat on the front porch and scratched out French and English tunes along with the polkas and waltzes.

Could this life of cows, food, music and deep sleep continue indefinitely? No, of course not. Yet, Donald, as I've said, knew that at least seventeen farms in as many square miles went under the auctioneer's hammer during his short years with the Verduns, but it was something he did not consider.

During the next three weeks, after the twilight milking, machine scrubbing, and barn cleaning, and after the cows were turned out to the sweet grass and dew of the pasture, Donald came into the house, ate some cold bread and lukewarm soup, took his fiddle off the piano, sat on the porch and played. Jack and his wife, Denise, were already asleep in bed as were the six children and the older folks. The fiddle scratched while the crickets chirped. A half hour later, Donald came inside, put his fiddle on the piano, went to his room off the kitchen and slept the brief hours before the early dawn.

Jack said nothing to Donald. While Donald kept up his work with the cows, the Verduns packed everything they had accumulated in the past sixty or so years.

On the Friday afternoon before the auction, Jack said to Donald, "Milk, tonight, like always. Milk tomorrow. After morning milking, auction start. We go Connec'cut tomorrow, late."

Donald, quiet as ever, went to his room and packed his clothes. After the morning chores, he, too, would go, but not to Connecticut, nor to another farm. But where?

That night, the family had not gone to sleep and gathered in the parlor. Donald walked to the piano to get his fiddle. Instead, he sat at the piano and started playing the polkas and waltzes he played during the winters; not just on the Verduns' piano, but on other pianos – pianos that went to antique dealers who followed closely the border farm auctions.

Gradually, Jack and Denise, the children, Denise's mother and Jack's father, and relatives Donald had not seen before – most from interior Quebec -- formed a circle around the piano. As Donald played the *St. Lawrence Waltz*, tears poured from their faces – generations of faces blended in North America for hundreds of years, when English was still a language across the ocean, not yet reaching our shores. He finished the waltzes on the never-tuned tinny piano. With fiddle in hand, he made his way through the faces, the French, the whiskey and cakes to one end of the front porch. He sat in darkness, the view overlooking a valley, where in the shadow of a bear-back looking mountain, Holsteins rested like boulders in the wet thin grass. He started to play – not a waltz, not a polka, but a jig – *Napoleon's Retreat*. The faces stayed in the parlor and before their tears had dried, they nodded up and down in tune with the jig.

As the fading notes of the jig echoed faintly across the moonlit valley, Donald got up, carried his fiddle through the sea of faces and retired to his room.

Jack had paid Donald earlier in the week, plus ten dollars extra. You would think that Donald would leave before the morning milking, before the auctioneer's crew came into the barn, shoo in the cows, and not let them return to the pasture. They would be sold before noon. But, Donald, as usual, herded the cows in from pasture, hooked up the milking machines, milked and then cleaned them. However, with the auctioneer's men milling around, the cows did not go out.

He went to the kitchen, poured himself a cup of coffee and ate a slice of dark bread. The family, outside, stood in the shade of several fully leafed trees. The auction crew set up a tent and chairs for the early birds who came for the sale. His hunger satisfied, he went to his room and got his suitcase and fiddle, now enclosed in a black leather case. He walked outside and started down the dirt road. No one had said a word to him. He looked back once and saw two men push the battered piano onto the porch where the night before he had played the jig.

Today is a long time from Donald and his windblown footprints in the dirt road…footprints that led away from the eighteenth farm sold from under him…footsteps during that middle of the Viet Nam war time, a time that made it easy for border families to go south and make planes, helicopters, weapons and ammunition…easy, except for the tearful memories of music and meals.

I can't see Donald working in those factories, and I can't see him milking cows when farms for miles around had vanished. Neither do I see him poking for cans like that woman in the Dumpster, or spending a dollar in a million dollar lottery. I don't know what I see. Where do people out of orphanages and off farms go? Where did Donald go after he walked the three miles in dirt before he hit the State asphalt?

Footprints vanish on asphalt.

DON'T BET YOUR MULES ON IT
By Bidgie Weber

It was another South Texas winter's day…brutally cold with a heavy, biting damp that kept old men inside and babies in warm beds. Even without the northern snowstorms, the icy fingers of the howling winds could freeze the breath into icicles.

Five old gray haired cronies with bushy whiskers hanging to their shirtfronts sat in a semicircle around the potbellied stove in the Raymondville feed store. All eyes were on the sixth man as he kicked a stool into his customary place so that he could be seen and heard by all.

"Tell us agen 'bout the picture of those mules ya got, Byrd. How'd ya come by such fine mules like them?"

Byrd Clements was a photographer by profession. He was not skilled in the fine art of horse or mule trading. Dude, Shep, Lee, and the boys knew this fact. However, this was a perfect afternoon for a good story. Even though they had heard it many times before, they became all ears again.

As Byrd scooted his stool closer to the stove, he leaned a bit to the left in order to warm his "other" side. "Now, boys, we all know that a prize set of mules standing over fifteen hands high is as good as gold in the bank," he began.

He shifted a little so he wasn't so close to the heat because he didn't want to singe his favorite wool shirt. He continued the tale. "That being the case, and me having TWO pair of mules, you can say that I have a "double digit account!"

He rubbed his hands together and let the friction warm them before he rolled his Bugler. Byrd's audience gave the usual round of belly laughs and the familiar response from Shep, "Guess that makes you' bout as rich as God, Byrd!"

"Right ya are, Shep. Right ya are!" Byrd opened the familiar blue pouch containing strong, sweet-smelling "tobackey". Years of practice made it easy for his yellow stained finger and thumb to pinch out the perfect amount to roll the pencil shaped cigarette. A quick swipe with his damp tongue to the tissue thin paper, a neat little twist to each end, and he was ready to fire it up. He leaned back to continue the story of the mules.

Before he sat down, he reverently removed the framed photo from the wall behind the counter. The soot outline of the frame marked its place of honor in the feed and seed store. Four shiny black mules, each standing fifteen and one half hands high, posed shoulder-to-shoulder dressed in their Sunday finest leather and iron.

"Ah..h.h," breathed Byrd. These were the stars of today's tale. They were his pride and joy.

A second look at the photo brought into focus a figure of a man dwarfed by the huge beasts. Cyris Fullbright stood about six feet behind his team. The knot of reins crowded his massive hands as they snaked over the rumps of the mules and connected to the bit of each animal.

"Lordy, lordy...just look at that Cyris," chuckled Lee.

Cyris, wearing his one and only suit, with his felt bowler placed at a cocky angle on his bald head was puffed up like a toad in a tight sweater. He was fairly busting out the seams of his jacket. He had a look of pride with a hint of arrogance. A feeling of importance shone in his eyes. However, fear overshadowed all the others.

Mutters could be heard from the boys...

"Don't you just know it"

"Oh,, man, ain't he a piece of work"

"Better him than me."

"My camera don't lie." Byrd let his audience absorb that moment in time captured by his camera.

Dude, having seen the picture countless times before, chimed in. "Just lookie at ole Cyris, standin' there...like he BIRTHED them mules all by hisself. He don't know what he's in for."

Byrd let the men enjoy the story a little more. Their looks showed how they felt. "We all know the man's in for the ride of is life."

The looks of admiration and appreciation proved just how much they enjoyed hearing the mule tale over and over again.

Lee, the quiet one of the bunch, took aim at the brass cuspidor in the corner. His aim proved true when he cut loose with a chaw of tobacco and hit the spittoon dead center. He leaned back and searched for a clean spot on his shirtsleeve. He found something that passed for a spot and swiped it across the yellow stained mustache. Hoping that he had cleared any lingering juice from it, he said, "Yep, that's fer sure. He's gonna have one hell-of-a-ride."

"AHHH, Lee, hush and let Byrd get on with it." This came from Dude who had taken it upon himself to be the assistant narrator.

"Y'all know how ole Cyris came to have those four beauties." The men nodded and grinned one and all.

"It's a fact he won them from Minor Hasket in a crooked poker game over at the Full House Saloon."

"He forgot he didn't know one durn thing about mules or horses or farming or log hauling or much of anything except gambling," one of the boys said.

"All ole Cyris could see was gold in his pocket," another one added.

Why, with a team that strong, he could hire out to haul stumps or equipment or clear land. He could hire out to plow fields at plantin' time. The gold would just pour into his pockets."

Anxious for the story to move along, Dude chimed in with, "Yeah, but he sure didn't want to pay a teamster. He was sure plumb dumb about that."

"Don't rush my story, Dude. I'll get to it. The devil's in the details now, ain't it?"

Properly chastised, Dude settled back in his warm spot to let Byrd get on with it.

"Yep, PAYING wasn't what Cyris had on his mind. BEING PAID was the order for his day," Byrd said.

"First he had to have a plan. He decided he'd have posters made up to advertise all over the county that he had the finest and strongest mule team for hire. They'd make short work of any job a person might have."

Byrd chuckled and continued, "Being's I'm the only professional photographer in this area, 'course he came to me to work a deal. I'd photograph those majestic beasts; he'd have the posters drawed up, and nail one on every fence post and barn in six counties. Then we'd split the cash.

Once again, Dude, who just couldn't stop his squirming, blurted out, "How dumb do ya have to be to not know ya just don't grab hold to the business end of a team of mules and take over like ya had good sense? Cyris don't know 'gitty up from sic 'um'." Pleased with his crack Dude waited for the expected chuckles from the group.

"Yep, Dude, that was another thing Cyris forgot," Byrd nodded, "and that's where his big mistake cost him dearly. The day came for the shoot. I loaded up my equipment—expensive equipment, I might add, hitched up my old grey and headed out. Hasket agreed to let me take the picture over at his place. When I got there, everything was all set up."

Byrd picked up the picture again and said, "If you look at this photo real close you can almost see the sweat rollin' down from under that felt hat Cyris had on. Look real close to how he's holding the reins."

"Look at that…his fingers are white as lilies," one of the boys said.

Another one added, "Yea…look at that big vein in his neck poking out above his collar."

Dude coughed. "He was so darn tight in his skin a strong wind could 'a blowed him to pieces.'"

"You gotta hand it to old Cyris though," Byrd continued. "He stood his ground with that team for almost a full two minutes."

The look on each man's face told the story. Each man was thinking the same thing. "Wonder just how long I'd-a been able to stand that ground."

"Ever seen a man talk without movin' his lips?" Byrd asked. "I heard ole Cyris, but I swear I never seen his lips movin'. He told me to shake a leg and do my job so he could relax. Guess ole Cyris didn't account for the time it takes to set up for a good photo.

"His legs were shaking so bad, his knees were knocking 'cause it took me so long to get things ready. And all that time those mules had been perfectly still. Those devils had created a plain and simple case of false security.

"I knew I was set up too close to those animals when I could smell the spit and polish from their leather riggings. But I was gonna get the perfect picture. When I looked up and was eyeball to eyeball with one of 'em, I understood I had placed myself right in the line of fire, ya might say.

"Bad judgment on my part…a last minute decision to shoot at a right angle probably saved me and my camera."

Byrd paused to think on that, but was brought back to the story by a voice, "Com'on, Byrd, what'd ya do then? Get on with it!"

" 'Hold it now!' I started the count down. '1…2…3' Man, when that black powder flashed, all hell broke loose!

"Those four mules reared back all together and bolted, bound for glory. All you could see was ole Cyris locked around the end of those reins. His hat flew off. His head snapped back. His body swung like a flag in a windstorm. Both his arms seemed to get longer right in front of my eyes."

"That musta been 'bout the craziest thing you ever seen, huh, Byrd. Sure wish I'd seen it."

"I can just see old Cyris," Lee chuckled. "He musta looked purty wild as he disappeared in a cloud of Texas dust."

"Yeah, that was quite a day," Byrd agreed. "I got my photo and Cyris got two broken arms, a broken rib, some crushed fingers, and a strained back. When the dust settled around ole Cyris, he made a deal with Minor Hasket on the spot to sell him those mules."

"Is that when ole Cyris went back to gambling?" Shep asked.

Byrd laughed, "Right...with one major change. Old man arthritis set in, and he was forced to deal honest poker hands!"

After a rousing round of belly laughs and backslaps, Byrd picked up the story where he left off. "But that wasn't all. "Must have been about a week after that when Hasket came to call on me. He had not only managed to end up with those mules, but he decided Cyris had a good idea for making money. So, we made the same deal as Cyris and I had.

"There was no way Hasket was going to leave himself open for a major catastrophe like the one he witnessed before. No sir-reee, he had a new plan. When I arrived at Hasket's place, he had those mules ready and all duded up in their Sunday-go-to-meetin' harnesses. It was then that I noticed, instead of holding the reins in his hands, Minor had tied them to the corner post on the frame of what was to become his brand new barn."

At this point in the story, Byrd could no longer talk through all the laughing. Knowing what was coming in the story, the boys were doubled over with belly laughs and foot stomps.

Lee caught his breath and demanded, "Go on, Byrd. Tell us the rest of it. That's the best part."

"Well, you boys oughta seen them mules when the powder went off again! Instead of old Cyris, they had the whole side of Hasket's barn frame in tow."

When the dust settled, there stood Hasket dumbfounded. At that point he announced, "I got some durn good animals and they're yours if ya want 'em and ya can catch 'em."

"And that, my friends, is how I ended up with four of the finest mules in six counties and a photo worth a thousand words!"

Family Reunion
By Robin Cate

You fed on my excitement.
Made me the family fun.
Filled my glass with bubbles
Relished in my troubles.
(And, you whispered.)

I jump started you.
Kept you going
Right through the
Closing' prayer.
(And, you whispered.)

All this until:
My son put a gun
To his head. Then,
You left me for dead.
(But, you whispered.)

Although I never hear from you,
Live in quiet joy, I do.

Heard you
Never leave your bed.
The prisoner of
Temper and clutter.

On dark, dark days
I want to whisper.

FAMILY SECRET
By Verne Wheelwright

There is something of a secret in our family, that I think is true. I'll probably never know all the details. Most of the older relatives deny the stories and seem embarrassed at the possibility there could be any truth in them. Certainly, it was scandalous when it happened nearly a century ago, and might be today.

Maria was still in her teens when she started working in the fields for the Williamson family near what is now Harlingen, Texas. In the early 1900s, the railroads were still laying tracks and building the big steel bridge over the Arroyo and water had started flowing into the Valley through the canals that Lon Hill had envisioned. He was right. The desert soil was fertile, and the Valley already produced crops, including cotton, small fruits and vegetables. Cotton and other Valley crops required a lot of labor to plant, care for and harvest, but field hands just seemed to appear where they were needed.

The border with Mexico was well defined by 1900, but there was little concern for who crossed the border in either direction, so labor from Mexico was natural and spread all over Texas. The landowners needed workers and the workers needed jobs. Maria appeared at the Williamson place and went to work in the fields. If she had a family somewhere, no one knew. Or cared. She spoke English and Spanish interchangeably, switching easily from one to the other.

Despite her youth, Maria proved to be a good worker. Like most of the field workers, she didn't say a lot, but she had a cheerful demeanor and was always in the fields when work was to be done. She wore a large straw hat into which she somehow pushed all her long, dark hair, a long sleeved men's blue work shirt and a long skirt, a field worker's uniform that protected her small form from the hot Valley sun. They were probably the only clothes she owned, as no one ever saw her in anything else. She lived with the other women in a "lean-to," a shed that extended from one side of the Williamson's barn. Whether she was hoeing weeds, planting seed or harvesting, she always worked steadily and usually accomplished more than the others. Not in a competitive sense as much as naturally efficient.

Harold and Jessie Williamson were hard working people. They treated their field workers well, provided good food and paid fair wages - no more than the other landowners near Harlingen, but no less. Their oldest child, Adelia, was already married with two children of her own. Harold, Jr. was also married but lived and worked on the Williamson farm. He worked mostly with the teams of horses, whether preparing the soil for planting or cultivating between rows.

"Jessie," Harold said, one evening not long after the harvest was complete, "we're in pretty good shape. We've got a good farm, money in the bank and no debt. We've given our kids good educations, and this farm should feed all of us well for the rest of our lives."

"Isn't that a satisfying feeling?" she asked. "We really don't have any wants. The good Lord has provided well for us."

"Well, he had a little help from you," he replied, chuckling. "You've worked hard, managing this house, the children, and the crews. All those people that work for us would do anything for you."

"We've been a good team," Jessie said.

Maria and the others had just finished their breakfast and were starting into the fields for the morning. "Miss Jessie?"

"Yes Maria."

"I'll be along in a minute. I need to stop at the shed."

"That's fine, Maria. Would you bring another roll of twine when you come out?"

Jessie went on with the field workers. Harold walked with them to the barn, then went in to hitch the horse to the wagon. He was going into town to talk to the banker, who was offering the Williamsons some adjacent land.

"I'll be back before supper."

Suppertime passed and Harold had not yet returned. Jessie was worried. She had one of the hired men saddle a horse to go see if Harold had broken down or gotten sick on the road. Nearly two hours later, the man returned, driving the wagon, his horse tied to the back. Alone.

"The wagon was at the train station, Miss Jessie. Mr. Harold left it there and took the train to Houston."

Jessie was baffled. Why? What could have happened?

Then she remembered. Maria had not returned to work that afternoon. She went to the shed. Only Maria's straw hat remained.

Maria had never ridden on a train before, and now she was on one, leaving the Valley and riding toward a new life. She was not sure what that new life might be, but she trusted Harold and would go wherever he took her. She wasn't going with him because of passion or a wild love affair. In fact they had never really been alone together for more than occasional conversation, and most of that was about the farm and work. Just two days ago he had talked to her in the field, away from the others.

"Maria, I have a secret. You can't tell anyone. OK?"

"Of course, Mr. Harold."

"I'm leaving. Leaving the family, the farm and the Valley. Starting over. Would you like to come with me?"

She hadn't asked why, but maybe she knew. The preacher had been showing up at the farm more frequently, staying for dinner and having long talks with Jessie. She had seen them near the barn one evening, standing very close, and she had wondered. But that was not her business, and she spoke to no one about it.

"Yes, Mr. Harold. I'll come with you." He was more than twice her age, but that made no difference to Maria. She knew him, trusted him.

"It will be a whole new life, Maria. We'll buy a farm and start from scratch, somewhere far away."

That morning, they waited at the new train depot as the northbound train came into the Harlingen station from Brownsville. It consisted of a steam locomotive, a coal car, one car for baggage and freight and two passenger cars. Leaving Harlingen, the two passenger cars were each just over half full.

Now, Maria was on a train going north toward Corpus Christi and Houston, places she knew very little about. Harold hadn't told her much more yet about their future, but she felt confident, and free. She could make a new life with Harold, or without him if things didn't work out, but she had a good feeling about him. Yet, there was a feeling of guilt that she was with another woman's husband, and really, she wondered, why had she come?

"Maria, we're going to be on this train the rest of the day. We don't really know each other all that well, so anything you want to know about me or where we're going, this is a good time to ask. Once we get to the end of this train ride, we're likely to be pretty busy for a long time."

"Was it because of the preacher?"

Of all the possible questions she might have asked, that was unexpected. He was a little stunned.

"Was it that obvious? I thought I was the only one who saw it, and I was never positive, but yes."

"I doubt anyone else ever thought about it," she said. "Will I be your wife?"

Thoughts streamed through his head. "Damn! She's sure right to the point. What's coming next?"

Gently, he answered. "Yes, Maria. You know, I'm still married, so we can't legally marry, but yes, I'd like you to be my wife. Whatever we build together will be ours, and in case something ever happens to me, it will be yours. I'll have a lawyer see to it."

It was Maria's turn to be surprised. "Mr. Harold, I'm not asking for anything."

"I know that, Maria, but I asked you to come with me, to be my partner and my wife. I don't want you cheated out of everything if something happens to me. You know, I'm almost forty-five, so you'll certainly outlive me. If we don't set it up right, whatever we build could end up with my oldest son. Also, no more 'Mister'. OK? Just Harold."

"OK. From now on, we'll take care of each other, Harold." Maria smiled and thought to herself that this was a good man.

"Maria, it was more than the preacher. That farm had been inherited from Jessie's father, so it was hers. She decided that if something happened to her, Junior would inherit the farm. That could leave me working for my son! I love him, but wouldn't want my life to depend on him."

To his relief, there were no more tough questions. As they rode, they talked, and he realized what a remarkable young woman she was. Barely twenty, she spoke and read English and Spanish. She was clearly intelligent and he already knew she could outwork nearly anyone in the field, man or woman. Moreover, she had a natural ability to lead. Other workers respected and followed her. Now he found that she was charming and interested in everything. She was unfashionably slender, not a "full figured" woman, but he found her beautiful.

They left the train in Angleton. Harold stepped down first then turned and reached up for her hand. Maria reached without hesitation, and as they walked through the station, she put her arm through his. He squeezed with his elbow and they each smiled. They left his bag at the railroad hotel and walked to the bank, where Harold had been introduced by his banker in Harlingen. There had already been some negotiation by mail and they soon chose the farm that would become their home.

A middle-aged woman, recently widowed, wanted to sell the farm and return to her parents' home in Tennessee. The two-story house was sound, with a screened porch. The barn was large and sturdy, and the fields were already fenced and under cultivation. There was enough equipment to get started, and the price was fair.

Almost a year after they settled in, Sallie was born. Two years later Harold Joseph, Jr., nick-named Joe arrived. It seemed no time at all and there were four children. Maria was very happy in her life, but occasionally the feelings of guilt returned. She asked herself why she should feel guilty. Did the pastor who preached the Commandments to his congregation and then flirted with Jessie feel guilt? Just lust. Both of them. Her judgment of the preacher and Jessie generally dispelled her doubts, but they returned from time to time.

Harold did not wait long to fulfill his first promise to Maria. His meeting with Ed Wolters became tense when the lawyer asked, "Why do you want to leave your land to a Mexican woman? Why not leave everything to your oldest son like Texas law suggests?"

Harold had to fight down the temptation to respond in anger. His face flushed briefly while he controlled his emotions then he responded quietly.

"First, this is my decision, not the state of Texas' decision. Second, Maria has never even been in Mexico. Her family was ranching in Texas before there was a Texas. She came to work for me when her oldest brother inherited their family ranch, so she understands Texas tradition. Ed, this woman is my partner in this farm and in every sense of the word.

"Now, there's something else that's really important in this conversation, Ed. I want you to be prepared to protect and fight for her if necessary. Her family will back you up if push comes to shove, but she'd prefer not to ask for help beyond yours. I don't want any bankers or neighbors or anyone else to ever feel they can push her around. Can I count on you?"

Wolters smiled, slightly embarrassed for his bad start. He liked having a client who knew his mind. He also liked having a client with the power to back the attorney's actions. "Harold, I was out of line and I'll not make that mistake again. I came here as an immigrant from Holland so I shouldn't be judging others. Yes, you can count on me in both respects."

"Just one other thing." Harold slid a folded piece of paper across the desk. "If something happens to Maria, and I'm not here, there's how to reach her family."

In the years that followed, Wolters proved himself a capable attorney and a reliable family friend.

Although they had a few bad years, for the most part they benefited from a long growing season with plenty of sunshine and rain. Some years there was just too much rain. They knew the risks. Galveston was not far from Angleton and had been completely wiped out by a hurricane just over a decade earlier.

Harold selected his crops well and usually had enough rice planted during the wet years to pull them through. Despite tough economic times in 1913, World War I gave him markets for everything he could raise. Then, when the war was ending the influenza epidemic came, and he nearly didn't survive. The whole family caught that flu, but Maria and the kids recovered quickly. Harold was very sick and took longer to recover. When he did, he quickly got back into the routine of the farm. He could even laugh when he heard the girls reciting as they jumped rope,

> *I had a little bird,*
> *Its name was Enza.*
> *I opened the window,*
> *And in-flu-enza.*

Walking behind the cultivator, Harold was happy. He had never minded working in the heat. He felt like he absorbed energy from the sun. His straw hat shaded his eyes and the soft leather of the reins looped over his head felt comfortable on the back of his neck.

He walked with both hands on the handles of the cultivator, guiding it as the big mule, Dandy, plodded forward, pulling the cultivator through the earth. Harold watched the cultivator as the tines broke the soil, loosening the weeds, pulling their roots free from the soil, and tearing open an animal's burrow. Before he saw it, Harold had stepped into the burrow.

He jerked his head back to stop the mule, but too late. He cried out from the pain as the forward momentum snapped his lower leg bones. The same force jerked the reins tight on Harold's neck and yanked his face into the cross bar of the cultivator. He never heard the sound of his neck breaking and was dead before his body fell to the ground.

Dandy stood in front of the cultivator, waiting for Harold's command, or the pop of the reins signaling him to move on.

When Harold didn't come in at midday, Maria walked out to remind him it was time to wash up and eat. Take a break from the heat.

Dandy was standing in front of the cultivator...then she saw the broken, lifeless Harold on the ground. She ran to him, too late. He had been gone for hours, but she held him, sobbing.

Maria had two men bring Harold's body to the house, where they put him on the bed. She sent one of the men into town to get a pine coffin, while she washed and dressed Harold. Afterward, she lay on the bed and held him, crying until she fell asleep, exhausted. "It wasn't fair," she told herself. He had survived the great influenza epidemic, though she had wondered if he would, and now this. Just because of a varmint's hole in the ground.

The neighbors came the next day, and the preacher asked, "Will you bury him here on the farm, Maria?"

"No, pastor, I'm taking him home to his family."

The preacher thought to himself that this was remarkable, and that Harold's parents must be quite elderly.

As she rode on the train with Joe, the words of a song kept passing though Maria's mind. The song was *In the Baggage Car Ahead,* and that's where Harold was. She couldn't stop remembering the lines:

As the train rolled onward, a husband sat in tears
Thinking of the happiness of just a few short years
Baby's face brings pictures of a cherished hope now dead
But baby's cries can't awaken her in the baggage car ahead.

She held back her tears with difficulty. Joe took his mother's hand, and from time to time they would both cry silently, holding each other. When he asked her why they were taking Daddy on the train, she told him that this was what she must do, that there were other people who loved him.

When they reached the station in Harlingen, a wagon was waiting for them and the pine casket was quickly loaded. Maria asked the driver to take them to Jessie's farm. Now, she became uneasy. She did not know what Jessie might say or do. She didn't know what she would say herself, but she knew she had to do this. As they rode in the wagon, she learned from the driver that Jessie had remarried several years ago, and not to the preacher.

Maria decided she should be prepared for anything to happen when she arrived, and told the wagon driver to turn the wagon in the loop in front of Jessie's home before he stopped the wagon. "Once we're stopped, get down quickly and unload the casket, then get back in the seat and be ready to go. We may be there a while, but we may have to leave in a hurry."

The driver was an older man, probably an ex-cowhand. He smiled and said, "Yes, Ma'am!" This day might be more interesting than he'd expected.

When they pulled into the farm, Maria could see people on the porch. As the wagon drew near, she could see Jessie, standing at the top of the three porch steps. The wagon stopped and Maria stepped down carefully, then held Joe's hand as he came down. They turned and walked toward the house.

Jessie moved quickly down the steps to confront Maria. She was clearly upset.

"Maria! What on earth are you doing here? I don't want you here!"

Maria looked into Jessie's blue eyes, then replied quietly," I don't want to be here and I don't want to hurt you, but it's Harold, Miss Jessie. In God's eyes, he's still married to you. I had to bring him back to you!"

Maria saw that the casket had already been unloaded, and the driver was climbing back into the wagon. No obvious haste. He just appeared efficient.

Jessie softened slightly. She saw the depth of sorrow in Maria's eyes, and understood the reasoning in her words. More, she didn't want to be asked about her re-marriage, so she replied in a more gentle tone, "Maria, we heard he had died years ago!"

They talked briefly, then Maria, still holding Joe's hand turned, climbed back up into the empty wagon and returned to Harlingen. The next day, she and Joe were on their way back to Angleton.

Reflecting on her encounter and knowing that Jessie had remarried long ago washed any remaining feelings of guilt from her mind. When she went away with Harold, she hadn't hurt Jessie, hadn't taken anything Jessie really wanted. Now she realized that Harold had always known that. She still grieved, but there were no more tears.

"I'll miss you, Harold, but we'll be okay."

Epilogue

Maria raised the four children and managed the farm until they were grown and married. She divided the farm equally between them. Maria lived with Sallie and her husband until she died in her early seventies. Her hair was still dark, with no hint of gray. Sallie, lived to over 100. Wolters, the attorney, did in fact protect Maria from men who sought to capitalize on her loss. He knew most of them and anticipated their moves with a warning before they could act, so they didn't.

In the early sixties, not long after Maria's death, Jessie's son Junior, now an old man, located and met Maria's son Joe, his half brother. Maria's family was not aware of Harold's first family, as Joe was very young when his father died and never clearly understood the implications of their trip. Junior died soon after meeting Joe, so the half brothers never met again. It was the next generation, Jessie's great-grandchildren, who researched the family tree. They discovered Harold's second family and contacted Maria's children and grandchildren in about 2000. After more than eighty years, Maria's descendents understood the family secret.

"FAT LOUIE"
By Charlene Moskal

I was probably six or seven and I remember the look on Mother's face at the end of a day out with Daddy—resigned and annoyed, a figurative shrug, headshake and sigh. On those days out, we would have just returned from visiting Daddy's friend, "Fat Louie."

"Fat Louie" was an enigma. He lived in a hotel suite near the flower district on the west side of Manhattan. Somehow, I associate the color green with him; maybe it was the color of the carpet, or curtains or bedspread. The room was large. It had a bed, a table, some chairs and a dresser. I see him sitting in a chair in front of an armature of sorts, which held a canvas. Next to it on a small table was a basket of colored yarns. There sat "Fat Louie" creating petit pointe.

"Fat Louie" lived up to his name. He was on the light side of being morbidly obese. His heavyset face had a swarthy complexion. He had dark eyes that were almost lost in fleshy cheeks. In addition, like my father, he had thinning black hair. His hands were pudgy. "Fat Louie" wore dark trousers, a long sleeved white dress shirt opened at the collar—an ensemble held together by suspenders.

As we visited he would select his yarn and work the needle with great speed and concentration turning the canvas fabric into a bouquet of multi-colored flowers. I guess it was therapeutic given the demands of his "real" job, whatever that was.

There were also other people in the room. There were a couple of large guys wearing hats. In my adult hindsight they probably were sporting revolvers in shoulder holsters. Present, too, were the sort of blonde ladies you see in cine noir films. They would fawn over me. I'd try on their red lipstick, they'd spritz me with perfume and paint my nails. There was always ice cream and music from the radio and lots of laughter. I really liked those ladies and wanted to be just like them when I grew up!

The men would be talking and laughing, too, but I never knew about what. Theirs was a secret world. It seems Daddy knew Louie from when they were kids in the Bronx or Perth Amboy. Louie had some connection to the florist business. I know that whenever we went to visit "Fat Louie" we would stop by a flower shop on the way home and bring Mother gladiolas that she would place in a tall crystal vase.

The gladiolas were like the Biblical sin offerings. Daddy knew Mom disapproved of his taking me with him on those visits. And it wasn't just removing the chocolate ice cream stains, the smell of cheap perfume, or the stale odor of cigars from my clothing that made her mouth turn down.

My Mother's acceptance of Daddy's "from the old days" friends was a mixed message. On one hand I assume there was this fascination with the seedier side of my accountant father, and on the other hand, there was the denial of us being anything other than the All-American family.

Mother knew "Fat Louie" but not as well as I. She must have made his acquaintance at the flower shop because I seriously doubt that it was in the hotel room with his bleach bottle blonde floozies or his alleged bodyguards.

I remember a gift to my Mom. It was a set of earrings and a matching pendant. In each piece was a delicate red rose bud encased in clear resin with a black backing that made the roses look as if they were floating. They reminded me of flowers suspended in space, everlasting, always about to burst into full bloom. Those earrings and pendant were no larger than an inch in length. "Fat Louie" had made them. That amazed me. To this day I have no idea how those red roses were shaped and inserted so perfectly into the resin by those pudgy fingers.

A few years later, when I was about ten, Daddy and I were walking in the Theater District with Artie, another of Daddy's friends "from the old days." Artie was on his way to work at the Majestic Theater. We had just crossed Broadway and Artie said Louie was dead. He had died from lead poisoning.

"Lead poisoning?" my Father said.

"Yeah. Some car pulled up alongside him and pumped him full of lead."

My Father made a "tch, tch" sound, looked sad for a moment and then he and Artie laughed.

I don't recall my immediate reaction to the news. It must have been strong, disturbing. To this day I have a vivid memory of that conversation. There's a picture in my mind: a black car with men rolling down the window, "Fat Louie" exiting the flower shop and splotches of blood on his white shirt…red as the roses in the resin.

FOO FIGHTERS
By Hugh Barlow

This is not my official report on the Foo Fighter phenomenon, but is instead a blog for use by those merely interested in the phenomena. The official draft will be completed upon the conclusion of my studies. This blog is merely a catalogue of my thoughts and experiences while I study this phenomena . As anyone who reads this report should know, Foo Fighters was the name given to unidentified flying objects that first started chasing aircraft during World War Two. The phenomenon had been identified as possibly being ball lightning, optical illusions created by light refraction through ice crystals, or attributed to poor eyesight due to looking into the sun while flying. It was reported that one gunner on a B-29 fired his weapon and hit one of the objects causing it to disintegrate. As the debris fell it set fire to several structures on the ground.

I have postulated that this one instance raises the question that the current belief that these so called "Foo Fighters" are not in fact electrostatic phenomenon as is currently accepted by the scientific community at large, but are in fact some sort of craft. An electrostatic phenomenon would not have disintegrated upon impact as it was reputed to have done in the one instance when gunfire was accurately directed at the phenomenon. Only a physical object would react in such a manner. An electrostatic charge would have been either unaffected or would have dissipated upon the impact of the weapon's fire.

There have been increased reports of this phenomena being sighted in the Rio Grande Valley of Deep South Texas. Since the prevalence of the phenomena has increased in the area and seems to be steady, I have been dispatched to study the phenomena to ascertain exactly what these objects truly are. I have been given the use of a military surplus aircraft and the required sensors that I need to study these objects at both close range and at a distance. I have spotters that have been hired to inform me of any sightings of these phenomena, and I have a hanger at the former Air Force base in the area. The former base has been converted to civilian use some time ago, and I have taken up residence in the hanger that I am renting for my base of operations and the maintenance of my aircraft. I will proceed to place sensors throughout the area on the ground to measure any electrostatic anomalies to help prove or eliminate the possibility that this is the cause of the phenomenon.

Day one of my studies:

I have calibrated the equipment on the ground in the several locations where the phenomenon has been sighted. I hope to get a few readings of the area when there is no reported activity. Barometric pressure, temperature wind speed and direction and electrostatic charge are all measured at each station. With a baseline from which to work, I hope to be able to predict the arrival of the phenomena and thus, place myself in the most advantageous place to witness it. Spotters are stationed near each instrument cluster with video recorders to capture any unusual activity should anything be noticed. It is too early to tell at this time what my readings will show, but I remain optimistic that I will be able to study this phenomena when and if it should show.

Day two:

There were no anomalous readings of the data and no sightings at this time. Temperature is normal for this time of year and the wind speed was from the southeast at 10 miles per hour. This looks like a good day for baseline readings as I had hoped.

Day three:

Another good day for baseline readings. No sightings, anomalous weather, or electrostatic readings.

Day four:

Today we had a thunderstorm that came from the northeast. Although the electrostatic recordings were high, there were no reported sightings of ball lightning or of the possible "Foo Fighters." Maybe tomorrow?

Day five:

Rain today, but no thunderstorms. The electrostatic charges were high again, but not as high as during the thunderstorms from yesterday. I have of course been keeping the data on disk for each station and I will proceed to break it down on charts using software. The data will be available to anyone who wishes to see it. I do not record this data in this report, since this is not my official documentation of the phenomenon.

Day six:

There was a possible sighting of a Foo Fighter today, but I was unable to get my aircraft into the air in time to study the phenomena. I hope to be able to get the aircraft off the ground faster in the future, or at least hope that the phenomena stays around longer to allow me some time to study it. There were reports of unusual electrostatic readings before the sighting and during it, so perhaps I will be able to anticipate the arrival of the phenomena in the future.

Day seven:

No anomalous activity today. This is a bit of a letdown from yesterday's excitement. I hope tomorrow brings better news.

Day eight:

No sightings in the targeted area, but there were some to the south of us in Mexico. I am sorry that I missed them, but I do not have the permission of the Mexican government to enter their airspace to conduct my studies. I hope that when I do finally get to study this phenomenon up close in the air, I will not be required to enter Mexican air space. If I do have to go that way, I will have to break pursuit.

Day nine:

More sightings in my area of study. There were several sightings reported by my spotters, and some that were reported by civilians, but I was still not able to get into the air on time. I was able to get more data on the anomalous electrostatic readings, so perhaps I can get enough data to anticipate the arrival of the phenomenon in the future.

Day ten:

More anomalous readings, but no reported sightings. Perhaps they were there, but we did not spot them.

Day eleven:

I had some luck today. I was able to get into the air in time to spot the phenomenon from a distance, but I was unable to get close. It seemed that the phenomena was evading me. From what I could see, it appeared to be an orange ball of light that traveled at a high rate of speed, and was able to perform maneuvers that defy the laws of physics. This matches reports that the phenomenon seems to be guided by intelligence, but as yet, I have been unable to confirm that. Still, it was an exhilarating experience.

Day twelve:

I was able to anticipate the arrival of the phenomenon today, and was successful in getting a close look at it. I was unable to get accurate readings from the plane however. What readings I did get were odd, and I will have to recalibrate my equipment. I hope that I get another chance to study the phenomenon tomorrow.

Day thirteen:

I was again able to anticipate the arrival of the phenomenon. There were several different types this time. I saw the familiar orange ball of light, but blue light and a green one joined it. They traveled together as if they were each attached to the point of a triangle, and they seemed to rotate about a central axis as they maneuvered. The experience was quite stunning, and I have some good video to study at my leisure. The anomalous readings were back despite my attempts to recalibrate the equipment. Perhaps this is due to some sort of interference by the phenomenon. The Foo Fighters seemed to follow my aircraft for a few minutes as I was studying them and then took off at a great rate of acceleration as if they were toying with me, or perhaps showing off. Once again, I must say that the phenomenon seemed to be guided by intelligence. One would think that an electrical charge such as what I seem to have discovered would be drawn to the metal body of the aircraft instead of just flying along beside it as this unexplained phenomenon seems to do. I have placed myself in a position to be struck on several occasions by now, but have not been. I will have to install a negative ion generator on the body of the aircraft to see if I can entice the phenomenon to come closer or perhaps to strike the craft. All of the instrumentation on board the craft has been hardened and insulated against high discharge electrical pulses, so I should be safe enough. My pilot agrees that there should be little risk of crash from the experiment, so I will proceed with it on our next flight.

Day fourteen:

We had a run of good luck for the past few days, but it did not extend to today. Although we did take to the air in anticipation of the phenomenon, we did not witness any activity today. Hopefully, tomorrow will be better.

Day fifteen:

One of the Foo Fighters was spotted today, but it was not the original orange one, nor the blue or green one that joined it a few days later. This orb was a bronze color that was almost silver. Call it a "gold" color. It was deeper in color near the center, with a lightening of the color toward the edges. This orb also seemed to toy with my aircraft, but did not come any closer than a few feet from its wingtip despite the negative ion generator. It circled my plane a couple of times before accelerating away at a high rate of speed toward Mexico. I had to break off pursuit once we reached the airspace over Mexico, although I was loathe to do so. I will try to positively charge the skin of the craft on our next encounter to see if that makes a difference in how the Foo Fighter reacts.

Day sixteen:

It has been just over three weeks since I started this experiment. I have had weekends off, of course, but still, I seem no closer to figuring out what these phenomenon are. Again, we have gone up in our aircraft to encounter these things and we were successful in getting close, but the positive charge did not seem to attract the Foo Fighters any more than the negative charge. The orange, green and blue spheres were back again today, and they seemed to react the same way they did before. They flew along side the craft for a short period of time before veering off in an impossible way and disappearing. The readings on the electrostatic sensors were just as anomalous as they have been on each encounter. Recalibration seems to make no difference. It is as if the phenomenon seems to emit random pulses of electrostatic charges designed to frustrate me.

Day seventeen:

Without a charge on the skin of the plane, we were struck by the bronze colored orb. Contact was brief, and it seemed as if the orb passed right through the aircraft. Despite the shielding of the equipment, most of it failed. We managed to land by "dead sticking" the plane into the airport. I will have to have the gauges and most of the electronics replaced before

I can fly the plane again. I will also have to hire a new pilot. My old one refuses to continue with the experiments. It will probably be a few days before I can get back up in the air again. All of the readings that I got today are lost, of course, so let's hope that I can get some better equipment and make a successful study with it.

Day eighteen:

Our Foo Fighters were back in the sky today. It was the orange, green and blue spheres that were flying around. Unfortunately, I was not. The plane was grounded for repairs, and the new pilot had not yet arrived. Maybe next time.

Day nineteen:

No significant activity today. I guess it is good, since the plane still has not been repaired. I was told that it should be ready for tomorrow, if needed. I just hope that my new friends have not forgotten me by then.

Day twenty:

I have a new pilot, and the plane was ready. The phenomenon was spotted today and we made an attempt to engage. We were successful. The bronze colored orb was back, and the plane was struck twice during our encounter. The total time that we spent studying the orb was less than 15 minutes, and it ended with the double contact of our hull, but we did not experience the same disabling of our equipment. The engine did stall during the encounter, but we were able to get it restarted once the Foo Fighter sped away. I was struck a glancing blow by the object and passed out. I have been hospitalized for observation but feel fine. Electronic equipment does seem to be affected by my presence however. My portable computer keeps cycling off as I attempt to use it, and I must type my report in with a separate keyboard. If I use the keyboard on the computer, it just starts flaking out. I guess that I have built up a significant electric charge from my exposure to the bronze colored Foo Fighter, but I cannot get any reliable readings from the equipment I had one of my assistants bring in to check me out. I seem to be experiencing a fluctuating charge similar to that of the Foo Fighter.

Day twenty-one:

I can't seem to get close to any electronic equipment today. All of the sensors that have been brought near me seem to go amok. I have been discharged from the hospital, since the doctors can find nothing wrong with me, and I feel fine. This inability to use electronics is frustrating though. I have had to hand write my report and have someone else type it for me. All four of the Foo Fighters that we have been studying were seen in the sky today, but since I could not get near the electronics, I was unable to fly to see them. Video equipment goes haywire around me as does my computer. I did not want to test the plane. Perhaps this symptom will resolve itself by tomorrow.

Day twenty-two:

Electronic equipment has become even more erratic when I am around. It seems that my electromagnetic influence is expanding. It almost seems that I am becoming like the Foo Fighters. Others tell me that I seem to glow, but that can't be right. Still, I wonder.

Day twenty-three:

There is definitely something going on. Everything that is not shielded from electrostatic discharge goes off when I am near. My staff tried to take me to the local hospital today, but there was no vehicle that could take me until they started up a diesel truck when I was not near, and drove me there in that. Even then, nothing electrical would work in the vehicle when I was near it. The glow that people told me about is plain to see even in daylight now. I was asked to leave the hospital since I was causing wide spread electrical problems while I was there, and the doctors have taken to studying me back at the hangar. The only light they have at night is chemical in nature. They use a lot of Coleman lanterns to work on me at night. They do not really seem to need it when they are close to me because the glow that I was experiencing seems to be getting brighter. My spotters report that the Foo Fighter activity seems to have increased while I am grounded. I no longer have any doubts...I am certain that the Foo Fighters are directed by some sort of intelligence. Unfortunately, I have no way to prove it.

Day twenty four:

My name is Agent Pierce. I am an officer of the FBI. The project has been temporarily closed. The director of the project has disappeared. He was in the hanger being attended by a nurse who said that he had just turned his back on the director for one minute and suddenly he was gone. After the director left the building, the lights came back on. Spotters at the remote ground stations reported seeing five different colored "Foo Fighters" take off from around the area near the airport. They reported gold, blue, green, orange, and red colored globes flitting about in a pentagonal shape that seemed to rotate about a central axis. There have been no reported sightings since. There is no valid scientific data that can explain what has happened during this study. What data we have makes no sense. Until we can decipher the data we have, we will not be putting any more money into this research. The search for the director of this project has gone nation wide. If anyone has any information as to his whereabouts, please report it to your local police or the FBI. Criminal charges may be leveled.

Entry ended.

For The Love Of The Land
By Bidgie Weber

Tennie came to the Valley from the lush growth of East Texas. The view from the dusty covered wagon caused her heart to stop. So unlike the familiar piney woods, this exotic landscape mesmerized her. From her perch it seemed as though every tree and bush had thorns. The green spiny clumps of, what she would soon recognize as cactus, looked deadly to her.

She marveled at her husband's stamina, energy, and determination during the journey south. It would take even more for him to mold this wild land into the paradise he envisioned.

At first, the awe of the land and the prospect of the dangers clouded her mind; but soon, her spirited nature won the day and she began to feel the excitement of conquest.

What a grand adventure!

A lifetime later, she sat at the kitchen window, sipping coffee, and looking down the dirt road. To a stranger traveling on the dirt farm road, the scene looks like a quiet plot of land with a white frame house in the center. However, like a good novel that comes to life only when the pages are turned and read, the acres come to life when that stranger crosses the boundary that separates the world of the farmhouse from the rest of the world. Nature's natural perfumes wrap around him. The breeze bathes his body in the sweet heady aroma of blooming orange blossoms. The pungent fragrance of lemon, lime, and grapefruit blossoms mingle with all the senses to create a veritable fruit salad.

This tickle of the senses opens the mind to appreciate other delightful aromas: freshly baled hay, coated with the lingering smell of recently turned soil; a trace of grain dust riding on the wind during harvest time....

And there is the cotton field. Do you know that a field of cotton has its own distinctive smell, of rich dark Valley soil mixed with the odor of sun-baked cotton bolls on the verge of exploding for picking?

A huge mulberry tree offers its branches for shade. Buried in the branches hang ripe juicy magenta berries ready to satisfy the most demanding palate. The sweet juice runs out the corners of the mouth and down the arm where it can be licked with a quick tongue.

What wonderful thoughts spun through Tennie's mind while the coffee cooled. Then her sons...had life been too hard on them? Had they suffered with the labor to create a life on the "foreign" land? She had become old too soon. Her dear husband had aged rapidly, also.

Her mind slipped to the memory of the row of shanties, built for the farmhands that helped bring life to the acres. She remembered the babies she had helped bring into the world. The sound of their cries was her reward for that care she offered to the young women. That row of shanties helped hold the little plot of ground separate from the rest of the world. Yes. Her sons had learned valuable lessons from the laborers.

She thought of the big white frame farmhouse as it stood for so many years. She could hear the stories carried on the wind: the cries of pain, the laughs of success, and the moans of sorrow. The familiar night sounds were the most remembered. One of the most comforting sounds was the window weights bumping together when a strong wind caused them to collide with the shiplap frame of the house. Hundreds of sounds with thousands of memories filled her mind often.

A movement from the far door pulled Tennie back to today. The old man, bent with age, strode into the kitchen. The love of this land carried him throughout these years. He worked hard to carve out his own paradise. He grinned at me. This was his favorite time of day. He wore his funny looking old felt hat with the net hanging from it. The patchy overall pants soiled from hours of work, and sweat stained gloves that said he was dressed to rob his beehives of nature's sweetest candy.

After watching him move to the outside to do his chores, Tennie slipped back into her memories. The fruit from the groves, the cattle, the products from the fields...all the acres belonged to the old man. He labored in the heat, rain, and cold to cut down the tough mesquite trees.

With mules, he dragged the tough mesquite trees away from what was to become life-giving fields and orchards.

For the love of the land, he cleared the cactus that attacked him as he struggled to open fields to harvest.

For the love of the land, he provided a better feeding ground to its former occupants: deer, wild hogs, bobcats, many kinds of birds, and other wild animals. This he gave back because they afforded him food for his family.

Tennie's heart jumped as she watched him move about the home they had built. What a wonderful adventure they had shared.

For the love of the land, he had carved out a good life for himself and his family.

For over a hundred years, there have been many more brave, adventuresome pioneers, who for the love of the land, followed in that old man's footsteps to this great adventure.

His legacy is a deep abiding love of the wild, rich, and ever-changing land found only in the Rio Grande Valley of Texas.

As the Texas sunset painted the western sky, Tennie put her memories to bed along with another glorious day in the Rio Grande Valley.

GRATITUDE
By Prenda E. Cook

So many things I'm grateful for:
My family, my friends,
A loving spouse, good health,
Some wealth.
My list, it never ends.

But when I wake up thirsty
In the middle of the night,
And everything is dark and cold
With not a speck of light,
Of all my many blessings
There is one that fills my head:
It's that little glass of water
On the table by my bed!

GROWING OLD
By Eunice Greenhaus

I'm growing old
How do I know?
I'm starting to ache
From my head to my toe

My skin is so wrinkled
It looks like a prune
My hearing is gone
My hair will be soon

My eyesight is dim
My legs are so weak
When I et up from a chair
My bones start to creak

The years went so fast
It just cannot be
When I look in the mirror
That it's me that I see

HA!
By Jack King

They would have called themselves Atheists Anonymous, but the boozers already had the acronym, so they settled for Heathens Anonymous. They weren't trying to quit like the boozers. They remained anonymous because they were merchants in a medium-size township in the middle of the Bible belt and knew that public knowledge of their unbelief would prompt boycotts, demonstrations, or even vandalism of their businesses. They met on Sunday mornings at the luxurious home of Helvinity Thorn, the wealthy heiress whose estate had fallen exclusively into her possession with the passing of her husband, a manufacturing magnate thirty years her senior. The group met not so much to keep the Sabbath holy as to keep it interesting. Helvi certainly knew how to keep things interesting.

On this particular Sunday morning, between nine and ten, the members of HA arrived individually at the mansion, left their cars in the spacious tree-ringed parking area in front, walked briskly to the main entrance, and rang the doorbell. Responding to each push of the button, a voice from the speaker above the door asked, "Who?", and when the visitor shouted, "Ha!" the door opened automatically. The system was so designed that if the visitor uttered anything but the correct password, a recorded message would tell him that a private worship service was in progress and would the visitor please come back in the afternoon.

After the who-ha ritual, nine members climbed the stairs to the chapel at the far end of the north wing, seated themselves at their customary places, and eagerly awaited the appearance of their high priestess. It was mid morning, but inside the chapel it seemed more like late evening. The only light in the room came through the small purple-and-green, stained-glass windows situated high on the walls.

The pews had been removed and replaced by an oak table with a chair at each end and four on each side. The only vacant seat now was at the head of the table. The pulpit had also been removed from the chapel and the low stage upon which it once stood was closed off by a purple velvet curtain. The men chatted among themselves as they waited for the signal, and at last, it came — a bright little one-note chime as if made by a microwave oven announcing the arrival of fresh popcorn. The purple curtains parted in a slow glide, and there on the stage under a soft warm spotlight stood Helvinity Thorn in a bright-red low-cut evening gown, her smooth bare arms reaching out to her congregation. A welcoming smile adorned her face and a slit up one side of her dress revealed one of the two most perfectly formed legs in all of Calvary County. The fingers on her outstretched hands beckoned in graceful undulations, and the men quickly approached the stage, queuing up to await their turns as the music began. One by one, they stepped onto the stage, each to enjoy twenty seconds of intoxicating slow-dance with the luscious Helvi. The little chime sounded at twenty second intervals to signal change of partners, and all sang along with the recorded music:

> *When the deeeep purple falls*
> *Over sleepy gar-den walls...*

As the music ended, Helvi's final dance partner lowered her body in a smooth dip, and that perfectly formed leg pointed straight up at the spotlight. Applause and whistles resonated through the room, and all took their seats at the table. The lights came up and the chapel shed its gloom. The kitchen staff had spread a tablecloth and set the table during the dance. At each place setting were a round cracker on a silver plate and six ounces of red wine in a long-stemmed glass. To the delight of the little congregation, the buffet offered several bottles of vintage grape from the renowned Thorn wine cellar, a variety of crackers, platters of fine cheeses, and bowls of Russian caviar.

"Communion will now commence," announced Helvi. "I request that each of you commune exclusively with the delightful reality of our freethinking fellowship. Let us now enjoy the providence of honest work and earnest commerce."

Each member lifted his glass adoringly to his hostess and then happily to his lips. One member, Jonathan Farley, exclaimed, "God, this is the best wine I've ever tasted!"

Helvi pushed her chair back and stood up. "What did you say, Jonathan?"

Jon set his glass down, his face flushed with embarrassment. "Sorry, I didn't mean to say that; it just sort of … slipped out."

Helvi smiled and sat back down. "Forget it, Jon; that little peccadillo is nothing compared with what I've learned about the activities of others seated at this table. When we're done with communion, we're going to have a little exercise in confession. Some of you boys have a bit of explaining to do… What the hell, let's start right now. Matthew, I hear you've turned your vacant building on Bethlehem Street into a Christian bookstore. Would you care to explain yourself?"

Matthew had been spreading caviar on a cracker and now carefully placed it on his plate and folded his hands onto his lap and looked at the hostess. "It was a business decision, Helvi. There are seven churches within two blocks of that building, and book sales are off to a good start. Yes, I sell Bibles and inspirational and spiritual books, but to balance any support that might give to theism, I have slipped onto the shelves a smattering of subversive literature that I think will prompt my customers, over time, to rethink their beliefs."

"You mean books by Darwin, or Dawkins, or Dennett?"

"No, and nothing so blatant as Hitchens or Harris either. Several of my customers, for example, have purchased Frank Ryan's Darwin's Blind Spot, assuming from the title that it's a rebuttal of Darwin's theory … but really it's about how evolution favors cooperation as much or even more than competition. Nature is not so much red in tooth and claw as rich in symbiotic embraces. The book has been particularly well received by those who preach love and generosity, and some, after reading the book, have abandoned the Biblical account of creation and accepted evolution as a logical and scientifically supported explanation of how we got here."

"Very good Matthew, you are absolved of your sin, at least for the moment." She turned to another member. "Jacob, you have been my financial adviser and have managed the assets of the Thorn estate since before my husband passed away. That arrangement could possibly terminate. I was in your office the other day while you were out, and I saw a number of astrological charts on your desk. No idiot who believes in astrology is going to manage my money. Do you believe in astrology, Jacob?

"Of course not, Helvi. I look primarily at market fundamentals, not superstitious nonsense like astrology, but occasionally something comes right out of the blue and knocks the markets for a loop. I attribute that phenomenon to superstitious people who invest by the stars. Some of them are wealthy and powerful enough to move the major markets, and their beliefs become self-fulfilling prophesy when they act in concert. These dingbats cannot be completely ignored. In the spring of 2000 for instance, there was a so-called grand alignment of the planets, which coincided perfectly with the beginning of that historic slide in stock prices, which came to be known as the Tech Wreck. I was going to move the Thorn investments out of stocks anyway because PE ratios and other fundamentals were way out of kilter, but all the publicity about the grand alignment was the clincher. I adjusted your portfolio accordingly, and in the ensuing slide, the market lost over half its value. Fortunately, I had liquidated your equities and moved you into Treasuries, which you know did exceedingly well during that period.

"Just as we atheists must be circumspect with regard to society's superstitions, an investment manager must be circumspect with regard to superstitions that affect the market. Don't you agree?"

"Yes, Jacob," said Helvi, "I do, and I hereby absolve you of all suspicion. Thank you for the explanation." She turned to another member of her flock. "Samuel, I was in your store the other day, and I noticed you were having a back-slapping good time with that notorious pack of Irish Protestant Bible thumpers. What was that all about? Have you lost your mind and gone over to the other side?"

"Not at all," said Samuel. "Here's what happened: I had stocked the soft-drink machine in my store with those notorious Dr. Pepper cans that display that excerpt from the Pledge of Allegiance —- you know, the one that says "One Nation – Indivisible", leaving out the words in between. Well, those guys came in and one of them went to the machine and got a can of Dr. Pepper and before I knew it, he was berating me about selling a product that leaves God out of the Pledge. I explained that "under God" wasn't even in the pledge until 1954 after the Knights of Columbus petitioned Congress to insert those words. Well, as soon as they realized who was behind the change, every one of them went to the machine and got a soft drink with that audacious Catholic insertion deleted, and we had a thumping good discussion."

"You disappoint me Samuel. Sectarian differences divide this world enough without you encouraging those kinds of rivalries," said Helvi.

"Divide and conquer," said Samuel.

"No, Samuel. Our goal is not to conquer, but to liberate."

Paul Fosdick piped up. "And didn't Eisenhower also want those words added to emphasize the difference between the U.S., which guarantees freedom of religion and Communist Russia, which did not?"

"Yes," said Helvi, "and I'm disappointed that he and Congress fell for that argument, because adding God to the Pledge violates the First Amendment and lessens our religious freedom. They should have known better. The 9th Circuit Court of Appeals declared the change unconstitutional because it advocates monotheism, but sadly, the Supreme Court lacks the fortitude to follow through and make a definitive decision in favor of the Constitution. Congress is deathly afraid to mess with the First Amendment on the one hand and afraid to take God out of the pledge on the other. So, the issue remains in limbo. Thomas Jefferson and John Adams must be turning over in their graves. Mark Twain must want his pen back, Mencken his typewriter back, and Colonel Robert Ingersoll his lecture circuit back. Lincoln must be kicking at the lid over his coffin so he can remind us that our government is of the people, by the people and for the people and not under any authority but our own. Some of the local ministers watch me closely when I attend an event where the Pledge is recited, and they've noticed that I stop reciting while everyone else says those two words. I even heard one say to another, 'I wonder what it is they worship at her private services'."

Helvi paused and smiled slyly. "But they won't say anything to me because they know I'll withdraw the monetary support I give to those church programs which I consider justifiable."

Her eyes scanned the group again. "David! I was four rows behind you at the football game Friday night and I noticed that you bowed your head during the invocation. Why did you do that?"

"Because," said David meekly, "I didn't bow my head the Friday before and a couple of young thugs accosted me after the game and accused me of being a dirty disrespectful little un-American atheist creep. They pushed me around and roughed me up and said if I didn't show some respect and bow my head next time, they were going beat the holy hell out of me. They were standing right behind me again at last Friday's game. That's why I bowed my head."

"Well, that's not going to happen again, David. Luther, as you know, is a plainclothes police detective, and I will personally pay the expense of having him or another officer stay nearby and watch over you while you enjoy the next game. He'll be just a few feet away as you walk to your car, and will follow discretely as you drive home. Is that agreeable to you, Luther?"

The man at the far end of the table answered, "Yes, and I'll be happy to do it myself, and I'll do it for free, Helvi ... and David, don't let me catch you bowing your head for the invocation."

"But isn't it disrespectful not to?" said David, meekly.

"No, David," said Luther. "Those men are disrespecting your right to think for yourself and act as you will as long as you do not break the law. And if I see them push you around or create a disturbance at the game, I will arrest them. Mass prayers are not conducted because some big magician in the sky will answer; their purpose is to draw others into the fold. If you ask people why they believe, especially young people, most will tell you it's because everyone else does, so that's why these social manipulators conduct those prayers at public events—to foster the illusion of universal belief. Those who don't take the cue from the crowd and bow their heads are systematically ostracized or subjected to abusive pressure to go along, just as you were. That's the way these religionists work. It's a political thing; it's about power over people. Helvi can tell you all about that; her father was a minister."

"Those tactics are in common use around here," added Helvi, "and we're going to resist them, aren't we, boys."

Samuel slammed the table with a fist. "Damn right!" he shouted.

Luther lifted his glass. "A toast to liberty!" he cried.

David sprang to his feet. "Give me liberty or give me death! We don't kiss no imaginary butt."

Helvi stood up and spoke sharply. "David! No more wine for you. Put the cork back in the bottle and behave yourself. You too, Samuel, or you'll both be drinking herb tea at the next meeting.

"And speaking of meetings, it is now time for the business meeting. Aaron, you chair the committee on church evaluation. Who's at the top of the good-works list this week?"

"That," said Aaron, "would be the House of Jesus on the corner of Nazareth and Bush. They are providing half-price day care for the children of poor working parents, and the church is struggling financially to keep the service available."

"They're not running the place like a militant Middle-East madrasa are they?"

"No, Helvi, as far as we can determine there is no brainwashing other than the standard children's Bible stories. The place is clean and well staffed, and the children are not mistreated in any way."

"Good, now whose turn is it to be Philanthropist of the Week?"

"That would be me," said Joseph, the man seated to Helvi's right."

"Mr. Treasurer," said Helvi, directing her attention to Jacob, "Send a five-hundred-dollar donation from my account to the House of Jesus in Joe's name. Stipulate that the money is to be used for the day-care program. Is there any other business?"

"No, but could we have another little dance before we adjourn?" asked Samuel.

"Sure, why not. Some of you boys are a little too tipsy to go out in public after allegedly attending a worship service, so I'll have the staff serve you some coffee while I change into my short shorts, and then we'll dance a little rumba or do some fast tango to work off the alcohol; how's that?"

"Even better than caviar," said Matthew, and whole group cheered.

After the dance, the members of HA went out to their cars and Helvi changed into conservative business attire. She walked through the mansion to the south wing where her 74-year-old mother had her own suite of rooms. Her mother was sitting in a chair in her bedroom, reading. She closed her Bible and looked up as Helvi appeared in the doorway.

"Why hello, Helvi dear, how did the prayer meeting go?"

"Just heavenly, Mother."

"Yes, I'm sure it was. I'm sorry that I never attend your services, but those stairs up to the chapel are just too much for me. You understand, don't you, dear?"

"Of course I do. Are you ready for lunch?"

"I'll just eat here in my room if you don't mind. Could you have the staff brew me a cup of tea and make me a turkey sandwich on wheat toast with mayo?

"Of course, Mother. I'll be right back with your meal."

As she turned and left the room, her mother called after her, "Your father would be so proud of you."

Taking off down the hallway, Helvi shouted over her shoulder, "Ha!"

HANNAH AND THE SWEETIES
By Verne Wheelwright

When the doorbell rang, I thought it would be the driver for DHL, bringing a package, but when I opened the door there was a very small girl standing on the front porch. She smiled big and I saw that her two front teeth were missing, so she must be about six years old.

"I'm Hannah, and I live there" she said, pointing at the new house next door. It had been under construction for nearly a year, and I had met Hannah's parents when they first visited the empty lot on the corner to plan their new home. They had built a beautiful, large home with a swimming pool and had finally moved in less than two weeks earlier, just in time for school to start.

"Hello, Hannah, I'm Verne. Welcome to the neighborhood!" I stepped out onto the porch and sat on the threshold, which brought me to just about eye level with her. "I'm glad you came to visit."

"My school is selling raffle tickets for a big-screen television set. Would you like to buy one? They're going to use the money to build some new classrooms."

"How much?"

"Ten dollars."

"Okay. Let me write you a check, then you won't have to worry if it gets lost."

I didn't tell Hannah that when I was her age, my school sent me out to sell something and I lost some of the money. I stepped inside to get my checkbook and came back to the porch to write out the check, which I made out to the school. Hannah carefully wrote me a receipt. It was mostly pre-printed, but she wrote in $10 and Hannah. For a six-year-old, she gave a real impression of responsibility.

"Thank you, Verne!" She flashed her no-front-teeth smile and ran out the driveway to the next house on the cul-de-sac.

Fall evenings are warm in Harlingen, usually with a breeze out of the southeast to cool the day's mid-ninety degree temperatures. My wife and I walk most evenings, traveling a two mile loop around the neighborhood. Whenever we saw Hannah she would call out, "Hi Verne!" and I would answer. With time and, apparently some parental prompting, she started calling me Mr. Wheelwright. Then Mr. Verne. Then just "Hi." I felt she had been intimidated by the demands of adult etiquette.

At first, we saw Hannah nearly every day. She would be shooting baskets in the driveway with her big brother, riding a scooter, playing hopscotch, drawing chalk pictures on the driveway, and even playing dress up or dolls with a friend.

One day I asked, 'Hannah, do you know what a palindrome is?" She had no idea. "It's a word that is spelled the same way forward and backward. Like Hannah." She smiled, with all her teeth now, but didn't seem certain what to say, but the smile was sufficient.

Hannah was not only energetic in nearly everything she did, she was also athletic. She was on the basketball and soccer teams in her class at school. Her parents both played golf, and she started taking golf lessons at the Country Club, which was just across the street.

She was a natural. Soon she played in her first tournament, and won in her age group. And her Dad was her caddy. Her parents were both proud of her and happy that she was having so much fun with her golf. For her ninth birthday, she received a package of twelve golf balls, each with a tiny red heart on one side and a number on the other. One through twelve.

Hannah was absolutely excited with her gift. "They're beautiful! I'm going to call them my 'Sweeties'!"

She kept them in the original box on her dresser, and when she went to play golf, she would take two with her. And she called them by name; Sweety Number One, Sweety Number Two and so on. She would talk to them like friends whenever she played golf. She would tee up one of her Sweeties, take a practice swing and say, "Here we go, Sweety!" and "Whack!"

On the greens, she'd carefully eye the distance and the slope, position herself over the ball, then, quietly, "Straight into the cup, Sweety."

Her Dad worried that Hannah would be upset when she lost one of her Sweeties, so he was a little prepared when she sliced Number Nine into the tall rough. He waited patiently while she walked back and forth through the tall grass, pushing clumps aside with her six iron and asking out loud, "Where are you Number Nine?" Then she saw him in an open spot between clumps, smiling at her. Smiling?

"Oh Dad, look! I've put a big cut in him! Right under his heart, but he looks like he's smiling!" So, Number Nine was retired to his place in the box on her dresser.

Hannah grew that summer. Straight up. She was only nine, but she was nearly as tall as her parents. The growth spurt affected her game in a number of ways, both mechanically and socially. Mechanically because as arms and legs grew, her personal geometry changed. She had to start using her mother's clubs, because her own were too short. She also found that the adults at the Club thought she was older and expected more of her. But Hannah is a quick learner and coped with all the changes very nicely. She continued to improve her game. Moreover, she still had all twelve Sweeties on her dresser.

Which worried her Dad. He knew she would eventually lose one of the Sweeties and was afraid she would be devastated. But even when he was sure she had lost one, she found it, calling, "Where are you, Sweety?"

Then Number Five went into the water. Dad knew that was it. That ball was gone. As they walked from the tee to the pond, Dad tried to prepare her. "Hannah, I don't think you'll find this one. I've put quite a few balls in that pond and never got one back."

"Number Five's been pretty lucky so far, Dad. And it looked like he went in close to the edge. Maybe we'll find him." She showed no signs of the devastation her father had expected. But the determination was clear.

Hannah walked to the edge of the pond, near where she thought Number Five had gone in. She could only see a few inches into the water, no matter how intently she stared. "Where ARE you, Number Five? I don't want to lose you."

She probed a clump of grass that was about a foot from the edge with an iron. He wasn't there. She circled to the left and then to the right. She spotted white! Hannah stepped into the water with one foot and retrieved the golf ball. But it wasn't Number Five. She tossed the ball to her dad. "Here, Dad. It's a brand new Nike!" But it wasn't number Five.

"Hannah, we're going to have to go. There are people playing behind us." She thought she saw something. It was like the water had cleared for just a moment, and she saw the red color. The heart. It must be Number Five. "Just one more minute, Dad!" She waded in, bent over where she had seen the red heart in the water and reached down, her face in the water, reaching for the bottom. Then she felt Number Five, grabbed him, stood up and waded ashore, wet from head to toe. Hannah didn't even look. She knew it was him. She tossed Number Five up onto the grass. "I'll play him from there."

Hannah's father was stunned! Flabbergasted! Relieved. He walked over to Hannah and hugged her, hard. " I can't believe you," he said, "But I do."

Later in the Clubhouse, people were talking about the girl who dove in the pond to get her golf ball. There were lots of jokes about the high price of golf balls and how some people will do anything to save a stroke. But Hannah wasn't at the Club. She was already home and Number Five was safely in his place in the box on her dresser.

During the winter, Hannah played on her class basketball team. Her father coached the team and had a great time. And Hannah and I had found something in common. Cookie dough. For the past two years her school had been selling frozen cookie dough. The first year I ordered raisin oatmeal cookie dough and managed to eat some of the dough before my wife baked the rest into cookies. Hannah said she liked the dough as well as the cookies and I told her I thought maybe the dough was better! But the cookies were good. Hannah knew she had a customer for as long as her school offered cookie dough!

That summer, as soon as school was out, Hannah's golf classes started again, every Tuesday afternoon. She had some close calls with her Sweeties, partly because she had to play faster now. Other players didn't want to wait while she looked for a lost ball. They weren't as patient as her Dad had been and would complain if she held up their game while she looked for a lost Sweety. So she made a decision.

At dinner, she announced to her family that she had been worrying too much about losing one of her Sweeties, so from now on she wasn't going to use them in practice or family games any more. She would save them for serious competition, like tournaments. And if she lost one, she would just have to accept that it was lost and keep playing. Hannah's mother and father were a little surprised at Hannah's announcement, because they knew she loved her Sweeties. But they admired the maturity of her decision.

A few weeks later, Hannah was starting her first tournament of the summer. She had three Sweeties in her bag; Number One, Number Two and Number Three. All freshly washed and shined. They looked like new. She was playing Number One, and they were doing very well. At every tee shot, she would quietly say, "Here we go, Sweety!" Then "Whack!"

It was on a sharp dog-leg around the water that Number One went into the deep rough, and Hannah wasn't sure she had seen where the ball had landed. She hoped her Dad had seen better. Confidently, "Daddy Caddy" led her to a spot just a little further than she thought she had seen the ball drop. But they could not find Number One. She walked back to where she thought the ball had landed, but still no luck.

"Hannah, you're going to have to play another ball and take the penalty. People are waiting."

She knew. Number One was gone. Her Dad handed her Number Two and she played out the hole and the rest of the tournament with him. She had the lowest score in her age group for that tournament, and won a handsome glass trophy. Her best one so far. She had a big smile when the reporter from the Valley Morning Star took her picture, and more smiles when people came to congratulate her.

In the cart on the way home, there were quiet tears. The kind that break a father's heart. Dinner was quiet, but after the kitchen was cleaned up. Hannah's father said, "Let's go take another look. The course is closed now and there's still light. I'll take a flashlight just in case." Hannah couldn't believe what she had heard. Silently, she hugged her Dad and they went out the door.

In the golf cart, Hannah's father drove across the street, took a short cut through a neighbor's yard and pulled onto a cart path. Hannah was so happy now she was giggling at anything her father said. She was certain they'd find Number One. Soon they were back in the tall grass and Bluebonnets where they had looked for Number One that afternoon.

In the summer, the South Texas sun stays up even later than golfers do, so they had plenty of light. They started at the point where they had searched in the afternoon and Hannah worked back in the direction from which she had hit the ball while her father looked in the other direction. The sun moved lower, then below the horizon, and the light was fading. As Hannah searched, she talked to Number One, telling him to stop hiding and let her see him. But he didn't, and she kept looking, thinking they might need the flashlight after all. She never did see him—she felt him.

Under her shoe. She knew it wasn't a rock, and when she moved her foot, there was Number One.

"Daddy! I found him! I found him! We must have walked right by him a hundred times!"

As they walked back to the cart, she thanked her father for bringing her back her to look for Number One, telling him how much she appreciated this and all the things he did for her, and held his hand as they walked, having no idea what she was doing to her father's heart. It would be years before he would tell her how important that moment was to him.

There was no announcement this time. Hanna simply retired the Sweeties to their box on the dresser. She'd take them out for putting practice, talking to them like old friends, but she wasn't taking any more chances with her Sweeties. Besides, she knew she might not play her best when there was a risk of losing one of the Sweeties. Even though she'd won the trophy that day, she thought she might have played better if she hadn't been worrying about losing Number One.

The morning of her Tenth birthday, there was a box on the breakfast table for her, but the family was nowhere to be seen. Maybe she was just up too early. So she waited. And decided that was one thing she was really not good at. She was good at golf and basketball and running, but she was not good at waiting. She liked action!

They came into the room singing, "Happy Birthday, Hannah." Even her brother was singing and smiling. Finally, her Mother urged her to open the box on the table. They all watched while Hannah unwrapped the package and opened the box.

It was another box of twelve golf balls, each with a bright red heart.

But no numbers.

The note said, "We are the second string, we have no names. It's OK if we get lost because someone will be happy to find us!"

"YESSSS!"

HARDHATS, HAMMERS AND HONOR
By Jack King

On Friday our framing crew finished the house on Sycamore Street and before we knocked off for the day, Oscar gave us the directions to the next jobsite. We on his crew variously knew Oscar as foreman, lead carpenter, safety officer, boss man, and big cheese. We didn't like him, but we respected him because he knew his geometry. He could grab a pencil and a square and lay out a stair stringer in sixty seconds flat or a rafter with a compound cut in fifteen. He informed us that the new job would be out in the middle of nowhere, a forty-minute drive from town. There was no electricity at the site, so we were to leave our power tools at home and bring hand tools.

The two handsaws I would need, a five-point for ripping and a ten-point for crosscutting were hanging on the wall in my garage. They needed to be in top shape for the days ahead, so I took them down and used steel wool to remove the light film of surface rust that had accumulated since I'd last used them. I set the teeth and sharpened them with my little triangular file, and I dug out my old block plane and sharpened its blade too. I subscribe to the old adage that a workman is only as good as his tools. My old brace with the crank handle got a proper oiling, and I dug out the old bits with the exaggerated spiral and the little screw-spur on the tip, and cleaned them up with a wire brush. I put all my power tools away including my 220-volt air compressor, pneumatic nail gun, power drill, and a worm-drive circular saw I had barely broken in. I was pleased at how light my toolbox had become. The old ways were better in one respect, at least.

Monday morning came, and after a bumpy drive down dirt and gravel roads, I found the jobsite right where Oscar said it would be. The wooden gate to the property was open, and I could see Oscar's truck about a hundred yards inside. The jobsite was situated on a gentle slope above a little spring-fed creek, and sure enough, there wasn't a light pole or a power line in sight. The lumber and other materials were stockpiled around the clearing where the house was to be built, and the batterboards were up and the lines stretched tight. The neat array of wooden stakes sticking out of the ground told me that Oscar had gotten in some overtime laying out the foundation over the weekend. He greeted Tommy and Frank and Jimmy and I with a curt, "Let's get to work boys," and gestured toward the four pairs of post-hole diggers that he'd stabbed into the ground where we were to begin digging the holes for the post-and-beam foundation. By the end of the day, we had aligned and set the creosoted posts, tamped them in deep and solid, and leveled and bolted the floor beams to them.

We put in the floor joists and most of the subfloor on Tuesday, and on Wednesday, we finished the subfloor and started framing the walls. On Thursday, we finished the wall framing and started nailing in the ceiling joists.

Tommy didn't show up for work on Friday. Oscar told us he had called in sick and headquarters was sending out another man. Oscar seemed unhappy. "I told them," he said, "to send out a real carpenter, not some greenhorn wood butcher that don't know a ten-penny nail from a two-by-four. I seen enough of those in my day."

Tommy's replacement showed up in his pickup at nine-thirty and introduced himself as Red Bonker. He was a tall, muscular, hard-featured fellow about thirty years of age. He had an angry look about him and seemed not to be the sort you'd want to joke around with. The man was all business; he strapped on his tool belt and went right to work. He nimbly mounted a stepladder, pulled a fistful of spikes out of his nail apron and hauled out his framing hammer. It was a big one with a long hickory handle, and we watched in admiration as he sank a sixteen-penny nail with a starting tap and two quick blows that left the head perfectly flush with the wood. He sank another and another in quick succession. Wow! This guy was a human nail gun. Although Frank and Jimmy and I were impressed, Oscar was frowning and that was a bad sign. He stepped up behind the ladder Red was standing on, unfolded his carpenter's rule, and waited. When Red dropped the hammer into the loop on his toolbelt and began checking the joist spacing, Oscar extended his rule upward, laying it alongside the hammer handle. "Hey, Red," he shouted. "Our insurance company requires that we use standard tools. A standard framing hammer has a sixteen-inch handle and yours is eighteen. Tomorrow you'll come to work with a standard hammer. Got it?"

Turning on the ladder and glaring down at Oscar, Red replied with a sneer, "And what if I don't?"

Oscar bristled. "Then I'll break that bastard handle off your goddamn hammer!"

In less than a heartbeat, Red shot back, "You do and I'll stick it up your goddamn ass!"

Oscar's jaw dropped and his face turned beet red. He was the foreman and no subordinate had ever talked to him like that. The new man turned back to his work, and Oscar reached up and flipped the hammer out of its loop. He caught it in mid-air, leaned over, and propped it against the nearest corner-post. He straightened up quickly and brought the heel of his right boot down hard, snapping the handle off just below the head.

Red came off the ladder like a laser-guided bomb, and Oscar hit the floor under the weight of a one-hundred-ninety-pound flailing maniac. The maniac undid Oscar's belt buckle in a flash, yanked his pants and undershorts down around his knees, and flipped him over on his stomach. He grabbed the broken hammer handle, and when Jimmy and Frank and I saw what he was about to do, we all piled into him at once. It took us a full minute to subdue him, and by the time we had him under control, Frank had a sprained thumb, I had a busted lip, and Jimmy's left eye was swelling shut. Oscar's rectum, however, was free of hickory.

Once Red had calmed down and promised to behave himself, we let him up and turned our attention to Oscar. Our lead carpenter and safety officer was beginning to come around. He'd had the wind knocked out of him, but otherwise he was okay. I heard some thumping and clattering behind me and turned to see Red tossing his tools into the back of his pickup. Seconds later he was behind the wheel, gunning the engine and throwing gravel at us from the rear tires. Oscar limped to his truck to call the dispatcher on his radio and have him send the sheriff out, but none of us ever saw Red Bonker again.

Frank and Jimmy and I stopped at the old Javalina Tavern on the way into town. Jimmy had been there before and recommended the place. The sign on the screen door said, "Dress Code: We smile on sweaty shirts, dusty jeans, and scuffed boots. High faluters in suits will be hanged with their neckties." We took a table near an open window and had the barkeep draw us a big pitcher of Lone Star. We all lit cigarettes and hashed over the day's events as we blew smoke rings and guzzled our beer. We had some good laughs and Frank, the rookie on the crew, asked, "You think I could get away with ribbing Oscar a little tomorrow? You know, like teasing him about walking kind of funny?"

"Not unless you can walk straight with Oscar's boot up your ass," said Jimmy . We had a knee-slapping howl over that one, and it was Frank's turn, so he got the check.

No sooner had we arrived at the jobsite on Monday than Oscar stepped out of his truck and told us that Tommy was still sick, and headquarters was sending out a second replacement. "That must be him now," he said, nodding toward the gate. We looked out to see an old Dodge cargo van pulling in, and as soon as it was parked, the strangest- looking carpenter I had ever seen stepped out of it. He had oriental features, jet-black hair tied back in a ponytail, and a cannonball shape that must have tipped the scales at close to three hundred pounds. Strapping on his toolbelt as he strode toward us, he introduced himself: "Soshigawa Megabushi (at least that was what it sounded like). I'm the new man, and I'm ready to go."

Oscar seemed to be choking on the smoke from his Chesterfield. He jerked the cigarette out of his mouth and coughed and retched for about fifteen seconds and then did a second take at the newcomer. Regaining his composure, he coughed once more and spoke. "Well, let me tell you, fellow. I got some serious concerns here. First of all, we'll be framing a roof today, and I don't think the rafters will support a goddamn hippopotamus."

Soshigawa Megabushi looked at the stack of rafters we had cut the day before. "Two-by-six number one hemlock," he said. "They'll hold me just fine."

Oscar seemed somewhat taken aback by the man's self-assurance, but continued the affront. "As foreman and safety officer, I take pride in the precision and efficiency of my crew. We do the job right the first time and we do it fast. You got this mongoloid look about you, and to be honest, I don't think you're gonna measure up."

"I'll do fine."

"And while I'm on the topic of efficiency, that name of yours is about as unpronounceable a string of syllables as I've ever heard. If you stay, you'll answer to a name of my choosing."

"Call me whatever you like."

"Well, let's see now; you look like one of them fat Jap wrestlers I seen on TV, so I think I'll call you Sumo. The roof plans are on that sheet of plywood over there atop those sawhorses, so you go study them for a minute and then join the others topside."

Oscar and Frank stayed on the floor feeding the rafters up to us, and Jimmy and Sumo and I spiked them into place. We put up the hip, valley, and common rafters, along with the ridgepole, and then we nailed in the hip-jacks and valley-jacks. There was a complicated dormer on the east side of the roof and Sumo put it together with the easy assuredness of a man who had done it a thousand times. For a big man, he got around on the roof quite nimbly, and he did more than his share of the work. I told Oscar he ought to have named him Cat.

"I think you ought not to second-guess my decisions," said Oscar as he wound his new Bulova wristwatch.

Later, when all the roof framing was securely in place, Oscar snapped a chalk line across the rafter tails on the west side of the house and told Sumo to cut them off plumb while Frank and Jimmy and I cut them off on the north, south, and east sides. Sumo went to his van and came back with something that looked like a thin, elongated meat cleaver with teeth along the cutting edge. He placed a stepladder under the first rafter tail, marked it vertically using a torpedo level as a straightedge, and cut it off quick and clean. He moved the ladder to the next rafter and made another swift cut.

Oscar was frowning, and that was a bad sign.

Sumo moved the ladder again, and Oscar stepped up behind him as he sawed off another rafter tail. When he laid the saw down, Oscar snatched it from atop the stepladder and barked, "What kind of a bastard thing is this?"

"It's a traditional Japanese pull saw," said Sumo, looking down at Oscar.

"Well, it looks like some kind of freak foreign abortion to me, and if I see it on this job tomorrow, I'm going to rake the teeth across that pallet of patio bricks over there. You ever try to cut wood with a saw that's been used on bricks?"

Sumo looked at the saw in Oscar's hands, his previously placid face showing earnest concern for the first time since he'd arrived. He glared at Oscar and said, "You ever been castrated with a saw like that?"

Oscar looked as if he didn't know whether to move his bowels or wind his Bulova. His face turned a deep shade of crimson, and he turned resolutely toward the pallet of bricks. He had taken exactly three steps when the flying hippopotamus left the launch pad. The two men hit the ground with a heavy thud and slid for about five feet before Oscar's head slammed into the wooden pallet that held the bricks. Sumo quickly snatched the saw from Oscar's limp hand, and as Frank, Jimmy, and I sprinted toward him, he raised the saw high above his head, and it looked as if he intended to cut down anyone who got within reach. We stopped in our tracks.

"Listen up," said the angry Asian. "Frank, you go over to Oscar's truck and radio for an ambulance. You other two stand where you are and listen to what I have to say."

There was a long, pregnant pause during which Sumo seemed to be searching for the right words. When he finally spoke, his voice was calm and firm. "Nobody abuses this saw, least of all some jerk of a foreman who knows nothing about honor. This saw belonged to my great grandfather. He worked and saved and did without for a year just to have enough money to buy such a fine instrument. He used it to help build a Shinto shrine near Mount Fuji, and that shrine is still standing and will stand for centuries to come. He bequeathed this saw to my grandfather who made a living with it for forty years before he passed it along to my father. My father earned enough with this saw to immigrate to America, where I was born. And since I finished high school in Los Angeles, I have used this saw with diligence and cared for it with reverence. I come from a long line of craftsmen, and I have kept this saw as clean and sharp as my honor and my skills. I will protect it with all means at my disposal until the day that I pass it along to my son."

At this point, Oscar emitted a groan, and we saw that Frank was back from calling for an ambulance and was checking our foreman's pulse. Sumo calmly carried his tools to his van, loaded them, got in, and drove slowly out the gate. Frank asked if he should go back to Oscar's truck and call the sheriff. I said, "No," and he nodded.

The ambulance arrived and the attendants checked Oscar out and loaded him into the unit. "He's semiconscious," said the technician in charge. "His vitals are good, and he's moving his extremities, so he's probably going to be okay. That lump on his noggin tells me he's suffered a concussion, and he might also have a couple of cracked ribs, but my guess is that he'll probably be back on the job in a couple of weeks or so."

After the ambulance left with Oscar, I radioed the office to explain to them exactly what had happened, and then Frank and Jimmy and I loaded our gear and climbed into our pickups. I was the last one out, so I padlocked the gate. At the edge of town we convened at the Javalina Tavern again and were soon sitting at a table filling cool clean glasses from a gleaming pitcher of beer. We sipped our suds quietly, thinking about what Sumo had said, and finally Jimmy saw a sign that we hadn't noticed before over the front door and he read it aloud:

No tequila at any cantina
No highball at any marina
Can be any better
Nor colder nor wetter
Than a beer at the old Javalina

"I'll drink to that," said Frank and then he and Jimmy lit cigarettes and started competing to see who could blow the better smoke ring. After a minute or two of relative silence, Jimmy spoke. "We probably won't have a foreman tomorrow, and since we're ahead of schedule anyway, I think I'll take the day off and go fishing."

"Me too," said Frank. "I ain't been fishing in a long time."

"Well then," I said, "There's a pay phone on that far wall, so I'll step over there and call the office, and if it's okay with them, we'll all take the day off." Minutes later, I hung up the phone and walked back to the table. Frank and Jimmy had already started on the second pitcher. "Guess what!" I announced. "Oscar's tougher than we thought. He's already out of the hospital and we're going back to finish the job tomorrow. Headquarters has lined up the third replacement for Tommy and since we're ahead of schedule, you guys can still take the day off if you want."

"Who's the new man?" asked Jimmy.

"A big bad-tempered fellow named "Bull" Ripper. You've probably never met him, but I worked with him on a job in Fort Worth last year. He wears a hardhat with a little transistor radio installed inside it, and you have to communicate with him by sign language because he keeps the country music turned up loud while he works."

"Oscar's going to love that," said Frank.

"You guys still taking the day off to go fishing?" I asked.

Jimmy looked at Frank and then spoke for the two of them. "Are you kidding? The fish can wait. We wouldn't miss tomorrow for the world!"

HUEY TRODS THE TRAIL WITH A MANITOU
By Don Clifford

"Without a doubt, you are the tenderest tenderfoot that ever trod the trails of the Arroyo Colorado!"

Huey Langston cringed. He stood at attention while his Boy Scout patrol leader and would-be drill sergeant chewed him out. *Only Dimmy Michaels would use a phrase like "trod the trails." He was bright as a half-lit bulb. What did he expect? He joined the troop just two weeks ago and, technically, he wasn't yet a Boy Scout.* Huey shrugged and let the tongue lashing roll off his shoulders like rain falling off a roof.

"And that uniform! You find that at a flea market?"

"Belonged to my granddad," Huey said. "My folks thought it would be a nice tradition if I wore it."

"Khaki knickers? And that hat...twice the size of a dinner plate! I swear! You look like that Smokey Bear character dressed in a World War One sojer suit."

Huey could have crawled into a hole. Of course the wide brimmed hat and the flared knicker trousers were antiques. Back in 1945, money was tight – but that wasn't a patrol leader's problem. Even now, the recent "man-to-man" talk echoed in his mind. *"I know this transfer was sudden,"* his Dad said. *"Maybe this time we owe you one. In Jacksonville we let you join the Cub Scouts because we thought we were staying put."* Instead, the folks squeezed him and Sis into the jam-packed back seat of the old Chevy. It was goodbye Florida – hello Texas.

Just thinking about it made Huey scrunch up his shoulders. Actually, he looked quite sharp. With scissors, needle and thread, Mom made the old uniform fit in the right places. Some folded newspaper tucked into the hat's sweatband kept it from sliding over his eyes. His first meeting with the troop, though, was something else.

"Hey, a Smokey Bear!"

"Hi yuh, Smokey. Where'd yuh leave your shovel?"

At first, Huey rankled whenever someone called him "Smokey". He thought about it for a time, and then decided that "Smokey" was a good nickname. Like the uniform, the name fit. One of the few skills he learned in time for the coming jamboree was how to build a fire without burning his fingers — or the surrounding woods, for that matter.

"Pay attention!" Dimmy braced Huey like a new recruit. "If you expect to earn that Tenderfoot Badge in time for the Council Awards Ceremony, you have a lot of learning to do – the Scout Oath, the Scout Law, a couple of basic knots. When are you gonna get with it?"

He was right. I really want that badge and this might be my only chance. So many times I've started a project, but couldn't finish it. If the family transferred again…well, I wont think about it now.

Dimmy thrust his face into Huey's and snarled. "Assuming you hope to make Second Class rank, much less Eagle, show me what it means to 'Be Prepared'."

Huey fastened his mess kit, canteen, knife, flashlight, hatchet and compass to his surplus Army belt and snapped it around his waist. With each step he clanked — a situation sort of like the knee bone connected to the leg bone and so on; only here, the mess kit clanked against the canteen that rattled against the hatchet, which banged against the flashlight and the knife, while the compass dangled from his neck on a string and clacked against wherever it bounced.

Dimmy groaned. "How ya gonna sneak up on a rabbit dressed like a walking kitchen?"

Maybe if I trod the trail on tiptoe?

The boys of Troop 94 worked hard during the summer of 1945 in preparation for their annual jamboree at the Camp Perry Campground in South Texas. The campground overlooked a river named the Arroyo Colorado — Spanish for Red Creek. During the day, tugboats towed barges and chugged up and down the Arroyo. A skipper would blast his foghorn at a passing boat or when a scout waved at him from the bank.

At night, a tug's bright spotlight would rake the river's shore and freeze a deer in mid-stride along the water's edge.

Army surplus pup tents swelled and flapped in the breeze. Huey and the boys huddled around Scoutmaster Gomez. "We invited an Indian Medicine Man from the Kickapoo Nation to join our Council Fire tonight," he said. "Maybe he can conjure up a Manitou."

A sea of blank faces stared back. Three heartbeats later, a chorus of questions swamped the Scoutmaster.

"What's a Man-ee-too?"

"Is it a spirit?"

"Like a ghost?"

"No way, dummy! Ain't no such thing as ghosts."

"Is that right, Mr. Gomez?"

The Scoutmaster laughed and held up his hands for quiet. "Boys, I can't say one way or another." With that, he got to his feet and said, "If we're to go canoeing before dark, let's get to doing what needs to be done."

The scouts scattered to their assigned tasks.

Soon, Huey's stomach growled. Inside his pup tent, he snapped shut the Boy Scout Manual that Dimmy ordered him to study and strapped on his camp gear. *"Be Prepared" the Manual says…never says be prepared for what.* Besides, he wasn't about to leave anything behind. Dimmy kept hammering into him, "If you lose your gear, don't blame anyone but yourself…your responsibility." *Well, I can't lose it if I'm using it.* He crawled outside, stood, and looked around for his troop mates who were nowhere in sight. *Reckon they forgot I was with them, being a new guy and all.*

His stomach growled louder. He clanked over to the cook tent where a short fat man wearing a soiled apron piled foodstuffs on a table that served as a makeshift counter.

"Nice suit," the man said. "Haven't seen one of those in years."

"Got anything to eat?" Huey asked, ignoring the comment about his uniform.

"Missed the word, huh, Kid? On arrival day, we don't provide meals until supper."

"Oh." Huey managed his best-abandoned sheep dog look. "I didn't know."

"Wait a minute." The cook rummaged in a box. "Can you make a fire?"

Huey nodded.

The cook pulled out two soggy hot dogs. "Bon Appétit!"

Huey gathered twigs and small blow down limbs and set them in an assigned fire pit. In minutes, burning wood crackled merrily. He arranged the hot dogs in his mess kit and placed them over the fire.

"Smells good," Dimmy said, out of the blue. "Wondered where you were."

So that's how he sneaks up on rabbits.

Dimmy hunkered down next to Huey and watched the dogs sizzle. At length he reached into a sack and handed Huey two raw chicken wings. "Here, Smokey. Figured a tenderfoot like you might need something like this."

"Gee, thanks." Huey plopped the wings along side the hot dogs. Dimmy stood, and like a precision drill team of one, spun on his heel and marched away. *Hmmph! Bet he learned that from a John Wayne movie. He didn't say how long I should cook them.*

He didn't wait long. The dogs were overcooked – burnt; the wings were undercooked – pink. He wolfed both down with equal gusto.

That evening, the pungent smell of wood smoke drifted over to Huey's tent site and curled up his nose. Supper was out of the question. The queasy ache in his stomach grew into a lump of molten lead.

He was sick.

He had to barf.

He clanked to the nearby brush and with a loud gut wrenching "Aar –uUU-ga!" threw up behind a mesquite tree.

Maybe I should've cooked the chicken longer.

He clanked furtively through the shadows to his tent. *Can't let them see me…they'd laugh…never make Eagle…go to bed…maybe feel better, later.*

He crawled in, spread a blanket and pulled it over him.

Chills…can't stop s-shaking…this outing isn't fun any more. Close eyes… uh-oh…tent's spinning…Yuhh…gotta get outside…

"Aar-UU-ga!"

Dry heave…can't sleep…maybe feel better at the Council Fire.

The assembled scouts sat grouped in noisy bunches around a massive pile of burning logs. The roaring fire launched ribbons of flame into the inky blackness. A spark jumped out of the fire and landed on the knee of one scout. "Ouch!" he yelled, jumping up and slapping his leg with both hands. Others around him scrambled to safer seats.

By the time Huey had worked his way to the assembly area, a hush had settled over the group. He hid in the shadows and shivered under the olive green Army blanket draped over his head. Sweat dripped from his forehead and slid down his nose. *Doesn't feel much better here, either.*

The Medicine Man stood in the flickering firelight, his face to the sky. Buffalo horns crowned his fur-covered head. An owl-shaped shield decked with porcupine quills and a dangling eagle feather covered one arm. He began the dance. His body twisted and turned as he dodged in and out of the billowing smoke. The night got spookier with each chink-chink-chink of the olive-shaped clamshells tied around his ankles.

Huey was fascinated. The only Native Americans he ever saw were the Hollywood variety that chased wagon trains all around the silver screen. In spite of his fascination, the stomach spasms wouldn't quit. He was ready to run for the brush if he had to barf.

The Medicine Man stopped and pointed the shield toward the stars. Two glassy button eyes lit up and thin twin spotlights pierced the night sky. He raised his arms toward the rising moon. "Great Manitou," he prayed. "Show us the path through the wilderness of life."

"Bar-uUu-ga!"

The Indian's outstretched arms dipped. His head turned toward the sound. Nervous khaki-clad bodies squirmed and giggled. Huey's stomach quavered and sweat drenched his shivering body. *How embarrassing! Boy Scouts don't get sick...master woodsmen, thrive in the open air...like Indians. Yeah...Indians trod trails...earn Tenderfoot badges, too.*

The Medicine Man resumed the mesmerizing dance and the murmuring audience settled down. When the hypnotic chink-chink-chink reached a new peak, he threw his arms to the sky. "O Great Manitou! Give us a sign!"

"Bar-uuU-ga!"

A mesquite log flared and cast a bright orange glow on Huey.

"What's that?" Panicky scouts turned heads and craned necks to see what made the sound.

"A Manitou!"

Startled, Huey dashed out of the shadow to look. "Where?"

"There it is!" Fingers pointed at him.

A frantic Huey spun around and around. "Where? Where?"

At that moment, a tugboat's horn blasted the night. Its roving spotlight fastened on a spinning spectacle. Spooked scouts and adults jumped to their feet. Someone near Huey yelled, "Over here!"

A cold clammy feeling at the base of Huey's spine crawled up his back and raised the hairs on his neck. Scared blue, he broke into a run. "Ahhh! Don't let him get me!"

His ghostly shape clanked full speed through the darkness. *Oh, Lordy! That beady-eyed devil is after me. I'll never make Eagle. Dad will transfer without me.* Without warning, the moon did an abrupt somersault and faded into a fuzzy black.

Later, Huey woke with a start. He was home, in his own bed, with a cool damp cloth over his forehead. "Food poisoning...," he heard his mother say.

Poison? Heck of a way to treat a new guy.

"The doctor says you will be all right..."

Remnants of a weird dream whizzed through the daze. *A head of horns...spotlight eyes...this kid is sick...*

"You bumped your noggin in the dark."

Better trod him home...trod?

"Scoutmaster Gomez and a nice man dressed like an Indian brought you home."

"My badge!" Huey jerked up. "I was supposed to get my Tenderfoot badge!"

"Easy does it." Gentle hands pushed him back.

Oh, no...that was my last chance. Dad transfers so many times...so many unfinished...how will I ever become an Eagle Scout...

Still weak from his ordeal, Huey dozed off. When he woke again, Mr. Gomez, Dimmy, and Mom and Dad stood beside the bed.

Mr. Gomez said with a somber face, "You caused quite a stir during the Council Fire."

Huey's stomach sank. That's not what he wanted to hear.

The Scoutmaster couldn't keep a straight face and burst out laughing. "Best show we ever had."

Dimmy held up the Tenderfoot badge snugged between his thumb and forefinger.

"Since you missed the Investiture Ceremony," Mr. Gomez said, "Your troop mates insisted we bring this to you. The badge means you completed the first step on the long road to Eagle Scout." He grinned. "There's no doubt that you are a tried and true tenderfoot."

A few months later, Huey's family had moved to a post near Butte, Montana. While hitching a saddle to a horse, his newfound friend complained. "You gotta be the most gol-danged tenderfoot I ever did see."

Huey's chest swelled with pride. "Yup," he said. "And I've trod the trails to prove it. Wanna see my badge?"

HURRICANE
By Robin Cate

The Valley, buttoned up
Like the wool coat of winter,
Bowed its head in
Deference to Nature's will,
Burrowed in shelters,
Some mighty,
Most meager,
Fed on the last hot supper,
Lit candles with images of saints
Smiling through cheap glass holders,
Slept, dreaming of Life's storms,
Of being unprepared,
Of Mercy.

I TASTE HER LIPS
By Beto Conde

I taste her lips
And I sleep

Lying on my cot alone in my small room, I stare at the ceiling.
I'm surrounded by three walls of block and cement,
Walls covered with a gray shade of loneliness.
The other wall offers an absurd view of others like me,
Sitting in their cells. They wait,
They dream dreams that will never be.
I look at them through steel bars that keep my future
From going anywhere beyond these four walls.

I remember my life…once upon a time,
Somewhere hidden deep in the shadows of my memory,
Way back in the fading pictures of my mind,
I think of that girl,
I find her there.
I remember soft kisses.
I feel her small waist in my hands as
I taste her lips.

As I drift into sleep,
I think of that girl who years ago forgot my name,
I find her there,
Way back somewhere in the fading pictures of my mind.

Every morning, along with many other broken souls,
I walk down several fights of stairs made of steel,
Human souls protected by hard street armor,
Armor built up with many years of lessons learned the hard way.
I look back up to the top of the stairs where she waits for me.
And that makes me strong.
I talk tough and I act tough.
I'm well protected by street armor picked up as a boy in tough barrio
streets.
I have hardened even more, here in this forsaken human warehouse
Where modern society hides it's mistakes and it's ignorance.

As familiar strangers slap what might pass for food
On a tray faded by long years,
I go through the motions of the day.
She beckons me gently,
She is never far from me.

All day long, all I want to do is go back to my cell
Where she waits for me,
The only love I ever knew,
Soft kisses from a girl
To a boy who never had a chance.

At night when all is quiet,
When I hear no angry voices,
No painful groans from frightened dreamers…
For a long time, I stare at the ceiling,
Then I close my eyes forgetting cement walls and steel bars.
She comes to my rescue.
I fly to somewhere far away in my mind where love is real.
I hold her waist in my hands
And I taste her lips.

When I forget, I dream of the day I will look at her once again,
But the slamming of steel doors at the end of the day
Remind me that will never be

There was
No prom,
No graduation,
No wedding day,
No baby to hold in my arms,
Only a girl with brown eyes and soft lips
Who, many years ago, forgot
My kiss.

INTERNATIONAL PEACE
By Robin Cate

As I stand on my good leg
In a line at Starbuck's…
"Got my other leg blown off…
In Viet Nam."
I tell the kid who is serving coffee,
"Make that a tall, please."

He answers in a French accent…
Mentions he grew up in Da Nang.

He comps my order,
I accept.

Seated, I huff into the coffee.
Still some Agent Orange in the lungs,
And I break into tears.

My son leaves for Iraq next week.
If he gets back, who will serve him
Peace?

Melvin's Wondrous Wednesday
By Jack King

Melvin Thigpen had eight hours comp time coming, so on Wednesday he took the day off. Arising at daybreak, he dressed himself and went directly to the back yard to make a round in his primary source of solace: his garden. Melvin was a single, middle-aged man with little in the way of personality and even less in the way of looks. He hated his job, he hated his name, and he hated his plain looks, but most of all he hated the fact that people did not find him interesting. If only he could matter to others as much as his little collection of plants mattered to him. His plants made him happy and they weren't even sentient beings. Why couldn't he, an intelligent, caring member of the most evolved species on earth, make someone happy? Why didn't people find his practical jokes as entertaining as he did? He watered his precious plants, pulled out a dozen emerging weed seedlings and went back in the house for his usual morning coffee and bowl of cereal. Today, as he had done on other occasions when he was feeling down, he decided to drive over to the Royal Hospitality Hotel, his favorite watering hole. He'd never stayed at the Royal, but had walked past the front desk many times on his way back to the patio bar, which afforded a clear view of the magnificent tropical garden directly behind the main building. It was the ideal place to relax, savor the scenery, and enjoy a drink.

He noticed on his way down the main hallway that the hotel was hosting another convention. Every guest he saw was wearing a nametag displaying not only his name but the name of the city he was from. There was a Bob from Dallas, a Richard from Seattle, a Tony from Chicago, and so on. As he exited the rear door and stepped into the patio bar, he noticed that more than half the seating was empty, not unusual this early in the day, even during a convention. He took a seat at a small table near a flowerbed that bordered the patio and looked out on the luxuriously landscaped grounds. "How beautiful," he thought. He looked back toward the array of tables and noticed that the hookers were working the bar as they always did during a big convention attended by men from out of town. "How sad," he thought. One of the girls was sitting at the adjacent table with a Harold from Boston. Harold was telling her that for one hundred dollars an hour, she had better be damn good. She said she was, and Harold said "We'll see," and snapped his fingers for the check. When the waiter arrived, he said, "Put it on my room tab: Harold Hastings, 421." He then grabbed the girl by the hand and headed toward the elevator.

A different waiter took Melvin's order for a scotch and water and asked him if he wanted to run a tab. "Yes," said Melvin. "Harold Hastings, room 421."

"Very good," said the waiter, and he took off to get the drink as Melvin turned again to view the well-manicured landscape. A lush emerald lawn dotted with palms and flowerbeds sloped downward to a large crescent-shaped pond. The tips of the crescent curved around either side of the hotel, and the water was bordered all around with some of the biggest, greenest, elephant-ear plants he had ever seen. In the middle of the lake, a fountain sprayed water into the air in a continuously changing pattern.

Next to the water, a little dark-skinned fellow in jeans and a T-shirt was pulling the spent marigolds out of a flowerbed and throwing them into a wheelbarrow. Melvin wondered why he wasn't wearing a hat or gloves. "Must be newly arrived from across the border with only the clothes on his back," he surmised. The man dumped a bag of something, possibly peat moss or composted cow manure, onto the now-empty flowerbed, spread it around with a shovel, and began spading it into the soil. A lawn tractor pulling a small trailer loaded with flats of bedding plants pulled alongside and stopped. A sunburned gringo in a big straw hat and a colorful Hawaiian-style shirt, not unlike the shirt Melvin was wearing, hopped off the tractor and started waving his arms around and yelling angrily at the little Mexican. A hose had been left running in another flowerbed and the water had flooded it and was now running onto a nearby sidewalk. The little Mexican ran over and moved the hose, then came back and unloaded the fresh bedding plants from the trailer while the man in the straw hat stood watching with hands on hips. "What a jerk," thought Melvin. His thoughts were suddenly interrupted when a man sat down in the chair on the opposite side of his table. The nametag said he was Stanley from Colorado Springs. Stanley seemed very excited. "I urgently need your help," he said to Melvin. "I recognize that man in the straw hat. His name is George Blackerby and he's wanted for murder in Colorado. He was my neighbor and he strangled his wife and disappeared before they could arrest him. I'm going to find a phone and call the FBI, and I want you to keep an eye on that man till I get back. Okay? We can't let this killer get away again! Oh, and I'll bet you a dollar that guy working with him is an illegal alien or worse. I heard somebody ask him for his social security card this morning and he shrugged and said, 'Me no got.' I'm going to call the border patrol too."

"I'll watch the man in the hat, and if he leaves I'll try to see where he goes," said Melvin . His day was starting to get interesting. Stanley from Colorado Springs took off through the glass doors that opened into the hallway, and Melvin ordered another scotch and water to be charged to Harold in 421. He then resumed his surveillance of the man in the straw hat who was still supervising the transplanting of the bedding plants.

The border patrol showed up first — two agents in uniform. When the little Mexican saw them strolling toward him, he dropped his shovel, took a flying leap into the pond and swam furiously across. He charged through the elephant ears on the other side, ran up the gently sloping bank, then climbed the steeper bank of a high earthen levee and disappeared over the top. One of the agents grabbed his radio, spoke a few words into it and put it back on his belt. Then both turned around and strolled back through the hotel patio and continued in the direction from whence they had come. The man in the straw hat stood shaking his head, then knelt next to a flowerbed and continued the transplanting himself. He didn't notice the FBI agents until they flanked him on either side. As they brought him toward the patio bar, the bartender stepped in front of them and asked "Why are you taking Mr. Stone away in handcuffs?"

On of the agents flashed a badge. "Step aside, Sir."

"Please, I insist! So that you do not upset our guests, could you at least take him around the building and not down the main hallway and past the front desk?"

"Can do," said the agent, and he took his prisoner by the arm and steered him down the walkway that led around the building. The second agent followed behind.

The excitement now over and done with, Melvin looked out again on the beautifully landscaped grounds. The hose had flooded another flowerbed, and the water was running onto the sidewalk again, so he quickly downed what was left of his drink, trotted over to the hose, and moved it to the area that had just received a new installation of bedding plants. Then he saw the hat. Mr. Stone or Blackerby or whatever his name was had lost it while he was being handcuffed. Melvin picked it up and looked inside. Printed on the sweatband with a permanent marker were the following words: This hat belongs to Hiram Stone, chief groundskeeper at the Royal Hospitality Hotel.

"Well now it belongs to Melvin Thigpen," said Melvin, and he placed it on his head. He noticed that one flat of bedding plants was still sitting beside a newly spaded flowerbed and the little plants were starting to wilt in the heat. He thought he should save them. He knelt beside the flowerbed, grabbed a trowel and started separating the petunias and planting them. When he was about halfway done, he noticed the approach of a young woman he had seen at the front desk as he came in. He stood up as she stopped to address him. "Mr. Stone, I presume. I guess your cell isn't working. The salesman from the landscaping service called. He'll be here in a few minutes for you to show him how you want the plantings modified. Now that I know where you are, I'll direct him right to this spot, so don't go anywhere, okay?

"Okay," said Melvin.

Ten minutes later, the salesman from the landscaping service showed up and stuck out his right hand. The label on his shirt said Plant Kingdom Inc., Worldwide Landscaping Operations.

"Mr. Stone?"

"Yes," said Melvin Thigpen, "I'm Hiram Stone."

"Joe Wesley, Sir, at your service. I'm with the Plant Kingdom. What did you have in mind with regard to your landscaping upgrade?"

Melvin shook the hand and looked around before he spoke. "Well for starters, this is the Royal Hospitality Hotel, so I think we ought to take out those Washingtonia palms and replace them with Royals. And I want them all to be at least thirty feet tall."

Mr. Wesley took the pen off his clipboard and pointed it at each palm as he counted. "You've got fourteen Washingtonias here. A thirty foot Royal Palm will run you about 140 dollars per foot. We have to ship them in from our tree farm in Puerto Rico, and that price doesn't include the removal of the Washingtonias or the professional installation of the Royals. That's quite a large investment, sir."

"That's our concern, not yours," said Melvin, "and I also want a generous planting of exotic water lilies in assorted colors all the way around the lake just inside the elephant ear border. Go heavy on the tropicals; I like the way the flowers stand above the water on those long stems."

"You are very creative, Sir. Would you like to add something more?"

"Yes, take out that row of wispy-looking Phoenix palms along the sidewalk there and replace them with something with more character — something more distinctive and robust. I think bottle palms would be ideal."

"A very wise choice, Sir. Anything else?

"Not at this time."

Mr. Wesley removed a calculator from his shirt pocket and pecked away at the keys. "Very well sir, we should have the job completed in less than a month, and we provide a one year guarantee on all our plants. If the total cost here runs over one hundred twenty thousand, our company will absorb the difference. Would that be satisfactory?

"Quite," said Melvin "A hundred twenty grand is a reasonable price."

Mr. Wesley entered some notes and figures onto the document on his clipboard, and handed it to Melvin. "Then sign here."

Melvin signed the contract, and Mr. Wesley shook his hand vigorously, thanked him for the business, and took off up the sidewalk with a spring in his step. Melvin smiled and said quietly to himself, "I do love to make people happy."

Migrating Jewels
By Brenda Nettles Riojas

Jewels from our mother's treasure chest,
Winged rubies and emeralds
Dazzle our front yard

On their way further south,
The ruby throated hummingbirds
Collect their nectar,

Pausing at each red bristle
On our crimson bottle brush tree,
A rest stop before they continue

On their Migration route.

NACHO
By Bidgie Weber

Isn't it strange how one person who passes through our lives can leave an indelible mark? At seventy years of age, I still bear one such mark in my memory — the mark of a remarkable man called "Nacho."

No one knew where he came from, who his parents were, where he spent his childhood, or for that matter, where he spent his nights. He appeared in our world like a character from an old folk tale. He brought nothing with him when he came and he took nothing with him when he passed, leaving only lasting memories for everyone who's path he crossed.

The only thing I knew about him was his name. Nacho. Later, as people got to know him, they called him "Barefoot" Nacho regardless of summer, winter, rain or blistering sun. Maybe he never wore shoes; maybe he just liked feeling the earth beneath his feet.

I guess his feet were what fascinated me the most. They looked like worn out dark brown shoes. His skin looked like a shoe with no sole and the leather just draped around his ankles like baggy socks. From the top of his round heels, the skin was always cracked, dry and dirty. As a child, I used to wonder if he could walk over flames and never feel the heat.

He was probably of Mexican descent. Heritage had provided the color of his skin and nature had accented it with the rich chocolate glow that comes from hours in the hot Texas sun. No one ever determined his age. It was impossible to tell, tired and weatherworn from years lived.

His whiskers fascinated me. As a little girl, the only whiskered faces I had ever touched belonged to men in my family. Soft grey whiskers that tickled my fingers were my grandfather's. Black short stiff whiskers meant my dad didn't get to shave that morning. My uncles both had mustaches on their upper lips that felt entirely different from dad's and granddad's facial hair. Touching Nacho's face was something I would have never done so I can only imagine how they would have felt.

Hog hair!

I can see it as hog hair because we had owned hogs at one time, and Nacho's hair looked like that. It was dark, black, and wiry, and always the same length. Nacho's beard covered his lower face like soot from a campfire made from damp logs. The hair on his head was coal black except for a few stray white hairs that would catch the sun light at the most unexpected times. Sometimes, for a fraction of a second, they would shimmer then disappear. Random mats of stiff hair sprang out in all directions from his large head. Hair grew wild from his scalp down the back of his short neck. I imagined it spread across his shoulders like blot of spilled black ink.

If the eyes are the window to a soul, Nacho's eyes needed a good cleaning with Windex. Huge dark brown eyes, cow eyes as we used to call them, floated in a large sea of coffee-tinted cream. Lips are most interesting to me, so Nacho's are easy to describe. Take an inner tube, stretch it out as far as it will go, and those were Nacho's lips, in miniature of course. In all the years of his life in our town, those lips never uttered a word. Maybe he never had or needed a reason to speak. Maybe he couldn't. The only time he surely should have had something to say, but didn't, was during the last days of his life.

He always wore a pair of blue denim overalls and had a red handkerchief in his back pocket. For some reason he never buttoned the side openings of his overalls. As hard as I try, I cannot remember what kind of shirt he wore. He wore his pant legs rolled up half way between his ankles and his knees.

Bath time for Nacho came from the afternoon rains, rare here in the Valley. Swarms of gnats were constant companions for him, as they were for everyone else. He did not seem to mind them flying up his nose, playing in his ears or getting in his eyes because he never bothered to shoo them away. Like many other things, Nacho accepted gnats as just a part of life and he dealt with it.

As a kid, we learned early on to snort them out of our nose, blink them away from our eyes, or slap them out of our ears. They were nasty little pests whose only purpose in life was (and still is) to spread the dreaded "sore eye" or "pink eye" that spoiled afternoon games of baseball or hide-n-seek. Direct sunlight is extremely painful to anyone who suffers with "sore eye".

Summer time, when the Valley is hot and humid and perspiration flows like honey, is still the favorite time for gnats to torment a victim. Many were the times when I would yawn, cough, or just try to talk, only to suck what would feel like an entire swarm of the nasty little buggers down my throat!

But Nacho never seemed to mind those or any other discomforts. He was always walking, always going somewhere and always at the same pace. Not ambling, not rushing, just keeping a determined pace as if he knew where he was going and what time he had to be there.

The only things he owned were the clothes on his back. He never carried a sack, pushed or pulled a cart like the homeless do today. He ate somewhere every day. He seemed portly and in acceptable health, but his weight might have been an illusion. Dressed as he was, in loose fitting overalls, the wide pant legs rolled above those big weatherworn feet and the oversized head to complete "the look", we might have easily assumed he was heavy set.

Some days he walked by our house and stopped under the same tall date palm. There he would sit down and wait till my Granny Brooks brought him lunch. Each day at noon she looked out to make sure he was under the palm, then she fixed him a lunch plate and took it out to him.

Spoons and forks were "unknowns" to Nacho because he never used them. Everything from mashed potatoes to pot roast was finger food to him, no doubt seasoned by remnants of the day's adventures clinging to his fingers.

He finished his meal, never acknowledging it as a good deed, nor duty on Granny's part. He continued his journey. His mythical destination at the end of the "yellow brick road" led him to the edge of town and to the limit of his perception. An orchard on the outskirts of Lyford housed swarms of honeybees that needed Nacho's attention.

Maybe he made sure a family of skunks was safely hidden from stray dogs. Maybe this was a part of the world Nacho held in his head, safe from all intruders. I remember one blistery winter day Granny Brooks gave him a warm coat. Nacho accepted the coat, placed it over his arm then continued on his journey, never looking left or right, just straight ahead. I never saw him wear it, never saw him carry it again. I often wondered where it was.

Years, miles, and many changes brought me back to my childhood roots. Stories from old timers reached me and enchanted me. Nacho's last story, as told to me by Peto Cantu was one such story.

"I remember that Señor Nacho began to look bad. He had not been walking the roads. No one knew where he spent his nights or his days, so we could not check on him. He ended up at my door one day, all bent over and holding his stomach. I didn't know what was wrong and he couldn't tell me. I took him to your Granny Brooks for help. We got him to old Doc Minger's office. For about two days, Nacho was in terrible pain, but he never said a word. He just rolled around on the bed, bit his lips, and the tears ran down his face. We knew he hurt bad, but we didn't know what to do for him."

Old Doc Minger was the only doctor in town and he was good for broken arms, cracked ribs, and belly aches from too much spicy Mexican food.

He could give the required inoculations for the babies of our town, but at the ripe old age of eighty-eight, those were about the only things he could be counted on for. Symptoms of this sort were far above his head so, with no other doctor and no hospital any where near Lyford, Doc declared Nacho was just plain loco.

What happened next was inexcusable.

"When Señor Nacho started to fight, they tied him up in one of those straight jackets so he wouldn't hurt someone," Peto said. "He was so scared when they strapped him on a gurney and put him in that ambulance. Your Señora Granny had tears in her eyes too." No doubt that was the first time he ever rode in a motor vehicle.

"Madre de Dios," Peto whispered as he crossed his heart with the sign of the cross. "Before the ambulance got to the King Ranch, Nacho was dead." Once again, Peto bowed and made the sign of the cross.

We learned later that his appendix broke and he died in the back of the ambulance, in the straight jacket, alone in his mysterious, silent world.

Nacho could not utter the words that could have saved his life. He died in a strange place on his way to a place he could never have imagined existed. He left a "barefoot print" in the history of the small town of Lyford, Texas.

As it was seventy plus years ago, so it is today. Ask any old timer from town, "Who do you remember most from Lyford?" and chances are he will tell you the story of Nacho. The story you might hear could end something like: "That would be 'Barefoot Nacho'". He lived around here back in the thirties and forties. He died on the way to Austin because of some dumb doctor who couldn't figure out he had appendicitis. Died right there in the ambulance…a dirty rotten shame, too. That old boy never did anything to anybody."

NOCTURNAL JOURNEYS
By Julieta Corpus

Last night, while I slept,
My spirit transformed itself
Into a small, grey finch,
Which took flight towards the ocean.
Perhaps it wanted to dance
With the seagulls under the radiant
Constellations of an August sky.
Or perhaps, it was merely
Responding to a beckoning call
By playful, salty breezes whose vice
Was to whisper mischievous enticements
To small, fragile birds.

"Fly high above the waves, little one!
Let us ruffle your soft feathers
With our cool breath!
Now, get closer to the hypnotizing
Rhythms of the ocean and lose
Your tiny being in its depths.
Trust us, precious bird.
You've nothing to fear.
We'll cradle you and
Care for you on the way down!"

Trapped inside the rapid beating
Heart of that innocent finch, I
Could not issue a warning.
I wanted to scream at the
Deceiving breezes to LEAVE US IN PEACE!
I wanted to scream at my winged host
Not to get any closer to that ocean.
It was a trap. A clever sacrifice by
The breezes to romance the waters
And to thrill the stars,

But…
Perhaps my spirit had wanted to soar
On that night, of all nights,
Under the gorgeous constellations
Of an August sky.
It could be that it was merely responding
To the beckoning calls by those treacherous,
Playful, salty breezes.
Nonetheless, it should never have taken
The shape of a foolish, brainless bird, which,
Operating on sheer impulse, flew towards
The ocean and was immediately devoured
By enormous, hungry waves.

Tonight, I'll pray that my spirit morphs
Into something with a fully functional brain
Before it decides to venture out into a
Dream world in which breezes are conniving
And oceans are ravenous.

ODE TO THE HUMMINGBIRD
By Nelly Venselaar

You beautiful thing!
Did you know that you came just in time?
To cheer up this human being?
Is this your aim in life?

You were hanging there, in front of my window
As if trying to make up your mind: Where to go?

Feeding from the bright, blue delphiniums,
Decorating my view to its maximum
With cedars as background.

Your long pointed bill probing for nectar
Your droning and humming of your wings.
Your dazzling iridescent colors
Give us much joy and enchantment in life.

Not only here in the North.
I am sure I met you down South
Hovering in and out of the peach, red and yellow hibiscus.
Flowers shaped like a drinking cup
And treated by the hummer with love and respect
As if drinking from the Chalice.

Ode To The Valley
By Eunice Greenhaus

The Rio Grande Valley, what a wonderful place
Friendliness beams from each person's face
No "Snowbirds" are found anyplace here
"Hello Winter Texans" is everyone's cheer

The weather is warm, the sea breeze cools
All around us Mother Nature rules
The palm trees rustle in the air
Flowers and shrubs bloom everywhere

Fat lazy cattle graze in the fields
Many crops the fertile farmland yields
Birdwatchers come to see the migrations
Of flocks that fly in from the southern nations

People and animals all cross the border
Back and forth they traverse the water
But a great big wall that's under construction
May change my Valley to one big obstruction

ONE MIDWIFE'S STORY
By Janice Workman

Pain streaked from her back to her lower abdomen with such intensity that she gasped and grabbed the table so she wouldn't fall. Just as suddenly, there was a gush of water that soaked her skirt in a pink-stained flood and filled the small room with a familiar astringent odor. "I have to push!" Lucy said, trying to catch her breath. "The baby's coming."

I eased her down to the waiting pallet. Theresa brought a steaming pan from the stove closer so I could easily reach whatever I might need.

"Help me, Doña, please!" Lucy groaned from the bed, as more damp curls showed themselves with each push.

I held a flannel cloth soaked with warm olive oil under the baby's head to relax Lucia's muscles and allow a new life to slip more easily into my hands.

"It'th a girl!" Theresa exclaimed, her lisp pronounced from excitement, as she leaned in close to watch. My fingers nimbly tied string around the cord before separating mom and baby with a snip.

After methodically winding a bellyband snuggly around the coin covering the umbilical stump to keep the belly button flat, I pinned a diaper securely into place. Last, I wrapped the chubby pink baby papoose style in a soft clean blanket before handing her to a tired, but content Lucia.

I guess this is as good a time as any to introduce myself. I am Doña de la Luz. The perfect name for a midwife, don't you think? My mother died in childbirth with just enough breath to name me "Maria Natividad." I did not want to attend women in labor with a name I associated so closely with death, so after my sixteenth year, I became "Doña de la Luz". Many times I've encouraged women in labor with, *"Da le luz a el niño!"* (Give the light to the child). So beautiful, those words, but no one uses them anymore.

I came here from Mexico, long before there were bridges and laws to by-pass. For more than 40 years I've been helping babies into the world, following the path my own grandmother laid before me. It seemed a natural transition to go from being the one who boiled water, held the lantern and washed linens to being the one who made teas, eased the child from the womb and cut the cord.

It is an honor to be present for this miracle. Most of the time it is such a lovely miracle, but, life being what it is, there are sad times too. Oh, the stories I could tell you…give me a moment while I sort my thoughts…

San Juanita… She came to me from a distant rancho one early July morning in a buckboard driven by her oldest son. Her blankets were soaked in blood and her face was pale with fear, pain and shock.

"Something's wrong! It's not time," she whispered, as we half carried her into my house. "I don't know what to do. Franco is gone. The bleeding started this morning. Oh, it's like a knife…"

I quickly set a pan on the stove to boil water. People joke about this all the time, "You tell the husbands to do that to keep them out of the way…" or "It's to make a cup of tea when you're done." But there are several good reasons to have it ready. Boiling water can sterilize string and scissors as well as other equipment. I can steep teas that relax the womb, ease pain, bring on sleep, slow bleeding, or encourage labor. Hot water helps prevent infections by keeping hands clean, sanitizing linens, bathing babies, washing private parts, and returning the birthing area to it's spotless condition.

"Find Theresa," I ordered Franco Junior, needing my helper and wanting him out of the room.

Pulling back the blankets, I saw two tiny feet inching slowly forward. "Juana, when is your baby due?" I asked quietly, trying to keep things calm.

"I'm not sure, I think October. This one has been different from the beginning. The other three - I never felt bad. I've been so tired. I don't have anything ready. Franco will be upset he wasn't here. I hope it's a girl."

In moments I could see Juana's desire for a girl would be fulfilled, but she would never put ribbons in her hair or sew her a doll baby. "Easy now," I coaxed her. "Just a little more." My hand supported the still, dusky baby as the head slipped free.

"Juana," I said, holding her eyes with mine. "She is very tiny. Her little lungs weren't ready for this world." Gently I wrapped the baby in a piece of flannel and handed her to Juanita.

"My baby…" She howled, with the grief of every mother who has lost a child.

Theresa came through the door with a look of expectation. "Baby not crying?" She asked, heading toward the bed.

"No, *mija* (daughter)," I told her, holding her shoulder to keep her at my side. "Baby is in heaven."

"Oh." was all she said, looking into my tear-streaked face with almond shaped eyes that held a depth few people gave her credit for.

I've always said, "Midwifery is about life's happiest moments and the saddest ones." Here's the story of my happiest one.

I never met a man who understood my need to care for women, work for my own money and be gone from the house at all hours of the day and night. As a result, I never had children of my own. At least, not until Theresa was born.

Eighteen and a-half years ago a couple knocked on my door. Her belly was round and full with life.

"It's my time," she said, with a peaceful smile of one who has done this before and has no fear of the process. Not like today where women expect childbirth without pain, shots to sleep through the labor and numbness from the waist down.

Her husband stepped outside, turning his hat in his hands. Nervous, I thought, because he had no work to do. "Mari, I wouldn't mind another son," he shouted over his shoulder. "With four girls and three boys, I can use more help with the cotton."

"I didn't tell him it was another girl," she told me, as she paced the small room, hands holding the small of her back. "Anna, the youngest, has been so fussy. I think she's jealous already."

Moving quickly, I made up the bed, putting plastic under the sheets and fluffing pillows to support her back.

"Okay, okay…" she panted. "I'm ready. Give me a cloth to bite so she doesn't go back up after I push."

Wordlessly I handed her a washcloth, knowing it would also stifle loud noises she didn't want her husband to hear.

She pulled her clothes out of the way, leaving a red string around her bulging waist that protected her from the evil eye for nine months and would stay there until the required forty days after delivery. A shiny metal key, dangled near her belly button, suspended from the string by a safety pin. This talisman prevented birth defects caused by eclipse of the sun or moon.

With a single throaty grunt, the baby's head became visible. Another push. I gently eased a loop of cord from around the child's neck before wiping mucus and fluid from the mouth. Without a sound she slid into the world, eyes wide open. "You were right, Mari", I said, placing her child in her arms. "It's a girl."

Her husband, unable to contain his excitement, rushed into the room and stared into the baby's face. "No! It can't be!" he exclaimed with distress that didn't fit the situation.

"Girls can help around the farm just as well as boys," I said, and handed him the child so I could help Mari clean up.

I took the soiled sheets, towels and rags to the back laundry area to soak. Bloody items in the cold bleach water, others in warm water with soap. I was humming wordlessly when I returned to the birth room, pleased by how easily everything had gone.

The bed was empty, the rocker next to it was empty, and the kitchen was empty. No one was on the front porch or even in the yard. Was this all just a dream? I saw movement in the laundry basket by the birth room door. Looking down, I gazed into the almond shaped eyes of the baby I delivered just two hours before. Her round, flat face had a solemn look as though she knew what was happening. I caught her chubby right hand in mine and opening the fist, saw a single straight line crossing her palm, and understood. She was mongoloid. Nowadays they call it "Down Syndrome" or some chromosomal something or other, but regardless, she was a baby and she had been abandoned.

No one had any idea who the couple might have been, and no one wanted to adopt the baby either. I took her as my own and named her Theresa, after my grandmother. She calls me "Momma." As I said before, "Midwifery brings some of the happiest moments."

There isn't much call for my skills these days. Folks want to go to the hospital. They want all the new fangled machines and medicines. There are too many rules saying what I can and can't do, regardless of my experience. That's okay. I've wanted to slow down any way. My bones get tired, muscles get sore and my garden needs tending.

Sometimes I get asked to help turn a baby since doctors don't like delivering them any way but head first. Occasionally someone wants a tea to help start labor or sleep better in the weeks before. Theresa has healing hands and can give a backrub that takes away knots and nightmares.

Now and then young midwives will come for a visit. There's always a lot of laughter. Theresa brings herbal tea and cookies out to the porch and sits nearby. We both smile when someone asks "Please Doña, tell me a story. Tell me a birth tale from your life."

OPIE EATS TORTILLAS
By Rudy H. Garcia

I am Opie Taylor, the little *guerito* boy who ran around the Carolina country town of Mayberry, in his black high Top Converse, playing cowboys and Indians in the back yard of my *Mexiquito* home, with Beaver the Cleaver and my big brother Wa-Wa.

I used to gallop barefooted, straddling my trusted stick horse "Palo Pinto", riding the western wind with Fury and Silver, wearing a Hopalong Cassidy white hat, tracking and fighting the unshaven bad guys in dusty black hats.

I chased cottontail rabbits and squirrelly squirrels and cooked darting white wings on a stick in the *Palangana Ponderosa* with my collie Lassie, accompanied by my favorite canine, *el Sergento*, Rin-Tin-Tin, the "fastest greatest dog that ever lived"; and I laughed for hours and hours with Tom and Jerry, *La Chilindrina* and her best friend *Chespirito*.

Captain Kangaroo and Mr. Green Jeans got me ready for Miss Garza's *esquelita*, school each morning. They ate Post-Toastees and drank Anita Bryant's orange juice while I ate *tortilla de harina con mantequilla* and washed it down with a cold glass of Elsie the Cow milk.

When I graduated from kindergarden to the *escuela Catolica* 1st grade class, I learned all about Jane the girl, Bill the boy, their dad with a brief case, wearing a fedora, suit and tie, and their stay at two-story home mother, cleaning house with a vacuum cleaner and cooking with a toaster, wearing a string of pearls, high heel stilettos, and a pretty pink fluffy, size five, can-can dress on black and white television. I always wondered what

Bill's dad carried inside the brief case because he never opened it…Bill wondered, too.

I had a little black cocker spaniel named Rover that used to follow me to school each day…after pulling spiny *espina del diablo* sticker burrs out of his furry dog hair with his four front teeth in the cool shade under a date palm. He would go back home to guard the house until 3:00 o'clock, when it was time for him to come get me, walk me back home, and chase cars along the way.

He understood and spoke English and Spanish just like me. And like me, he loved to eat *arroz con pollo*, but his two favorite foods were *papas con huevo* and *papas con carne*. We ate a lot of *papas* with everything, like little Ricky Ricardo and Dennis the Menace did, except, we never picked at our food during mealtime like they did. We wiped our plates squeaky clean with the last piece of flour or *maize tortilla, gordita de manteca*.

Rover especially loved the leftover *tortilla* scraps, soaked wet with *guisado* gravy and *chile piquin, salsa del barrio* dog treats, he got for supper every evening.

I am the *Chavo del Ocho, Cantinflas* named Adam, Hoss, little Joe Cartwright, fighting the *pinche* big *vatos* with Charlie Chan whiskers in Sister Perpetual Help's fourth grade class during recess…because they wanted me to give them my refried bean tacos, my mother had made for me, so that I could eat lunch.

I am the Oblate altar boy, who prayed the Holy Rosary daily… obediently kneeling in front of the *Virgin de Guadalupe*, the *Virgin De San Juan*, the Mary virgin mother of God and all the saints in both Spanish and English, till my knees tingled with a million *piquetes de hormiga* and my lower back felt hot and numb — like my calves used to feel when Mother Superior, Sister "Bulldog", spanked me almost daily — and often several times daily — with her evil ½ inch by 1 inch by 36 inch, yard stick.

One day, after school when Sister Bulldog had gone to the convent, to go to the bathroom or to visit Father Fanning, or something, Charlie Hamburger and me decided we had had enough of that devil stick and stole it. We made a little campfire with it in some small *montecito*-woods, next to the haunted house where we used to hunt birds, lizards and horned frogs. The old *bruja, Doña Pepa cara de Crepa* used to get mad at us, because she said the *montecito*-woods belonged to her, and to leave her lizards and birds alone. We roasted several Caw-Cawk sparrows on a mesquite stick like marshmallows with the *vara*-stick from hell, sparking embers. They were the best tasting Caw-Cawks, we ever done had!

I must confess, however, that being the good, devoted altar boy that I was, I confessed my sins to the semi-retired priest, Father McDermit, snoozing and nodding on the other side of the confessional screen, during my weekly obligatory Saturday afternoon confessions. I confessed that I had spoken some bad words like "*pinche*" and "*pendejo*", and that I told my mother a few little "white lies", like scrubbing good with soap and shampoo instead of just plain water during bath time…and that I fought with my older sister, Alma, and that I pushed my little sister, Melba, knocking her down for no reason, except that she was smaller than me.

I later heard my mother, tell my father, that the reason I had pushed my baby sister, making her cry, was because I was mad at her, because she had done the "*lo tumbo la burra*" to me.

Also, on my rehearsed list of things to confess, I confessed that I had thrown some rocks at Rita, Nina, Eva, Dolores and some of the other prissy-missy girls from school, but that I didn't hit them. I could have, if I wanted to, but I didn't. I was a dead shot rock thrower and could hit anything, right on the bulls' eye within 100 feet. I only threw the rocks close enough to scare them, and make them scream their girly-girl scream. Charlie Hamburger and me always got a thrill at hearing the missy girls let out their prissy yells. They knew we weren't going to hit them. It was a daily ritual that we went through each day on our way home after school. It was routine. It was pre-puberty behavior.

When classes let out, Charlie and me would be the first ones to charge out of class, run as fast as we could for two town blocks to a vacant lot that served as one of our many hideouts. The lot was perfect for hiding. It had chest high Johnson grass and many old majestic mesquite trees and lots of flowering prickly pear cactus. We waited there in ambush for the girls to pass.

The next day, as soon as they got to school, they ran straight to Mother Superior, who stood on her favorite look out spot over looking the play ground like an English sheep dog watching over its flock, to tattle-tale what me and Charlie Hamburger done to them the day before. Then they'd stick out their pink pudgy tongues at us as they walked back past us. They would put their clean, plumpy hands over their soft *Color de Rosa* lips and giggle, hiding their flirty smiles, like girls always do when they know they got you! They would run with their funny girl run to their favorite part of the side walk to skip "hot peppers" double-dutch jump rope, holding down their pleated plaid skirts with one hand so that when the rope and the gusty wind hit them, the skirts wouldn't lift, showing their white cotton under wear, because they knew Charlie Hamburger and me were waiting for that friendly gust of air or for the teasing rope to come up on them just right, so that we could catch even a tiny glimpse of their undies. Sister Bulldog was watching them too.

Unfortunately for us, they were extremely skilled at sensing the next rush of wind, and they also knew when they had landed on a spot off center and that the rope was going to hit their skirt on the way up, so they would bring both hands down, hold the skirt and skip out of the way.

But that day, when the bell rang calling us to lessons, Sister Bulldog couldn't spank us. She couldn't spank us because she couldn't find her wicked stick. So, in frustration, she shook us violently, pulled our ears and pinched our arms instead. She tried to pull our hair but she couldn't. She couldn't because our parents always kept our hair cut shorter than an army crew cut. They said they kept our hair cut short because "*los pelones no crean piojos.*" Instead, she gave us some *coscorrones* with her boney knuckles and sent us to the broom and coat closet to kneel in penance isolation… and we had no recess that day.

And I confessed that I had killed some little birds, but as always, I told the tired priest, that I had eaten the little birds, so it really wasn't a sin? I also confessed that it was me and Charlie Hamburger that stole Mother Superior's whipping stick and used it to make a fire to cook the little birds. It cost my young callused knees twenty Hail Marys, twenty Our Fathers, and one Act of Contrition, on the hard wood floor in front of Saint Francis of Assisi. But it was worth it! Besides, I had become an accustomed expert at kneeling for long periods of time. I had developed a technique. Kneeling had become second nature to me.

I even learned some Latin words like "*mea culpa, mea culpa, mea verdadera culpa*", "*Dominom du bisco*" *las nalgas te pelisco*, from a tobacco pipe smoking Irish priest named Father Fanning who drank beer at the church Kermes. He had a boxer bulldog named Carla. Some kids swore that Carla and Sister Bulldog were related. Not me. I knew better; but I wondered sometimes. There was an eerie facial and vocal resemblance about them.

I am the little boy who had two girl friends. One of them was Ellie May Clampet, a long-legged blonde swimming in the cool cement pond of her ritzy Beverly Hills mansion. The other one was *la niña bonita* with the *monillo colorado* and her *mochila azul*. She had long curly *Lucerito* hair and round bright *Palomita* eyes. During Charro Days, her mother used to dress her in a beautiful *China Poblana* dress with a *charra sombero*. She lived down the street from me.

I am the little boy who grew up loving and pledged to one country and having deep ancestral roots in another country, and because of this, I lived the better of two worlds.

I am the all American boy, who grew up to become a fine Latino, Chicano, Mexican-American, Hispanic made in the U.S.A., *Estados Unidos de America*!

PABLO, THE SPACESUIT AND THE CHUPACABRA
By Jack King

Pedro and Pablo Calaveras were brothers who lived on opposite sides of the Rio Grande. Their mother had given birth to Pedro at the family goat ranch in the Mexican state of Coahuila and to Pablo, sixteen months later, at the hospital in Del Rio, Texas. Twenty-five years later, Pedro was running the ranch in Mexico, and Pablo, a U.S. citizen, was working as a forklift operator at a NASA warehouse complex in Houston.

One day some men came into the warehouse where Pablo was working and announced that they were going to do a complete inventory of everything in the building. They would need his assistance. Pablo obliged, using the forklift to take large crates down from their racks as the men requested. He assisted in the opening of the crates, and he watched as the men took various items out and catalogued them. One of the crates contained several obsolete spacesuits that had been used by astronauts in the early years of the space program. Another crate contained several heavy-duty wall-size murals rolled up on a long hollow spool. When they were unrolled on the floor, the murals each measured a full ten feet square. Pablo liked the picture of the lunar landscape and the one that showed the shuttle on the pad, ready for launch.

When the men had completed their inventory and left the warehouse, Pablo turned to his friend and co-worker, Cecil Benson. "Hey Cecil," he said, "Let's get those murals out and hang a couple of them right over there, and then let's pull out one of those spacesuits. You can help me get into it, and then you can take a picture of me in the spacesuit in front of each mural."

Cecil looked a little uneasy. "We're not going to get into any trouble, are we?"

"Of course not. We're not going to steal anything. We'll have everything back where it belongs in a matter of minutes."

An hour a half later, they had everything back where it was. With the aid of the forklift, the murals had been easy to hang, but getting in and out of the spacesuit had been difficult. Pablo would never have been able to do it without Cecil's help, but eventually he got into the suit and later, back out of it. He would soon have a photo of himself on the lunar landscape wearing the complete spacesuit, and another photo of himself in front of the space shuttle with the helmet under his arm and his head sticking out of the steel ring that locked the helmet onto the suit. He also had a big look-at-me smile on his face.

Ten days later, he went to Mexico to visit his brother, Pedro; but before he left Houston, he bought a silver-gray flight jacket and had the NASA logo embroidered prominently on the back. On the front, he had the words, SPACE COMMAND, embroidered on the right breast and the words, CAPTAIN CALAVERAS sewn onto the left breast in the style of a military nametag. He had always dressed with imagination and style, and often said that clothes make the man. He also bought a pair of aviator-style sunglasses, and he went to a barbershop and had his jet-black mustache trimmed to crisp perfection. Then he went to Mexico.

Pablo's brother, Pedro, had a soft spot in his heart for his goats and hated to see them killed for their meat, so he had switched to angora goats, which are not slaughtered, but sheared periodically for the mohair. When Pablo arrived at the ranch wearing his new flight jacket and aviation sunglasses, the shearing was in progress, and much to his delight, several of the goat shearers were young women. He showed them the photos and told them he was an astronaut.

When the day's work was done, Pedro invited the shearing crew to the ranch house for the evening meal, and after supper, the pretty senoritas gathered around Pablo and asked him what it was like to be an astronaut. He told them that NASA had many secret programs that the public did not know about and that he had been involved in space exploration not only on the moon, but also throughout the solar system and even far beyond. He gave lurid accounts of battles he had fought in the steamy jungles of Jupiter, treasure chests recovered from the oceans of Neptune after bloody sea battles with flying submarines, and a battle of wits he'd won against the Vampire Queen of Venus who had tried unsuccessfully to lure him into her bed. The girls hung on his every word; listening to his tales with such eager delight and bright-eyed wonder that Pablo almost began to believe the stories himself. The weekend at the ranch ended far too quickly, and on Monday Pablo was back in Houston, running the noisy diesel forklift in the dismal NASA warehouse.

A month later, he got a call from the ranch. Pedro's voice conveyed a sense of worry and apprehension. "Pablo, do you still have the spacesuit that you wore in those photos?"

"Well, yes, it's still there in the warehouse, but it doesn't belong to me; it belongs to NASA."

"Is there any chance you could smuggle it out and bring it here to the ranch?"

"It would be very difficult, and it might cost me my job, and it might even land me in jail, but I suppose I could do it if it were really, really important."

"Pablo, I hate to tell you this, but it's really, really important. My future and the future of my beloved ranch depend on it. You must come here immediately and bring the spacesuit with you. I beg of you, please. Please come and bring the suit. I'll explain when you get here."

"Well, I do have two weeks vacation coming. I'll come the very minute they allow me to leave, and I'll try to bring the suit."

"Pablo, don't even bother to come if you can't bring the suit." And with that, Pedro hung up the phone.

Two days later, Pablo was on his way to Coahuila in his vintage Corvette. As he drove down the interstate, he daydreamed of the pretty *chicas* he had met on his previous visit, and he hoped he would get to see them again. When he arrived at the border, he called his brother. "Pedro", he said, "I'm here in Del Rio with the spacesuit in the trunk of my car. How am I supposed to get it across the bridge without having it confiscated by Mexican customs?"

"Don't worry, *mi hermano*. Our dear cousin, Arturo, is a Mexican customs agent. He is working the bridge today and is expecting you. You will have no problem at all. Come quickly, please."

After a one-hour delay at the Mexican customs office, Pablo was on his way again, and two hours later, he parked the Corvette in front of the ranch house. His brother came out immediately and escorted him inside. "*Bienvenidos*, Pablo. Arturo called and said you have the spacesuit. I am so happy. Seat yourself at the table, and I'll explain everything over coffee." Pablo sat down with Pedro, and Pedro's wife, Maribel, poured the coffee. Pedro took a quick sip and then spoke. "I know you will find it hard to believe what I have to tell you, but I'll come right out with it. A terrible and vicious *Chupacabra* has taken up residence here on the ranch and is killing my goats—not only mine but the goats of the other ranchers as well. If we don't stop this monster soon, we will all be ruined."

Pedro's eyes widened. "And you need a spacesuit to stop the *chupacabra?*"

"No, Pablo, we need you inside the spacesuit. The *chupacabra* spends the daylight hours inside that big thorny thicket at the four corners where my ranch meets the Alaniz ranch, the Gonzales ranch and the Galvan ranch. He comes out every night, and all of us here in these parts have lost dozens of our livestock to the hideous beast. We continue to lose animals at the rate of four or five a night. None of us have been able to get inside the thicket. It is infested with large rattlesnakes that can raise their heads and sink their fangs into your leg well above your boot tops, and there is also a huge hive of killer bees inside the thicket. Any kind of loud or unusual noise incites them to attack. Señor Alaniz just got out of the hospital after going in with his 30-30 saddle gun and suffering almost two hundred bee-stings, and Señor Galvan is still in the hospital after suffering a terrible snakebite to his right thigh. Mr. Gonzales posted a sentry to watch over his goats one night, and the next morning the man was found dead along with three goats, every drop of blood drained from each of the four bodies.

"We need a man with some kind of high-tech protective garb to go in and kill the monster. The girls who listened to your fantastic fabrications of space adventure have suggested to me that you are the man for the job. They approached me with such earnest and innocent and hopeful eyes that I didn't have the heart to tell them the truth about you, Pablo. At first I thought their idea was utterly ridiculous, but the more I thought about it the more plausible the proposition became. I am sure that the rich U.S. government makes a very strong and protective suit for its astronauts. It should certainly protect you against something as ordinary as thorny brush and cactus, bee stings, and even rattlesnake bites. Perhaps it will even protect you from the fangs and claws of the *chupacabra*. I would put on the suit myself, but I don't think it would fit me. I have seen your photographs, and so I know that the suit fits you. It is already four in the afternoon, Pablo. I will help you into the spacesuit, and I will lend you my twelve-gauge pump shotgun, and I will drive you to the thicket straightaway before the approaching darkness awakens the *chupacabra*. He is big and terrible, he is dangerous, and he is very very quick. It is said that he can see a bullet coming and catch it in his teeth, so it is imperative that you find him and kill him before he awakens. Come, let us get you into the spacesuit."

Pablo's eyes widened and he stuttered as he spoke. "Oh, n-n-no," he protested. "You know me, Pedro. I'm a lover, not a fighter. I brought the suit. You can find someone else to wear it into that cursed thicket."

"Pablo, you told me once that clothes make the man. Now put on the suit and be a man."

Pablo closed his eyes, trying desperately to come up with some excuse to refuse the frightful mission his brother was attempting to force upon him. "The oxygen tanks are empty," he said.

"Arturo had them refilled," said Pedro. "What do you think he was doing during that hour you sat in the customs office?"

Abruptly, the front door opened and Maribel entered bringing the spacesuit in from the Corvette. Right behind her were four pretty senoritas from the goat-shearing squad. They addressed Pablo excitedly as they hurried to his side. "Oh, *Capitan*, we are so happy that you are here to save us. We know it is asking a lot, but would you be so generous as to give each one of us a hug and a little kiss so that we can tell our friends and families and perhaps even our grandchildren someday that our lips once touched the lips of the brave astronaut who came to this humble place to battle the hideous *chupacabra?* It would make us so happy."

At this point, Pablo knew there was no way out, but his fear was dampened by a sweet pang of elation as he looked at the pretty young women waiting before him for his hugs and kisses. He arose, stretched himself up to his maximum height, and turned to Pedro. "Yes, my brother, I will accept this dangerous assignment. I, Captain Pablo Calaveras, will battle the mighty *chupacabra*. But before I don my warrior's armor, I must fulfill the request of these beautiful young ladies." Then one by one, he took each girl in his arms and kissed her with such tender and lingering passion that one would think that these were the last kisses he ever expected to get.

An hour later, Pedro was driving his pickup across the scrubby landscape, and Pablo was sitting beside him in the spacesuit with the helmet in his lap. The backpack containing the oxygen tanks had forced Pablo into a rather uncomfortable position, but he said nothing. Other vehicles were falling in behind them. The brothers traveled without speaking for several minutes, and then Pedro broke the silence. "There it is," he said, and he cut the engine and coasted to a stop beside a dry, rocky creek bed that led directly into the thicket about a hundred meters ahead. The other vehicles stopped too, and everybody stepped out into the fresh evening air. They all began to gather around Pedro's truck. Pedro smiled at them and announced, "It appears that you have all heard the good news. My brother, Pablo, has volunteered to go in and kill the *chubacabra*." He turned to his brother and handed him the shotgun. "I have to tell you, Pablo, that I'm not a deer hunter but a quail hunter, so the gun is loaded not with buckshot, but with birdshot. You will have to get in close before you pull the trigger or the pellets will only sting the beast and anger it."

"Yes," said another voice. "If the *chubacabra* is awake when you meet it, do not look into its eyes as you draw near. It will hypnotize you, and you will not be able to pull the trigger."

"Señor Galvan!" cried Pedro. "You're out of the hospital! You've recovered from the snakebite!"

"And it appears I'm here just in time," said the middle-aged man approaching slowly on crutches. "There are several things this brave young man needs to know before he goes in after the monster." Stepping up to Pablo and facing him directly, he said, "So that you have an idea of what to expect, let me tell you exactly what happened to me in there." The group fell silent as Señor Galvan continued. "I followed this rocky draw until I came to the thicket. It is the only way in. I stooped low as I made my way under the overhanging branches. The path to the *chupacabra's* lair is like a tunnel with the uneven stone of the creek bed underfoot and a canopy of thorny branches overhead. Once I was inside, I was able to stand up again, but even though it was the middle of the day, I found myself in a dusky world of spooky shadows; the canopy overhead blocked out most of the sunlight. There were a number of rattlesnakes crawling among the rocks and just enough room for me to maneuver around them as I made my way into the gloomy tunnel. They raised their heads and rattled their tails as I slipped past them. Then suddenly there was the monster, thirty meters straight ahead and coming directly toward me. I cocked my rifle, took the safety off, and waited, trying to keep one eye on the rattlers and the other on the approaching *chupacabra*. As it drew nearer, I noticed that it walked on two legs like a man, and its hide was covered not with hair, but with spines like a cactus. But what really caught my attention were the eyes. They were a glowing yellow, and the pupils were like black spirals that rotated slowly in opposite directions like a pair of windmills in a gentle breeze. I tried to raise the rifle to my shoulder but I couldn't. The eyes hypnotized me! I stood there frozen in place like a statue, watching the monster approach and unable to move a muscle or take my eyes off the hideous face. I had totally forgotten about the rattlesnakes, and I could not raise my gun to fire at the monster. As it drew nearer, I could see its mouth, not a big mouth full of sharp teeth, as I'd been led to expect, but a little round mouth with something flicking in and out of it like a serpent's tongue. But it wasn't forked or flexible like a serpent's tongue. It was rigid and tapered to a point, like a soda straw at the base and a hypodermic needle at the tip, something that could be used with equal facility to inject venom or suck blood.

"I was still paralyzed when it seized me by the shoulders and cocked its head to one side, I knew that it was about to sink its soda-straw fang into my neck, but I could not move. In the remnants of my shell-shocked mind, I recited a prayer and waited for the fang to stab into my neck. That's when the rattlesnake struck. It sank its fangs into the back of my right thigh just above the knee. I was still holding the rifle, and by some miracle reflex, the bite caused me to jerk and pull the trigger. The monster let go of my shoulders and fell back, howling in pain. The bullet had struck it in the left leg and blood was spurting from the hole. As it turned, it averted its eyes from mine to gaze at its wound. The spell was suddenly broken, and I regained the ability to move. The snake withdrew its fangs and coiled for another strike. I turned and fired into its open jaws, and the blast threw it back in a quivering heap. The gunshot had startled the bees and I could hear them swarming up the tunnel toward me. I dropped the rifle and ran back toward the place where I'd entered the thicket, leaping over rocks and dodging thorny branches and rattlesnakes. I looked back once and I could see the *chupacabra* lying quietly on the ground. I didn't know if it had passed out or was just playing possum to avoid the notice of the bees.

"My right leg was throbbing in pain from the snakebite, and I fell twice as I approached my vehicle. I got inside and slammed the door just as the bees swarmed over the truck. By the time I got back to the ranch house, my right leg was in such bad shape that I couldn't lift my foot to apply the brakes. My left leg wouldn't work right either. Unable to depress the brake pedal or even the clutch, I turned off the ignition and crammed the grinding gears into low. My vehicle slowed but not quickly enough. I had to swerve to avoid a goat. I hit the outhouse and knocked it off the pit, and the collision brought my truck to a stop. My family came running out of the house, and the last thing I remember was being lifted out of my vehicle. I woke up later in the hospital…I was just released this morning."

"*Chiiiiihuahua!*" said a voice in the crowd.

"*Carramba!*" said another.

Beads of perspiration had popped out on Pablo's forehead and he reached for the pocket where he customarily kept a handkerchief. There was no pocket. Pedro saw his brother's fumbling motion and exclaimed, "Your spacesuit has no pockets! I have some extra shotgun shells I was going to give you, but where are you going to carry them?"

"I have a nail apron in my pickup," said one of the ranch hands. "I'll get it." He brought the apron, and one of the girls placed it around Pablo's waist and tied it with a slipknot in the back.

Pedro filled the pockets with shotgun shells and spoke. "The gun holds four cartridges and it's already loaded. The safety lever is there on the side, and the safety is on. Don't forget to flip the safety off before you fire. It's getting late, Pablo. Let's get your helmet on."

Pablo handed the helmet to his brother and dropped to one knee as if he expected to be crowned or knighted. Pedro lowered the helmet over Pablo's head and locked the helmet neck ring onto the neck ring of the suit. He turned on the oxygen and Pablo nodded as he rose to a standing position. Pedro put his hands on his brother's shoulders as if he were about to kiss him on the cheeks, but instead he roughly turned him so that he faced the menacing thicket that loomed a hundred meters down the draw. Shouting loud enough that Pablo could hear him through the sealed suit, he cried, "Good luck, my brave brother. Here, take this machete with you too. We will wait here by the trucks until you return with the head of the *chupacabra.*"

Pablo wanted to say something, but he knew that the airtight helmet would prevent anyone from hearing his words clearly, so with shotgun in right hand and machete in left hand and a nail apron full of birdshot cartridges around his waist, he stepped out in the direction of the thicket trying his best to maintain a dignified posture and a confident gait in a clumsy spacesuit that had been designed not for battling *chupacabras* in a thorny thicket, but for floating in the zero-gravity vacuum of space. Ten meters from the thicket, he stepped down into the dry creek bed and began to pick his away along the rocky bottom. He tripped and fell twice and each time as he got back up, he thought he heard a ripple of laughter emanating from the crowd of spectators, but he convinced himself that his imagination was playing tricks.

Advancing along the bottom of the creek bed, he arrived at the thicket, ducked his head and plunged through the branches. He could hear the thorns scraping the helmet and the fabric of his suit. He stopped to examine the sleeves, but could see no tears or punctures. So far, so good.

He was now in the tunnel, and he strained his eyes to see. Thorny brush grew on either side of the rocky floor, and the branches closed overhead so that only a scant dappling of sunlight lit the way. The sharply winding course of the path permitted him to see only a few meters ahead. He'd advanced only a dozen steps when the first rattlesnake appeared. It was a big one, slithering down the center of the tunnel toward him. He stopped and began to back away. It came to a halt in the center of the path and coiled. It opened its jaws widely and he could see the pale pink lining of its mouth, and the two ivory upper fangs unfolded and dripped venom as they pointed straight at him. He felt a sudden impulse to turn and run back out of the thicket, but how could he bear the humiliation that would surely follow? He picked up a baseball-size rock and started to throw it at the snake but suddenly remembered that the *chupacabra* or the killer bees could be awakened or incited by noise. He waved the machete, but the rattlesnake held its ground. He slid the machete into the waistband formed by the nail apron and aimed the shotgun at the snake's head. It wasn't intimidated. He wondered if he could maneuver his way around it, as Señor Galvan had done. But what if it struck, and the spacesuit turned out not to be impervious to its stabbing fangs? A stinging drop of perspiration trickled into his right eye, and he suddenly realized there was no way to mop his brow. Due to his exertions, the spacesuit that had been relatively comfortable twenty minutes ago was now becoming a steaming sauna. The oxygen flow was sufficient for breathing, but not for cooling. He began to despise the thing for the trap it had become and the larger trap into which it had led him. He now had no choice but to suffer and sweat, stand his ground, and wait out the rattlesnake.

A minute later, it uncoiled itself and slithered away into the underbrush, and Pablo continued his nervous advance into the shadowy tunnel. Moments later, he heard a sound and turned to look behind him. There was the rattlesnake again, just a few steps back. He began to walk a little faster and turned to look back again. It was still there, following behind and urging him deeper into the thicket and closer to the monster . He found himself turning frequently to make sure the serpent wasn't getting too close. The turning wasn't easy because the helmet was attached to the suit and didn't turn when his head did. He had to turn his body around almost

180 degrees to get a good view of the area behind him, and sometimes it caused him to lose his footing and stumble.

The frequent turning was making him dizzy, and about the umpteenth time—he wasn't really counting—he turned to face forward again and… well, there it was—the *chupacabra*. And even though it had been the object and focus of his pursuit, he was still taken by surprise, and he dropped the shotgun and almost fainted on the spot.

He managed somehow, though, to maintain his awareness and found himself captivated by those yellow eyes with the rotating spiral pupils. Maybe hypnotized is a better word than captivated, even though he was indeed a captive. He was frozen in place and in a matter of seconds, the monster was upon him with its fore claws gripping his shoulders. And like Señor Galvan had been, Pablo was totally paralyzed. He could see the pointy, soda-straw fang flicking in and out of the little round mouth, and when the beast cocked its head to one side, Pablo knew it was all over. As the monster struck, he felt a dull blow to the inside top of his left shoulder and just knew the fang had pierced his jugular. But there was no pain—only a sound like a snapping twig and a sudden piercing shriek from the *chupacabra*. It fell back holding its fore claws to its mouth.

Pablo felt a blow to the back of his right thigh and turned around to look. The rattlesnake's fangs had failed to penetrate the suit but had become entangled in the strings of the nail apron. As it drew back, it untied the slipknot that held the apron in place, and it separated from the waist of the spacesuit, spilling the shotgun shells onto the rocks as it fell. Pablo spotted the gun on the ground where he had dropped it. He bent forward, seized it, flipped the safety off, and fired at the snake. Miraculously, the shot found its mark and took off half the serpent's skull. It crumpled and lay writhing and twitching.

Pablo heard a buzzing drone coming from somewhere deep in the thicket and realized that the shotgun blast had caught the attention of the killer bees. The sound was getting progressively louder and more intense. Still holding its mouth, the *chupacabra* dropped to the ground between two large rocks and lay very still. Pablo suddenly found himself in the center of a swarm of angry bees, and he began to swing his arms desperately in an attempt to swat them away. The swarm only became thicker and angrier. He began to run back down the tunnel toward the entrance. He screamed as he stepped on another rattlesnake, but he suffered no bite, and suddenly realized that he had not felt a single sting. The suit was actually protecting him.

He stopped in his tracks, a million disjointed thoughts racing through his head. As his mind began to settle, his thoughts became more cogent. What was he afraid of? Neither the snakes nor the bees could penetrate the suit, and the *chupacabra* had apparently broken its soda-straw fang on the steel collar-ring of the helmet. What to do now? He turned around and began to walk back toward the spot where he had lost the nail apron. If the *chupacabra* was still there, dead or playing possum, he would retrieve the machete, chop the monster's head off, and deliver to Pedro the trophy he expected.

The swarm of bees, still trying to get into the suit, accompanied Pablo back to the spot where he had lost the apron. The swarm was so thick now that he could barely find his way, but eventually he spotted the white apron lying among the dark stones. He picked it up and attempted to retie the strings around his waist. The gloves that were part of the suit made it very difficult, and after dropping the apron and picking it up again several times, he finally managed to get it tied, not in a slipknot, but a good tight square knot. He slid the apron around so that the pockets were in the front, and he began to pick up the shotgun shells and place them back in their compartments. When he'd retrieved the last cartridge, he looked around once more to make sure he hadn't left anything. He noticed a thin ivory-colored object lying beside the machete. It was the soda-straw fang of the *chupacabra*. He picked it up, dropped it into the apron with the cartridges, and retrieved the machete.

He looked around for the *chupacabra* and found it still lying quietly, belly down and face turned sideways, between the two large rocks. He raised his right arm, and holding the machete above his head, he cautiously approached the monster. As he drew near, the beast opened one glowing yellow eye, and Pablo averted his gaze and stopped in his tracks. The shotgun! Where was the shotgun? He stumbled around among the rocks until he found it. He dropped the machete, retrieved the gun, and had taken exactly three steps back toward the beast when it suddenly sprang to its feet and looked directly at Pablo with both yellow eyes open and spinning hypnotically. Pablo averted his gaze and fired in the direction of the monster. He missed. He pumped another shell into the chamber, and the monster turned and attempted to run. Pablo saw that it was limping, probably because of the wound inflicted by Señor Galvan. It was headed off in the direction of the tunnel entrance, moving as fast as it could with one bad leg and swatting furiously at the swarm of bees that was swelling around it.

Pablo lifted the shotgun to his shoulder, aimed carefully, and fired again. The *chupacabra* emitted a shriek as the birdshot stung its backside, but it kept going. Pablo took off in pursuit, but stumbled and fell after just four steps. He saw that he had tripped over the body of the rattlesnake that he had shot just minutes before. He knelt and tied a dangling apron string tightly around the snake just behind what was left of its head and took off again after the *chupacabra,* the nine-foot body of the serpent dragging heavily behind him as he stumbled across the rocks. Even if the principal object of his pursuit should escape, he would still manage to bring back a trophy. The *chupacabra* was still limping, howling, and swatting when Pablo came within range again. He fired once, eliciting another shriek from the beast as it took another spray of birdshot. The gun was now empty, and Pablo stopped to reload. The suit was now more stifling than ever, and the dead weight of the rattlesnake dragging from his waist was becoming a real impediment to his progress. It took longer to catch up with the *chupacabra* after each reload. After the third reload, he caught up with the beast again and got off one more shot before the monster exited the tunnel.

By the orange glow of the setting sun, the spectators waiting next to their vehicles saw what was happening, and an eerie sight it was— two figures, each engulfed in a swarm of angry bees, one dressed as an astronaut and trailing a three-meter rattlesnake from his waistband, was blasting away with a shotgun at a cactus-spined, yellow eyed monster that was howling and shrieking and swatting bees as it took successive loads of birdshot from twenty meters behind. As the strange pair of apparitions drew near, the spectators jumped into their pickups and rolled up the windows to fend off the bees. They watched through their windshields as the *chupacabra* fell dead before their eyes, and they saw the astronaut drop the empty shotgun and raise his arms in victory.

And that's how a pretentious forklift operator from the Texas side of the Rio Grande lived up to his braggadocio and became a living legend among a humble group of goat ranchers in the Mexican border state of Coahuila.

And while Pablo never says it out loud any more, he still maintains to himself that in some situations, clothes do make the man.

Papa
By Irma Guadarrama

Tears that emerge from my dreams
Are as deep as a well and as fierce as
The sun itself; you look at me in your coldness
While I lay before you a story of loneliness;
One heart, one love and no one,
No one to give and to give back.

Just an empty cradle.
Longing for a mother and father that once held you
But were gone, disappeared into a black hole,
Leaving you naked, in despair, drowned in the
Deepest tears, and fears, and agony of a life that
Should have been right, not wrong.

I can't understand your pain, Papa,
Your falling curtains shut me off,
And I'm left with your soulful, empty fears
That burden you in the cloudiest nights,
That hurt you without telling you,
That silence you to a wailing, yelling mess.

If you could talk to me from your cold and
Bloody grave,
I would hear your anger forever gnawing at
My heels,
I would feel all over again what I see in my dreams,
A young girl tearfully speaking
To her once-orphaned father, that
She is the orphan and he, the ruler of her life.

PUSHED ASIDE
By Ruth E. Wagner

We see the wizened woman
With a cigarette butt in wrinkled mouth.

She nods and pushes her grocery cart.
He, about a half block behind her,
Pushes his cart.

They travel together:
Protection?
Companionship?

A week earlier another of the
"Pushed aside," she, older now,
With peppered hair,
Sitting on the stoop of an abandoned house
Lifts her hand and smiles at me.
She remembers years before, a car trip
To the hospital, leg bleeding.
She remembers that she's not always unseen,
Hasn't forgotten, hasn't forgotten,
That she isn't always a throwaway.

RENEWAL*
By Marianna Nelson

The man barely fit under the mesquite tree. Its droopy leaves brushed against his canvas hat. His chair of sorts—a pair of plastic crates—sagged under the weight of his body. Tucked into his tattered shorts is a T-shirt with H-E-B printed across the front. His long legs, tanned to the brown of the soil, end at the top of once-white socks and a pair of gray sneakers fastened with Velcro tabs. A backpack, a Stripes drink, and a crate filled with books and papers lie next to him. A small tent is pitched near a tree where a bird feeder swings from a branch.

The front-page picture on a newspaper he'd found catches his attention. The caption says, "A homeless man known as 'the quiet man' has been living next to a drainage ditch for at least two years. According to people in the area, he's never asked for food or money, but when offered anything, he accepts with a polite nod of his head. The man never speaks, and his past remains a mystery."

The man looked up and shaded his eyes from the intense sun. In the distance he made out a person pushing a bicycle. The woman stopped, picked up something from her bike basket, and looked through it. Her actions suggested she was a birder, perhaps looking for spring migrants.

After her husband's long illness and recent death, Norma was trying to renew her life. She wanted to learn new things. For starters, why not take up birding, she thought. After all, the Lower Rio Grande Valley, where she now resides, is an ideal place. She learned that species such as the Green Jay, Black-Bellied Whistling Duck, and the tiny, elusive Least

Grebe, uncommon or non-existent elsewhere, live here all year. But the birds she most wanted to see were the migrants that stop by briefly every spring on their way north. One of the most coveted finds for birders keeping a Life List is the Painted Bunting. Although these birds usually seek the protection of camouflaging thickets around fields, occasionally male Buntings become bold enough to perch and sing from exposed branches. That's when they can be seen in all their colorful glory—blue head, red breast, and a Chartreuse upper back that matches the yellow-green of the female.

Before setting out on her first birding adventure, Norma spread liberal amounts of #50 sun screen on her face and sprayed mosquito repellent on her exposed skin, clothes, and hair. She tucked the containers in her bike basket next to her water bottle, a pair of binoculars, a field guide, and her camera. Two miles from the mobile home park where she lived a resaca flowed near sugar cane fields—that's where she'll go today. Besides spotting new birds, perhaps she'll be lucky enough to see a cane field set afire. Not only would that be a thrill but she might also see a hawk or other birds of prey, either hovering over the field or perched on a nearby tree waiting to dive down and snatch critters escaping from the fire.

Friends had told her that in a field close to where she lives, the spiky green cane plants looked nearly mature enough for harvesting. They said a burning sugar cane field is quite a sight and not to be missed. If you waited until you saw smoke rising in the distance and then went on the chase, you would miss the fast-breaking excitement. In the Rio Grande Valley, cane growers burn their fields to clear the underbrush so workers can drive big tractors between the rows and harvest the crop, which itself doesn't burn. The plants reach maturity in about 18 months; harvesting is scheduled for times when little or no wind is predicted. Then a new crop is planted and a new growing cycle begins once again.

Norma pedaled her bike out of the mobile home park and along a paved country road to a dirt path that led to the *resaca* and cane fields. The dry cracked ground, a sign of the extended drought, made it impossible to ride her bike. She got off and pushed it along, looking down for snakes as she did. Suddenly, she heard a rustling noise. When she looked up, a man lumbered toward her through the grass on the side of the road. Now, who is this, she wondered. As he kept approaching she stepped back. When she did, her bike bumped out of her hands and crashed to the ground; her things bounced out of the basket.

She hadn't expected to find another human in this secluded spot, and it took a minute to regain her composure. But not much flustered Norma, at least not for long. Her parents had raised her to be independent and her career as a social worker molded her into a self-assured, resourceful person, capable of dealing with the many challenges both she and her clients faced.

Saying nothing, the man bent over, stood her bike up, and put her things back in the basket. She thanked him and started to talk non-stop in her usual manner. At the same time she noticed a tent and a few belongings under a tree behind him. Acting as if the situation were entirely normal, she asked, "What kinds of birds have you seen today?" His eyes showed a glimmer of understanding but he said nothing. Thinking he might not understand English, she thumbed through her guide and pointed to the Painted Bunting on page 312. He looked at the picture. His fingers started to undulate gracefully, like a bird flying; then he squatted down and in the dirt drew the shapes of what looked like low bushes with a few tall branches sticking up. He walked away from his campsite and beckoned her to follow. Hmmm, she thought, even though this fellow doesn't want to speak, maybe he can show me where to find birds I've never seen before, ones I can put on my Life List, especially the male Painted Bunting. She followed, pushing her bike through the scrub toward the sugar cane field.

At the sound of an engine roaring she stopped and glimpsed a yellow pick-up truck through the branches. It began to move around the sugar cane field in front of them. A voice from a loudspeaker yelled, "*Peligro, peligro!*" in Spanish and then, "Danger, danger!" in English. More words in Spanish and English warned that the field would be set afire momentarily. A worker, satisfied that the volume of the loudspeaker was turned up enough to frighten away critters living in the field—or any humans hiding there—got on a tractor. As the tractor circled the field, orange flames burst out of the tube mounted on it and quickly engulfed the entire field. Flames leapt up into the air looking like diabolical dancing dragons. Thick weeds growing between the rows of cane complained and crackled in the blaze.

Norma paused in awe. "What a spectacle!"

She turned toward the man. A look of terror spread over his face as tree branches began to sway the way they do when the wind changes direction. The wind increased and flames leapt toward the trees and grass not far from them. Workers rushed to uncoil fire hoses from a truck and spray the escaping flames. They spotted Norma and the man and shouted warnings at them. She grabbed her bike and tugged on his arm, urging him to leave with her. Fire sirens wailed. Finally reacting to the possible consequences of the spreading fire, he ran after her screaming. Then he yelled, "Don't let my research burn! Save my work!"

A few months later Norma went outside to pick up her Sunday paper in the driveway. She glanced at the headline, "THE QUIET MAN SPEAKS AGAIN." The picture caption read, "Mute and homeless for two years, ornithologist J.T. Rathburn, regains his ability to speak and returns to his life as a researcher and lecturer." She recognized the face. A contented expression replaced the look of terror she remembered seeing that fateful day.

Back inside, Norma read, "Two years ago Rathburn was trapped in a hotel fire while attending a conference. Although he suffered from smoke inhalation while waiting to be rescued, the mental trauma he suffered caused far more damage. 'It robbed me of the ability to speak and interact with people,' said Rathburn. 'I thought it best to disappear from the life I knew, so for the next two years I led a solitary existence living outdoors, studying and documenting the habits of birds. I wanted to speak but couldn't, and after a while I stopped trying. One day I was near a sugar cane field looking for migrating birds. Another birder was there. I didn't know it, but the field was scheduled for burning. When the blaze started, I froze. Something burst inside me when the flames spread and fire sirens wailed. The other person and I started running for our lives. I started screaming. The sound of my voice after two years of muteness came as a shock. After that, the ability to speak again and the brief contact with the other bird-lover—the first such encounter in a long time—made me realize how much I wanted, and needed, to return to my former life.'"

Norma turned to the picture on her computer screen. A male Painted Bunting perched on a branch. His bright red breast and blue head gleamed in the sunlight. His brilliance reminded her that much-needed renewal had returned not only in her life but also to J.T. and to the scorched sugar cane field where once again tender green shoots were pushing through the soil.

　* Based on a true story.

SOMEONE ELSE'S MEMORIES
By Bidgie Weber

The summer of 1999 scorched the hot Texas soil causing it to look like an over baked piecrust. Rivulets of cracked soil cut deep grooves in the ground's surface to form natural highways and byways for columns of Texas red ants, horned toads, and lizards. Nothing but "flat" for miles and miles, with the exception of the occasional cactus patch that broke the monotonous scene.

Terrance Whitmore stood next to his dirty beat up Ford pickup and studied the open area. He was so dirty he sweated mud. After twenty some years of road work, he was still unable to adjust to the heat.

On any other day, Terrance Whitmore would have been at home in this element, but today things were different, strange, unsettling.

The ghost of a breeze teased his face and neck. Suddenly, his heart pounded beneath his khaki shirt. His legs felt like his Levi jeans were blistering them. His yellow hard hat felt like a vise slowly closing around his head. The lines around his dark brown eyes deepened as his eyes closed to protect them from the penetrating rays of the sun. The red and white bandana around his neck was choking him.

"I'm only forty two years old and I'm going to die from a heart attack on this deserted asphalt road," was his only thought.

Maybe hours or maybe minutes later, he pulled his one hundred and seventy pounds through the pickup door into the cool cab. He learned from experience to leave his a/c running on these short check stops.

His heartbeat calmed, and he could breathe normally. The moment he removed his hard hat his head "reshaped" itself.

What just happened? The threat of a heart attack or sunstroke dissipated. Feeling nearly normal, he slipped the pickup into drive and headed the fifteen miles back to town.

By evening Terrance had rationalized the strange incident and filed it as the results of dehydration. Tomorrow he would be sure to take a good supply of water to the job.

This particular job was no different from dozens of others he had overseen. A simple little road widening project that would make driving safer for the huge trucks that hauled everything from oil to cotton seed to and from the Port of Brownsville.

As foreman, Terrance was on site and involved in every aspect of each project. Early morning found Terrance and his road crew on the job and ready to survey, mark right of ways, and bring in the heavy equipment needed to widen the road.

The very moment he stepped out of his truck Terrance felt the same unsettled feeling wash over him. After taking a large swig of cool water, he felt somewhat better. Just as he thought, "dehydration."

All morning things went well until the front loader's sharp jaws made its first bite into the dry earth. Suddenly all hell broke loose, at least it did for Terrance. A blinding light engulfed him. Bursts of explosive sound deafened him. A nanosecond later, he was out cold, wet and white as a sheet.

When he came to, Terrance realized where he was. Sheer determination propelled him to the safety of his truck.

Once again, in the cool cab, Terrance floated back to reality. At least that is what he thought before he realized some strange things were going on. His nose detected a sweet floral scent.

"What is that smell?" His brain almost grabbed a hold of it but, not quite…. "Wait! There, I've got it…it's ROSES!"

Before Terrance's brain could digest this new sensation, another scent assaulted him. "Now what?"

The rose scent had an underlying almost menacing odor, faintly familiar. Recognition hit like a shot. Black powder. The volatile powder used in TNT. While his brain tried to digest the latest onslaught of smells, he experienced another problem.

He could not open his eyes. He was going to die right there in the cab of his truck! Terrance was about to give up when he realized what he felt. His eyelids were being pressed down. It was not the pressure he noticed most. It was the cold. He panicked.

His last conscious memory was of a bright light that seemed to engulf him. He got a flickering sense of being near a flower garden. The next moment he was back.

"Hold still Mr. Terrance." Sanchez barked. "We put the rag there to make you come back."

Terrance, stretched out on the seat of his truck, stared up at the circle of very concerned faces of his crew.

"What the hell happened to you?" Sanchez asked.

"Danged if I know. The same thing almost happened yesterday when I came out to check this site."

The crew snickered among themselves. At last, Sanchez said, "If you think you live now, I guess we get back to work."

Terrance opened the cab door and took a few steps toward the upturned earth and hit the ground like a tall pine.

Out cold again.

Later, he managed to sit up and drove back to the air-conditioned trailer, a short distance from the site. Never in his entire life had he ever felt faint. How could he pass out twice in one hour? Fleeting images and disturbing sounds flooded his brain and then faded. Terrance was very uncomfortable in such uncharted territory. He fell into bed, asleep almost at the instant his head hit the pillow.

The next morning, Lou Walters, the Project Director, was a bit surprised when he saw Terrance come in. "Winding up a little early today, aren't you?"

"Got a minute Lou?"

"Got the rest of the day. Why? Got a problem?"

"Don't know for sure but I might have. Couple of days ago I had a spell out there on the road job. I blew it off as dehydration, but it happened again yesterday, and I know it wasn't from the lack of water. I passed out, Lou, like a woman! Fell flat on my butt. This ain't normal and I want to check things out."

"Might want to check it out with the doc."

"What I want is for you and me to go out there tonight. Maybe between us we can figure this out."

Evening found Lou and Terrance standing in the exact spot where the "fainting" incident happened. Lou had taken a couple of steps when his foot struck something in the path. He leaned down and picked up a strange looking object that looked like bone.

"Would you look at this Ter. Be darned if it don't look like a piece of skull!"

Terrance touched the bone. He saw a brilliant flash of light. He heard a loud explosion. He felt like he was being sucked skyward. Suddenly, as he started to fall to the ground, Lou grabbed him and leaned him against the truck.

"What in the world happened, Ter?" Lou was almost as white as Terrance.

"Same thing as before. Did you hear or see anything unusual?"

"Like what? I didn't hear or see a darn thing, what in the world are you talking about?"

"No bright light, nothing that sounded like a gun shot? NOTHING?

"Nothing but seeing you starting to look different, like someone else. What in the heck is going on with you? Whatever it is, I don't want any part of it."

Next day Terrance had his crew search the area where he and Lou were the night before. After an hour or so, the men uncovered a number of human bones. Mixed in with the bones were a few metal buttons, strips of what looked like leather and a belt buckle. The bones were boxed up and placed in the bed of Terrance's truck to be hauled into town for a thorough examination.

Terrance had no sooner hit the main highway when a strange sensation came over him. The brightest light he had ever seen nearly blinded him. He looked down at his hands. Not HIS hands. One hand was on the steering wheel and the other hand held a strange looking rifle. He could feel the gun's heat, so hot he tried in vain to drop it. Something hit him in the gut like a sledgehammer, knocking the breath out of him. When he caught his breath, he found himself out of this world and in another.

"God, I'm dead," he muttered. "I'm stuck between two worlds. The dead don't feel though do they?"

The unexpected reply startled him.

"You ain't dead and nope, the dead don't feel. But you're gonna be as dead as that Yankee over yonder if you don't move your butt."

In a flash, modern memories mixed with ancient knowledge washed over Terrance and he saw the complete picture. He was fighting in a battle. Union and Confederate soldiers surrounded him. This was the Civil War!

In that minute, he realized no one had received word that the war was over. They were fighting for their lives. Sheer panic overruled common sense and he stood straight up to shout what he knew. Before he got one word out a bullet tore through what was left of his dirty, holey, gray uniform burying itself in his heart. The impact of the lead slug threw him five feet back onto the hard, dry, sun baked Texas soil.

As he lay there bleeding out, he knew he was dying. His only thought was, "We have all died."

Morning found Terrance safe in his own bed with no memory of how he got there. His "dream" hung at the edge of his consciousness and prompted him to deliver his "find" to the Cameron County coroner's office to be examined.

Terrance leaned down and gently gathered the bones. He noticed a small lead ball roll out of the hollow formed by the ribcage. The moment his hand cradled the mini ball his heart began to beat an irregular rhythm. Something pulled his hand back and moved it over the ground.

"There it is. I knew it was here." A voice from within assured Terrance that he would indeed find something special.

The desiccated leather billfold was stiff and cracked with wear and age. He did not know how he recognized it as a pouch used so many years ago for the safe keeping of special treasures. He opened it carefully and saw the faint outline of what might have been a flower, a rose maybe, from a sweetheart or wife. Even a hundred years could not diminish the beauty and love it must have carried when he put it there. As Terrance held it to his heart, he was once again complete.

Later, a team of archeologists searched the site, which produced the remains of eleven more men. Terrance had directed them to the exact spot where he and Lou found the first bones. The archeologists were gearing up to leave the site when he felt pains in his stomach. Once again, he heard the gunshots and smelled the smoke from the gunpowder. He knew what he had to do.

"You can't leave now. There are fifteen more men here and you can't leave them."

As he pointed out the location of the other men, the archeologists were amazed that he knew exactly where to dig.

The final results confirmed, the old bones were from twenty-six men who died many years ago.

By the summer of 2000, all the remains of the men who fought in the last battle of the Civil War were moved to a shady corner in the little cemetery five miles from Brownsville city limits. This city on the Rio Grande River had a beautiful statue erected with the men of that last company buried next to it. A touching ceremony was held on one of the nicest summer days of the year.

As Terrance stood watching the dedication, a cool breeze hugged him and he felt the presence of an unknown spirit. But, this time, instead of the bright light, loud noise and the smell of gunpowder, he saw a soft golden glow drift before his eyes. A bugler somewhere played Taps, and the sweet scent of roses filled the air.

What ever happened to Terrance Whitmore that day remains a mystery. But, if in the shank of some evening, you find yourself alone, driving down Highway 4 toward Boca Chica Beach, and you feel a little off, you might give some thought to putting your car windows up tight. Tight enough to keep the "yesterdays" on the backside of time where they belong. Many things ride the night breezes. They hide in the shadows, waiting to hitch a ride to a "tomorrow".

The Bulldozer
By Jack King

Half tight and feeling his onions, he left the tavern at closing time and danced into Hank's 24-hour Cafe half a block down the street. He smiled at the big blonde waitress as she approached his table. "The prettiest smile" he thought, "on the prettiest face I've seen in a week…and the rest ain't bad either."

"Hi, Sugar. What'll it be?"

"Coffee," he said, "and I like it the way I like my women: blonde and sweet. So dip your finger in the cup and bring me some creamer." He looked at the name tag on her uniform. "Gertie," he said. "You wouldn't be the Dirty Gertie I heard about over at the tavern?

"Could be," she said. "A girl makes a couple of mistakes with guys who kiss and blab, and the next thing you know she's labeled for life."

"A couple of mistakes?" His eyes lit up like he'd just won the lottery. "How'd you like to go for three?"

"I'll get your coffee," she replied as she walked away. A minute later, she returned with the steaming cup and set it on the table. "I didn't get your name," she said.

"That's a secret known only to me and my birth certificate. My friends call me The Bulldozer. You can call me Bull."

"Hmmm…Well, you sort of look like a bulldozer: broad shoulders, big biceps…tight buns and thick thighs, the kind of build I go for. Promise to behave and I'll let you give me a ride home."

"You got a deal. What time you get off?"

"Seven," she said, "and one other thing. I also like the big thick sirloin at Rogelio's, the other 24-hour joint down the street, so don't forget your wallet."

A look of disappointment briefly clouded his face. "You mean they don't feed the help here at Hank's?"

"Not sirloin, Honey."

"And Rogelio's serves sirloin at seven in the morning?"

"For me they do." She leaned forward, a cheek brushing his as she whispered, "I'm something special."

"Well, I knew that the minute I laid eyes on you."

She winked and moved to another table, bending over to wipe it with a damp dishtowel. He gazed admiringly at her behind for a moment, then finished his coffee, left a five- dollar bill on the table, and went to the register. He paid for the coffee and stepped out onto the sidewalk still holding his wallet. He examined the contents under the streetlight and found exactly eleven dollars, not enough for two thick sirloins. He looked at his watch. It was a little after two. A sense of desperation began to well up inside him.

He had just moved into town with a highway construction crew, and his workmates had learned the hard way that lending money to The Bulldozer was not a wise thing to do. His pickup was parked at the curb. He opened the door and tilted the seat forward to see if what he wanted was still there. It was. In the storage space behind the seat was a tire iron and a ski mask he picked up while working with a crew near Aspen. He got in and roared off toward the far side of town.

He found a convenience store that had, conveniently enough, only one vehicle in the parking lot. It probably belonged to the store clerk. He continued down the street, turned left at the corner and came back through the alley, parking far enough back that the security cameras would not be a problem. He pulled on the ski mask. A minute later, he burst through the front door of the store and stopped directly across the counter from the night clerk, the tire iron raised above his head. "Open the cash drawer and give me the money!" he shouted.

Suddenly, the clerk was on his feet brandishing his own tire iron, and The Bulldozer saw that his intended victim was as big and muscular as he was. Both men swung at once and the irons met above the countertop with a sharp clang. The impact caused both tools to go flying. Before Bull could collect his wits, the big clerk vaulted the counter and had him by the throat with both hands. Bull punched him in the stomach and the man let go and fell back for a brief moment. He came charging back and wrapped both arms around Bull, and both men went crashing into an aisle display knocking cans and cartons onto the floor. Rolling on the floor, the two men punched, kicked, and grappled as each tried with a do-or-die fury to disable or pin down the other. Bottles and jars joined the disarray of dented cans and smashed cartons on the floor. Shelves splintered and bags of chips were crushed and ripped. Bull got up and tried to escape, but the clerk tackled him and they crashed against another shelf of merchandise. Bull got hold of a bottle and rapped the clerk across the top of the head and got a punch in the face for his trouble. It was a plastic ketchup bottle and the cap popped off, and the contents shot out in a crimson spurt. The tiles upon which they were struggling soon looked like a slaughterhouse floor. Bull groped a wine shelf and came up with a heavy glass bottle of Zinfandel. He swung again and caught the clerk in the middle of the forehead, and suddenly all was calm except for Bull's pounding heart and gasping breaths.

He staggered around the counter to the cash drawer, emptied it into a plastic shopping bag, bulldozed the door open with a hip and shoulder and raced to his truck. He started the engine and removed the ski mask, thankful that it had not been ripped off his head in the struggle. Forty minutes later, he was in the shower inside his rented trailer.

Coming out of the shower, he caught a glimpse of himself in the mirror and stopped for a closer look. The bruises on his face were not purple yet, but were still a little too red not to be noticed. He wished for that sirloin, not cooked but raw, so he could put it on his left eye. In the refrigerator was a pound of raw hamburger, so he took it out and mashed it into a large patty and lay down on the bed holding it to the left side of his face. At 5:45, he got up and looked at himself in the mirror again. The eye was a bit better, but there were two noticeable scratches, one on his nose and one on his right cheekbone. Band-aids would be even more noticeable than these minor cuts, so he left them alone. He put on his Sunday best, and at 6:50, he waltzed into Hank's again, his wallet bulging with cash. Gertie noticed him but did not come to the table until a few minutes later when the morning shift arrived and assumed its duties. Bull was sitting in a booth by a window. She slid in on the opposite side of the table with purse in hand.

"What happened to you? Don't tell me the bulldozer met his match?"

"That'll be the day. I had a little disagreement with a guy, but I walked away on my own and he didn't. You ready for that sirloin at Rogelio's?"

"I been ready for hours. Let's go!"

Fifteen minutes later, they were seated at a table in Rogelio's and an hour after that they were back in the truck again. "That was good," said Bull, "but the best is yet to come. Your place or mine?"

"How 'bout we go to my place first so I can freshen up, and then we'll go to your place."

"Sounds good to me, Babe; just point the way."

Bull followed Gertie's directions, and twenty minutes later, he pulled into a narrow driveway alongside a dilapidated frame house in a run-down neighborhood. Another pickup blocked the drive, so he parked behind it. Two rows of rose bushes, one along the side of the house, blocked passage around the left side of the truck, and one along the fence, blocked passage around the right side. "We can't go in the front door," said Gertie. "My brother sleeps in the front bedroom, and I'm afraid we might wake him. I know it's going to be hard, but we have to squeeze past those thorny roses and go in the kitchen door towards the back."

They made it past the rose bushes with only minor scratches, and Gertie opened the sagging screen door and unlocked the inner door. They slipped quietly inside. The air was warm and muggy, so she left the inner door open for ventilation. The screen door had three hook latches—one at the top, one in the middle, and one at the bottom. She latched all three, explaining that the door was warped, and she had installed the extra hooks to keep it tightly closed so the flies wouldn't get in. "There's a six-pack of Bud in the fridge," she said. "Just make yourself at home, and I'll be back as soon as I shower and change."

"Okay, but don't take too long."

She turned toward the hallway just as the hulking figure of a man in pajamas emerged and stepped into the kitchen. "I recognize that voice," said the hulk. A bandage was taped to his forehead, and a tire iron was clenched in his right fist. Below the bandage, two eyes blazed with a lust for vengeance. Gertie watched in utter astonishment as The Bulldozer sprang to his feet and performed a feat worthy of his moniker. He ran straight through the middle of the triple-latched screen door, mowed down five rose bushes and sheared an outside mirror off her brother's truck as he barreled toward his own. Backing out of the driveway with engine screaming, he bulldozed an old galvanized garbage can and landed on top of it as the truck bounced and jumped the curb. He cut the wheels to the right and roared off down the street with the can stuck under the truck, throwing a burgeoning shower of sparks as the can scraped the pavement beneath the accelerating vehicle.

Gertie's brother limped to her side and placed a hand on her shoulder. "You sure know how to pick 'em, Sis."

THE CHACHALACAS
By Brenda Nettles Riojas

Chachalacas, a name self selected,
Identifies our gregarious group.
This species, though, stitches.
So around the sewing nest we gather,
A flock of friends who come from all places.
We sit, we sew, we share.

Cha-cha-lac,
Cha-cha-lac,
Cha-cha-lac,
Stitch.

Weaving our fabric of friendship,
We stitch at our own pace -
Telling our stories, revealing snippets of our lives,
Passing on sewing tips, ideas, and patterns.
As the hours elapse, we *Chachalacas*
Thrive in the raucous of constant chatter.

Cha-cha-lac,
Cha-cha-lac,
Cha-cha-lac,
Stitch.

Later we peck at sweets and treats.
We then spread our wings,
Showcase our quilted creations.
Here in this nest, with loose threads connected,
We *Chachas* quilt warmth fused with fun
Into a sampler of inspiration.

Cha-cha-lac,
Cha-cha-lac,
Cha-cha-lac,
Stitch.

THE HITCHING OF BINGO JOE TO THE WIDOW WHEATLEY
By Don Clifford

Bingo Joe fell off the wagon so many times he left potholes in the street.

My home town sits on the edge of the Arroyo, an' I swear, all four thousand three hunnert and ninety-two of us got the crazy idea that Bingo Joe and the Widder Wheatley oughter be hitched. The idea was crazy 'cause we had no way of knowin' how a prim and proper librarian would mix with a town drunk.

I was in on the crazy idea right from the start. My boss, Pharmacist Jim Cooper an' his best friend Henry Bottomsworth, hatched the plan durin' a coffee break. They was sippin' a brew at the drug store's ice cream counter, where I jerk sodas durin' the summer, when Mr. Cooper says to Henry, "Those two must be the unhappiest folks in town."

"Yeah, an' you can see why," says Henry. "All he ever does is play Bingo at the VFW, have a few drinks an' then sleeps it off in that old boxcar he lives in down by the Arroyo. She's not much better. Ever since ol' man Wheatley died, she hides behind the librarian's desk durin' the day an', at night, disappears into her little room above Jacob's Grocery Store."

"Well, you're almost right; but I seen her at the VFW playin' Bingo, too."

"Yeah. An' every time he sits next to her, she gets up an' sits somewheres else."

I knowed what Henry was talkin' about. Once, when I went a-fishin' in the Arroyo, I seen Bingo Joe through the sliding door of his boxcar shack. Funny thing 'bout that boxcar. That big ol' thing washed off the track during the flood of '47. No one claimed it 'cause it floated too far away from the mainline an' landed on the bottomland that Bingo Joe inherited from his Paw. Natcherly, he cleaned 'er up and moved in.

Anyways, when I seen him, he kinda sways with the breeze, six sheets to the wind. I see him take a sip of somethin' from an open half-pint flask that he never held more'n six inches away from his mouth. Then he fumbles it back into an inside vest pocket—in his condition, a major achievement considerin' the several layers o' rags he wears rain or shine. Ya never want to stand downwind of Ol' Joe 'cause the brewery smell would knock you out like a whiff o' chloroform—at least that's what Mr. Cooper says. He should know, bein' a pharmacist an' all.

One day whilst I was cleanin' up the counter, Bingo Joe wanders into the drug store an' asks for a cup o' coffee. As I pours the brew, Mr. Cooper comes up.

"How's it goin', Joe?"

"O.k. I guess." He kinda slurred his words.

I set the brew on the counter before him an' says, "That'll be two-bits, Joe."

"O.K." He fumbles in his watch pocket for some change when a quarter slips out an' falls to the floor. He bends over an' fumbles some more, tryin' to pick it up. When he straightens up, he plops the quarter on the counter.

About that time, Mr. Cooper bends over. "What's that stuff on the floor?" he says. "Looks like spots of water."

Bingo Joe bends over to look an' another spot of liquid appears.

"Well I'll be jingoed," says Mr. Cooper. "Either we got a magic spring sproutin' through my floor or—what's in your vest pocket, Joe?"

Ol' Joe is somewhat flustered, but manages to undo some buttons an' pulls aside his jacket. There, sittin' high an' mighty in his vest pocket is a flask—with no top. Ever' time Ol' Joe bent over some of that clear liquid spilled out.

Mr. Cooper had a hard time tryin' not to laugh at the sheepish look on Ol' Joe's face. "Wait a minute, Joe. I think I can fix that." He went into the room where he measures out the pills an' comes back with a cork.

"Here," he says to Ol' Joe, an' stuffs the cork into the flask. "Maybe this'll keep you dry."

Bingo Joe grins in a shy sort of way. He mumbles his thanks an' sways out the door.

Mr. Cooper an' I laugh so hard that tears come to our eyes. After we both come down to Earth, he says to me, "Horatio, better clean it up."

I went an' fetched a mop. When I get back, Mr. Cooper has this serious look on his face. "We must do somethin' to help that poor man," he says. "Maybe he an' the Widder should get married. If that doesn't spark 'em up, at least they could be miserable together."

Next thing you know, Mr. Cooper an' Henry are hatchin' their plan.

"He'd be a nice lookin' man if he'd clean up a bit an' get rid of those old rags he wears," says Henry.

"I understand he had a rough time of it durin' the war—saw lots of dirty fightin', wounded in action several times, an' his girlfriend 'Dear John'd' him. When the war ended, he had nothin' to come home to 'cept that piece of bottomland his Paw used to farm."

"No wonder he hits the bottle."

Mr. Cooper thought a few minutes. "Y'know...maybe that's where we can begin—get him out of those rags, start weanin' him from the bottle, an' build up his self esteem."

Henry scratches his head an' says, "I've got a couple of suits I don't wear any more. We can get the ladies of the church to call on him with some homemade bread an' cookies...or somethin'."

"You think they'll go along with it?"

"Oh, yeah. I never met a biddy yet who don't enjoy a little nosey-in' an' match makin'. Once they know who an' for why we're doin' this, they'll jump at the chance to put this man on a straight path."

"Where'll the Widow Wheatley fit in?"

"She works with the church group whenever her library chores don't conflict. When Bingo Joe realizes that she's involved, I think he'll try to clean up his act."

"We can get the boys from the VFW to help an' start plantin' a rumor that Miz Wheatley might be more interested in him if he didn't smell like yesterday's beer."

A week or so later, the VFW adopts Bingo Joe as one of their projects. "He's one of us," they say. "We should-a took care o' him before he got this far along."

A week after that, the boys from the VFW swarm into Joe's boxcar, rip off his old clothes, an' throw him into the Arroyo with a bar of soap. One ol' boy set fire to his rags. He tole me later, that when he lit the match, them ol' rags nearly exploded 'cause they was so full of alcohol fumes. Another ol' boy give Joe a shave an' a haircut an' cleaned his fingernails for free. He says, when they finished, Bingo Joe looked downright respectable.

Of course, you couldn't very well throw the Widder Wheatley into the Arroyo, so Ol' Lady Teasley an' her church group got to workin' on her, usin' the mysterious ways of wimmin. They primp her; they perm her; an' they parfume her so that she ends up smellin' like my Aunt Hattie's lilac water.

That night was Bingo Night at the VFW. As usual Joe comes in, sees where the prim and proper Widder Wheatley is sittin', an' goes over to join her. Instead of gettin' up an' walkin' away, like usual, she says, "Joseph! How nice you look tonight." He just grins, an' they sit together for the rest of the Bingo session.

Things really begin movin'. Ever' time the ladies of the church took their bread an' cookies to the boxcar, they'd say Miz. Wheatley did this, or Miz. Wheatley did that. They'd drop not so subtle hints that Miz. Wheatley's a fine an' outstandin' librarian...a real asset to the community... that she's a prize catch waitin' for some respectable gent to whisk her away. Then they'd get together with the Widder herself an' gossip about Bingo Joe. They'd tell her about what a hero he was, an' all the things he done to fix up the place...an' himself, bein' a fine farmer an' all, able to keep a plate of food on the table...an' how someday some lucky girl would just snatch him up, now that he's back on the wagon.

Eventually, it happens. One night after Bingo, Ol' Joe asks the Widder Wheatley if she'd like to go to the pitcher show with him. She must've said yes, 'cause the next night I seen 'em leavin' the movie-house holdin' hands. It must've been a real tearjerker, 'cause she kept dabbin' her eyes with a hankie. An' he kept tryin' to comfort her by sayin', that was one slam-bang of a movie.

Pretty soon, they become a regular twosome. He leaves his flask at home an' starts farmin' the bottomland. She perks up while shelvin' books at the library; an' durin' the church social functions, you'd think she was Belle of the Ball. Like two peas in a pod, they play Bingo together; they go to the pitcher show three times a week; an' they even sit in the fourth pew from the front every Sunday at church—holdin' hands, mind you.

Of course, Mr. Cooper an' Henry Bottomsworth are all excited, an' hoppin' about like two Mexican jumpin' beans. Mr. Cooper says, "We need to make plans for a wedding."

"Easter'll be here, soon," says Henry. "All the spring flowers'll be in bloom an' the smell of orange blossoms in the air'll be just delightful."

"Why you old devil." says Mr. Cooper, smilin' like the Cheshire cat. "I never thought beneath that trim haberdasher's outfit lurked the soul of a true romantic."

Henry grins pleased as punch. "Well, you can't tell what's inside a book 'til you read it."

So they both orders a cup o' brew an' put their heads together for the next phase of their plan. The VFW boys was to drop hints that the Widder Wheatley is ready for hitchin'. The ladies would drop coy bits of gossip, sayin' that Lucy Mae Goodridge, over in Arroyo City, is flashin' her eyes at Ol' Joe, and that she needs to tie the knot before Lucy Mae snags him.

Then disaster struck.

Ol' Lady Teasley found the Widder down in the dumps, in her former miserable self at the library. Jason Todd found Bingo Joe stretched out behind the VFW club passed out drunk—smellin' worse than a skunk with two tails.

Seems the two lovebirds got into a big fight over where they's to live after gettin' hitched, an' all. She says she wer'nt no hobo and ain't about to live in a boxcar; and he says he wer'nt no city dude and ain't about to live in her dinky apartment above Jacob's Grocery Store. The argument got heated. They split.

Mr. Cooper an' Henry Bottomsworth had a 'mergency meeting at the drug store. "What're we gonna to do now?" says Henry. "Easter is only a few weeks away."

"At this point, I don't know," Mr. Cooper says. "We don't seem to have too many options."

It so happens that Carlos Santana of Santana Realty was sittin' at the other end of the counter. He brings his cup o' coffee with him an' comes up to us, sayin', "Couldn't help but over hear you boys. I might have a solution to your problem."

"Be happy to hear it," says Mr. Cooper.

"I've got this nice piece of property down toward the Arroyo, sittin' on the edge of town," says Carlos. "It's a little run-down but wouldn't take much to fix 'er up…make a nice place for a couple just startin' out."

"Sounds good," says Henry. "Are you plannin' on givin' it away?"

Carlos shakes his head. "Oh, no," he says. "But I could let it go pretty cheap."

"They don't have any money to buy a house," Mr. Cooper says. "That's partly why the argument started in the first place."

I chime in. "Maybe we could take up a collection."

All three men kinda groan an' take another sip of their brew. As Henry's settin' his cup down, a thinkin' look comes into his eyes. "Wait a minute," he says. "That may not be such a bad idea."

Natcherly, I just beamed.

"We could raise enough money for the down payment by goin' door to door," says Henry. "Most ever' one in town knows about our project to get them two hitched."

"Yeah," says Mr. Cooper. "I'll even sweeten the pot an' offer each person who kicks in a free chocolate sundae—double dip."

"That sounds pretty good," says Carlos. "But how're they gonna make the mortgage payments?"

"That's easy," says Henry. "We'll get Rudy Rodriguez at the bank to make them an agriculture loan. When Bingo Joe harvests an' sells his first crops, he should have enough money to start payin' off the note."

Wal', that new plan is just enough for the three men to take off an' get the project goin'. Henry gets with Ol' Lady Teasley to stir up the women folk. Mr. Cooper convinces the boys at the VFW Club the plan is just another aspect of takin' Bingo Joe under their wing. Carlos begins puttin' together the necessary paper work. My job, as usual, is wash the cups an' clean the counter.

Sure enough, the ladies get the Widder Wheatley to realize it's just a lover's spat an' that all will soon blow over. The boys from the VFW swarm into the boxcar again an' toss Bingo Joe into the Arroyo with another bar of soap. Wal', to make a long story short, most ever'one in town pitches in and gets their free double dip chocolate sundae—an' it don't matter if you kicked in with ten cents or ten dollars.

One day, when all is said an' done, both parties gather at the farmstead on the edge of town. It's the first time they seen each other since the spat. The Widder Wheatley looks edgy. Bingo Joe is up tight. After a few shy glances at one another, they both rush into each other's arms, cryin' "I'm sorry! No, I'm sorry!" It went on that way until Ol' Joe just grabs the Widder, bends her back'ards, an' plants on her mouth one of the longest kisses in the history of our town. Of course, ever'one in the crowd cheers an' hollers.

When the excitement settles down, Carlos hands them the keys an' tells 'em the house is theirs. Bingo Joe gets a worried look on his face. The Widder grips his arm almost in a panic. "This is nice," he says, "but how're we gonna pay for it?"

Rudy Rodriguez jumps in an' says, "It's all taken care of." He goes on an' explains the financial arrangements that'd been made.

With big smiles of relief and gratitude on their faces, the lovebirds then take a tour of the farmstead. Of course, ever'one follows, ooh'n and aah'n all over the place. When it's over, a teary eyed Bingo Joe holds his arm around the Widder's waist. He tugs her to him an' says, "I don't know how we're ever gonna pay back all you folks. But we will find a way."

On the day after Easter, the town closed all its stores an' shops like it was a federal holiday. The wedding was on, an' what a gala event it turned out to be—one the townsfolk still talk about. Henry Bottomsworth blushed more than the bride did when he give her away. Mr. Cooper stood tall an' proud as the Best Man. I was Custodian of the Ring. When it came time to pass the ring to Mr. Cooper, I got flustered an' nearly drop it. But it wer'nt no biggie an' ever'one just smiled.

The years passed. I'm no longer a soda jerk. Mr. Cooper says I should consider bein' a pharmacist. Bingo Joe an' the former Widow Wheatley live happily on the edge of town where she's close enough to continue workin' at the library, an' he's close enough to farm the bottomland. He converted the boxcar into a big tool shed an' tractor barn. He usually grows a cash crop like cotton or soybeans an', so far, is able to meet the annual agriculture note.

They even found a way to help pay back the townsfolk for their generosity. Every year, Ol' Joe plants a vegetable patch on the homestead. After he an' his wife take what they need, they offer the rest of the crops to the townsfolk free of charge—even to Bert Jacob who promptly puts the vegetables up for sale in his grocery store.

The rest of their lives is like a fairy tale. Y'know…no more potholes, an' they live happy ever after. I should know. I got hitched to their eldest daughter, an'…that's another story for another time.

THE NEW DEACON
By Milo Kearney

Charley Bumblewood was such a congenial fellow! It seemed a shame that he had to be dropped from the board of deacons at his church. And it was all the fault of World War II.

Brownsville's First Baptist Church extended arms of welcome to Charley's family in the summer of 1941, when they had just bought their modest farm out on Military Highway. Charley's wife, Sarah Ann, joined the Ladies' Bible Study on Monday evenings; their older son, Johnny, attended the youth group; and their younger boy, Terry, enjoyed listening to stories in his Sunday school class.

The church members formed a close-knit support group. Pastors came and went, but the pillars of the church stood firm. The deacons provided supervision—all men, of course. All the same, the most effective overseers of congregational behavior were two staunch matriarchs: Grandma Johnson and Grandma Jackson (as everyone called them). No secret, no matter how small or how private, escaped their hearing. No impropriety failed to come to their attention. The flaming sword of the angel that guarded the Garden of Eden burned no more fiercely than their pronouncements. The flock was well protected by these two sexagenarians, as weighty in judgment as they were in flesh.

The church, built in 1926, was in need of members willing to tithe so they could pay off the cost of their new brick church with its beautiful stained glass windows, on Elizabeth and Sixth Street. The Great Depression made it difficult to liquidate the debt incurred in its construction. Money was so tight that the church treasurer went from door to door asking contributions to pay the pastor's salary. Only in 1944 would the debt be paid.

So it was that, despite some qualms, Charley was invited to join the board of deacons. It's not that he disputed any of the church's doctrinal interpretations, either religious or political. Nor was he lacking as a husband, father, and bread-winner. He was a hard enough worker on his farm. It was just that he was always kidding around. It was futile to try to hold a serious discussion with Charley about sin and the Devil; he'd always turn it into a joke. And forget about trying to get him to hand out Bible tracts. Before you knew it, he would be exchanging anecdotes with some stranger, with the tracts blowing around in the wind. But his heart seemed to be in the right place, and so deacon he became.

Soon, the church dominated the social life of the Bumblewoods, with Monday night Bible studies, Tuesday night visitations to homes of new attendees, Wednesday night prayer meetings, and Thursday night choir practice, plus frequent (home-made) ice cream socials and other get-togethers. His wholesome life on the farm also helped to keep Charley in line.

The farm lacked many of the amenities, as was frequently the case in the 1940s. Food preparation, drawn from the crops and chickens of the Bumblewood's farm, required a lot of time. They still had to go out behind the back yard to an outhouse. Their refrigerator was an icebox, cooled by a block of ice in the bottom compartment. When "northers" blew in, heated bricks wrapped in towels were placed between the bed covers to warm them. Their garage was a converted stable located behind the house, and their car had running boards—another holdover from the carriage days— on which Terry enjoyed riding, holding on to an open window. Writing with a pen was tedious, requiring constant dipping into an ink-well.

With this life style, virtually every minute of the week was spoken for, and there seemed to be little that could go wrong at the church. But Charley did love to have a good time, to shoot the breeze, and have a hearty laugh. Seemingly harmless, this proclivity laid many a hidden trap for the poor deacon.

One of Charley's duties was to stand in the Church vestibule, greet the people coming in, and hand out church bulletins. The first test of his abilities in this post came when Mrs. Aldridge's sister Lucy Belle came to visit her. Lucy Belle was an unrepentant floozie, whose escapades had made her a special object of prayer by the Ladies' Bible Study group. As Lucy kaleidoscoped from man to man and place to place, Mr. and Mrs.

Aldridge were raising her son. The men in the church had been alerted to be on their guard around Lucy Belle. But poor Brother Charley could not avert his eyes when that bulging bosom came through the door, barely contained underneath the plunging neckline of that tight-fitting, swiveling dress, with perfume permeating the air, and a soft voice cooing "Hi!" from a slanted, knowing smile. His natural friendliness found no room for even a hint of disapproval or reserve as he awarded the shameless hussy a warm welcome. Grandma Johnson's eagle eyes caught the scene, and Charley caught heck. It was an inauspicious start.

Nor did Charley do any better in dealing with the juvenile delinquents in the church. Rusty and Bert were the ringleaders. One Sunday evening, on their way to Baptist Training Union, the two boys came across a bottle of Lord Calvert whiskey at the side of the sidewalk, with a fifth of its contents still in it. Being late for B.T.U., they had no time to sample it on the spot, and so took the bottle along with them. When they entered the sanctuary, the other children were sitting on the first three rows, and the lesson had just begun. Rusty and Bert sat in the back row. Called to join their friends in the front, they declined, and, feeling too busy to argue (and a bit relieved to hold their influence at a distance), the teacher had let them be. Scooting way down in their seats, they started to take turns drinking.

This was the boys' opportunity to see what whiskey tasted like. They had heard the evils of drink condemned for years from the pulpit, but had never had the occasion to see for themselves. Now they could see what all the fuss was about. There might have been no problem, had Bert only been fair. But he began keeping the bottle longer than his rightful share, forcing Rusty to have to pull it away from him. Indeed, he held the bottle so tenaciously that when Rusty jerked it away, it flew out of his hands and loudly banged on the floor, spilling its contents. Brother Charley, who was helping to corral the kids, rushed to the back to investigate. Taking the boys outside, he started to chastise them. But, deep down, Charley found the incident amusing, and he had to admit a fondness for these mischievous lads. He could not resist ending his warning with the observation that he hoped the boys had learned their lesson—that liquor truly is an evil, especially when you have such a greedy friend as Bert.

It did not escape the church members that Charley's handling of Rusty and Bert had by no means reformed their behavior. This was shown soon after, when the church was advertising for a new pastor, and a young applicant was invited to present a sample service on a hot summer Sunday morning. He was nervous and sweaty (there was no air conditioning in those days, and the hand fans supplied by Charley in the vestibule were waving frantically all over the sanctuary). It did not help that Rusty and Bert were sitting right on the front row. They were out of parental control, since Rusty's parents were a bit sick at home and Bert's parents had been called out of town and left him with Rusty's family.

When the preacher expounded on Ezekiel 23:20, the parable of Aholah (Israel) portrayed as having defiled herself with 'whoredom' activities with Egyptians "whose flesh is as the flesh of asses," neither of the boys could hold back guffaws. Harsh frowns followed from all corners of the church. The preacher glanced nervously at the boys, and Rusty and Bert took a deep breath and forced their faces back into a serious mode. If only the sermon could have been modified to avoid these words! But the fateful phrase recurred, as the discombobulated speaker banged his fist on the pulpit and shouted at the top of his voice, "whose flesh is as the asses of...." Searching in vain for the correct word, he hesitated for a moment and then screamed, red-faced, "asses!" At this point, the boys doubled over in peals of laughter, and were promptly escorted out of the church—but not by Charley.

It wasn't just that Charley proved faulty in training the youth. He turned out to be a failure as the church photographer, as well. When the church held a summer picnic in Washington Park, Charley herded everyone together in front of the big central fountain for a group picture. Everybody was eager to receive a copy, but when the picture came back, there was Grandma Johnson with her bulk planted authoritatively in the front center. The problem was, she had forgotten (an affliction of age) to put on her slip that morning, and the glare of the bright summer sun melted away the appearance of her thin, silk dress, making it seem as if she wore nothing beside two scanty pieces of undergarments. Charley felt obliged to give copies to selected responsible people in the congregation, to prove why he could not make the picture generally known. Perhaps it should not have been held against him that the picture enjoyed such a general distribution—but it was.

However, World War II provided the last straw. From the Sunday morning in December 1941, when the radio announced that the Japanese had attacked Pearl Harbor, the church prayed for the Lord's help, and especially for His protection for the two young men from the congregation who were serving in the armed forces. Prayers of thanks were offered for every battle the Americans won, right down to the summer of 1945.

Then came that Sunday evening early in August 1945. The pastor was in the middle of a sermon about the prodigal son. All attention was focused on the speaker as he poignantly described how the wayward fellow rushed home to his father, when in burst Charley Bumblewood. To everyone's horror, he ran down the aisle, interrupting the sermon with shouts of, "Stop! Stop!" What he announced changed their focus in an instant.

"The war is over!"

"How do you know?" asked the pastor.

"Everybody's talking about it over at Piggly Wiggly," Charley explained. Now Charley was supposed to stay at his post by the church entrance as the Greeter for late stragglers, who joined the rest of the congregation, in listening to the sermon himself from the vestibule. Yet someone reported that he had been seen, repeatedly, slipping out to the Piggly Wiggly Grocery Store down the street, at the corner of Elizabeth and Eighth, to buy a snack and to chat with the folks there. He had been warned that such behavior was unbefitting of a deacon, and he had promised to reform his ways. But here he was, telling the whole church that he had left during yet another sermon to hang out at the grocery store.

As it turned out, the congregational relief at the news was so great that Charley's latest transgression was forgotten in the emotion of the moment. The pastor led the faithful in a heartfelt outburst of thanksgiving prayers and hymns of joy. First one person gave a prayer, and then another, and then another. How long these praise offerings might have gone on, Heaven only knows.

However, Charley interrupted the church proceedings still one more time. Again, he made his way down the aisle, but, this time, slowly, with a hang-dog look. In a low voice, he explained that he had returned to Piggly Wiggly, only to be told that the news of the war's ending was a premature report. It was all a mistake!

That Sunday evening, the war did not end, but Charley's term as deacon did.

THE SAGA OF NEPTALI'S JOURNEY
By LeRoy Overstreet

In the middle of June, Neptalí Castillo Herrera arrived in Piedras Negras, Mexico, just across the Rio Grande River from Eagle Pass Texas. Three long hard months ago, he had left his home in El Negrito, Honduras to walk and hitchhike the 2000 miles across Honduras, Guatemala and Mexico. A couple of times he found small jobs and bought bus tickets as far as the few pesos he had earned would take him. He begged for food along the way and slept in the streets or in the countryside. He had to find a way to enter the United States, the Promised Land, without getting caught.

Quite a few prospective immigrants probed the border there at Piedras Negras. He listened to their stories and tried to formulate a plan to cross The Rio Grande that he felt would be successful. After talking to some waiting their chance and some who had been caught and deported by "La Migra", as they called the U. S. Border Patrol, he decided to head downstream toward Nuevo Laredo in search of a better place to cross.

Five years before, he had entered the United States through the desert west of Nogales, Arizona with his older brother Santiago, his cousin Cecilia and her husband. They had joined with a man and his wife who said that he knew the way across the desert and where the water holes were. He had been working in Arizona but returned to Mexico to bring his wife back with him.

Most of the water holes had dried up and the "illegals" got lost and nearly died of thirst and starvation. They walked more than 100 miles before they finally stumbled through a mountain pass and saw an irrigated pepper field down below where a lot of workers were harvesting peppers. The emaciated woman looked exhausted and hungry.

The harvesters gave them water and food and a place to sleep. Neptalí and his companions joined the laborers and traveled with them from place to place, harvesting peppers and other crops. Neptalí stayed with his brother for three years, but became homesick. He bought an airplane ticket and went home to Honduras.

He could not find any good jobs in Honduras, and soon he used up all his savings. The best jobs he found only paid the equivalent of about $3.50 per day.

His brother and cousin had such traumatic experiences crossing the desert that they didn't want to leave the United States and risk having to cross the border again. They knew they would not be satisfied trying to make a living in Honduras.

Santiago now had a good job in Immokalee, Florida. Cecilia and her husband had gone north to work in Minnesota. They all kept in touch with each other and Neptalí had both their phone numbers.

About 30 miles upstream from Nuevo Laredo, Neptalí found the spot where he would attempt to enter through Texas, the big rich Promised Land that lay just across the river a short 150 feet away. He knew it would not be easy. With only a small amount of food and water and no money, he would have to choose begging in Mexico or begging in Texas. He chose Texas.

A power line crossed the Rio Grande and a road ran along side it due north. He put all his clothes and his *mochila,* his small backpack, in a plastic bag that he had salvaged from a garbage dump. He swam across the river at 2:00 o'clock in the morning of July 4. He had learned during his previous stay while working in the United States, that all the workers were given a day off on Independence Day. He hoped that "La Migra" would be distracted with plans to celebrate this important holiday, and perhaps they would be less attentive to their job of protecting the border.

On the Texas side, a smooth dirt road ran parallel to the river—smooth because the Border Patrol dragged it at the beginning of each shift so that they could see the footprints of any one who crossed it.

He broke a bushy limb from a mesquite tree and crossed the road walking backward while erasing his tracks with the limb. Before he could head north, he saw the lights of a car approaching. He ran as fast as he could toward a small thicket.

Two Border Patrol agents were in the car. One drove watching the road for footprints while the other looked out the window with his infrared night vision glasses. The agent fixed his scan on a target and said, "Stop the car and turn out the lights. I see a man running through the brush."

The driver stopped and put on his night vision equipment. "I see him. He's running toward that thicket."

Neptalí ran into the thicket and lay down in a small gully about three feet deep. He hoped that it was deep enough so that the heat from his body would not be visible to the agents through their infrared equipment. His rush into the thicket spooked three deer that ran onto the road and into the night. The driver saw them and shook his head, "Just some deer. They ran straight away from you and you just thought it was a man."

"I know what a man looks like and I know what a deer looks like. It was a man! Turn up the power line road; we can get closer."

They turned up the power line road and stopped near the thicket, close enough so that Neptalí could hear every word. They had quite a discussion about whether to hunt further out into the brush, but finally decided to return to their car. If they had gone just a few steps further, Neptalí would have been plainly visible to the agents with their infrared equipment.

After the agents left, Neptalí started walking north through the brush that stretched alongside the power line road, careful not to leave any foot prints. He walked through the night and early morning. By noon the next day, the temperature was well over 100 degrees. He had only brought a couple of corn tortillas and a quart of water and they were long since gone. His thirst was unbearable, but he kept on walking.

Just before dark, the rattlesnakes started crawling out of their holes. The snakes didn't worry him as much as the coyotes. He wore high top lace up boots and two pair of pants that he thought would give him ample protection from the snakes. He found a good stout limb to use as a weapon in case of an attack. Actually, the snakes were a lot more dangerous than the coyotes, but his parents had told him about some of his ancestors who had been attacked and killed by wild animals during their migrations in Honduras and these stories had made quite an impression on him.

Early in the morning of July 5, a Border Patrol helicopter came by; flying so low its landing gear seemed to skim the tops of the mesquites. Neptali dived under some brush. After circling around a while the helicopter hovered over a spot about a hundred yards ahead of where he was hiding. Three Border Patrol cars came up the power line road at a high rate of speed and stopped under the helicopter. As he watched from the brush, agents rounded up a group of men, none of whom he recognized, loaded them up and left the way they had come. The helicopter circled a while longer and finally worked its way out of sight.

Neptalí started walking again and when he came to the place where the helicopter had, circled, he found a gallon jug and a quart bottle of water that someone in the group caught by the Border Patrol had abandoned. He drank the quart on the spot and put the gallon jug in his *mochila*. Exhausted, he found a place a little farther along where he could hide in some thick brush, and lay down to rest.

He thought about his parents, two small sisters and little brother. They were all suffering. The money that Santiago sent home was barely enough to feed them. His father had had a heart attack recently and was unable to work. The doctor said that he must have an operation before he would be able to go back to work.

Neptalí promised himself that as soon as he got to where Santiago was working, he would get a job and send home the money for his father's operation and also enough to buy the school uniforms for his siblings so they could enroll in school again. As of now, the family spent a lot of time scouring the country side looking for bananas, plantains, mangos and coconuts, and chasing down iguanas to augment the meager supplies of rice and black beans that his mother was able to purchase with the money that was left after buying his father's medicines. Perhaps today there would be enough to buy a small piece of meat for soup. With this hopeful thought, he fell asleep.

He woke up about noon thirsty, hungry and sweaty. He drank from the jug and started walking again. He walked all afternoon and all night. With the coyotes howling all around, he was afraid to lie down.

On the morning of July, 6 he saw a small house at the end of a dirt road that intersected from the west. An old Mexican woman was at home and she gave him water and a tortilla wrapped around some refried beans. She was not very friendly. She told him that he better get away from there as quick as he could because it was time for her son to come home and he was a lot worse than the Border Patrol. She said he would tie up any "illegals" to that big mesquite tree out there until the Border Patrol came by to pick them up.

Neptalí found some thick brush a few hours later and lay down to rest during the hottest part of the day and that night. The next day, he walked until dark when he came to Highway 83. He crossed it and the dirt road that ran parallel to the fence on the other side, careful not to leave any footprints. The coyotes started howling. He clutched his club to defend himself, but they didn't come near him. He walked on through the night squatting down in the grass when cars came by so that nobody could see him. He ran out of water early that morning. He had nothing to eat in 36 hours. He had to keep going until he could find water.

Just after noon on July 7, Horton Williams left Brownsville towing his RV trailer behind his pickup truck. He was a widower and a retired farmer. He had decided to head west along the border and tour the Big Bend National Park. All his life he heard stories about the Big Bend. About the ranchers who raised longhorn cattle there and drove them over land up the Chisholm Trail almost 2000 miles to sell them in Wichita, Kansas. He bought the RV trailer when he retired at age 72. Now that he was approaching 80, this was the first trip of any consequence that he had been able to take with it. He had no schedule. He would stay as long as he liked and return whenever he got ready.

Sadly, he remembered when his wife's health began to fail shortly before he retired. Her condition deteriorated until she died last winter. She never felt like going anywhere. She just wanted to stay at home and rest.

Williams traveled north on Highway 83 through Laredo, and a little before dark he found a roadside park on the east side of the road. He decided, with its large parking area, that this would be a good place to spend the night. He parked near the fence a long way from the road, orienting the trailer so that the wind blew through it from one side to the other when the windows were open. The temperature was well over 100 degrees but it didn't bother him. He had lived half his life before he ever heard of air conditioning, which half the time he didn't use. He fixed a bite to eat, turned out the lights and opened all the curtains so the wind could blow through. He made sure that his trusty Ruger 357 magnum revolver was within reach. He stripped down to his shorts and set up a 12-volt fan to blow across his body.

He turned on the radio and found a Mexican station playing the beautiful *corridos* and *rancheras* of José Alfredo Jiménez, Vicente Fernández and other *conjunto* artists. It was so beautiful! The guitar playing was fantastic! Each presentation sounded better than the last. The announcer said the temperature was 38 degrees Centigrade. That translated to 106 degrees Fahrenheit.

By 10:00 o'clock the temperature had cooled down considerably and he was getting sleepy, but the music was so pretty he couldn't bear to turn the off radio.

He woke up with a start. It was after midnight and someone was outside the window asking for help in Spanish. His hand closed over the Ruger. He answered in Spanish and asked the man if he was by himself or with a group. The man assured Williams that he was by himself and he desperately needed some water.

Williams slipped into a pair of Levi's and told the man to come around to the door. He turned on the outside light so he could look him over. He handed him a glass of water with his left hand while he kept his right hand on the Ruger in his back pocket. The man drank it right down and asked for another. Williams looked the man over and decided the stranger did not pose much of a threat, so he invited him inside and advised him to sit down and drink slowly as it might make him sick if he drank too fast.

He asked the man if he was hungry. The stranger said that he had not eaten in three days except a tortilla yesterday morning. So, while Williams fixed something to eat the visitor told his story in acceptable English. He said that he needed to get to a telephone to call his brother to come get him. He heard the Spanish music on the radio and thought that Williams was Mexican and, therefore, safe to talk to.

Williams told him that he would not turn him over to the Border Patrol. After all, he had worked illegals all his life on his farm. It would have been impossible to raise vegetable crops competitively without their help, but he had no intention of breaking the law at this stage in his life and getting caught.

He told Neptalí to find a place for the night and come back after daylight for some breakfast.

About an hour later a Border Patrol agent stopped and shined his lights all around the park. He called in William's license tag number to find out who he was. He knocked on the door and Williams answered. The agent said: "I suppose that you are Horton Williams because that's whose name the truck is registered to. I just want to warn you. We have reason to believe that illegal aliens are in the area. I'd advise you not to answer your door if any of them show up here . Do you have a cell phone?"

"Yes, I have a cell phone."

"I'll give you this card. It has the number of the Border Patrol station at Carrizo Springs. Call us if you see or hear anything."

Meanwhile, Neptalí crouched down behind some brush less than a hundred feet away. His heart pounded! He heard everything said. Williams had not handed him over to the Border Patrol, but what would happen if the agent decided to use the infrared night vision device? After the agent left, Neptalí moved further back from the park and prepared to wait for daylight. He decided that he would rather risk an encounter with the coyotes than the Border Patrol.

At dawn, Williams invited Neptalí in for breakfast. Again, he told Williams that he needed to get to a telephone so he could call his brother for money.

They got in the pickup and headed north on Highway 83. When the truck got to Catarina, Williams pulled into a country store filling station with a public telephone out front and a Border Patrol car parked right beside it. Neptalí said he did not want to stop, so Williams drove on to another roadside park a couple of miles past Catarina. He felt that Neptalí needed to work on his plan a little bit. "Neptalí," he said, "Let's go back to the RV and make us another cup of coffee. We need to talk."

When they sat down to drink their coffee, Williams said, "If you call your brother, how is he going to send you money? There's no Western Union out here and there's a main Border Patrol station at Carrizo Springs and they probably have check points set up on the roads going in and out of there. I don't mind helping you, but I sure don't want to get caught breaking the law."

Neptalí said, "I need to get to a town somewhere. I'll have to find somebody who will help me and let my brother send the money to him because I don't have the identification that Western Union requires in order for me to collect the money."

A sudden knock on the door startled them both. Williams motioned Neptalí to go in the bathroom and shut the door. He answered the knock. A Hispanic woman, who had stopped at the park to attend to one of her three small children, asked him if he had some jumper cables. Her car would not start.

He raised the hood on her car and saw that the battery cable connections were badly corroded. He got some wrenches out of his toolbox and proceeded to clean the connections.

While he worked, she told him that she lived in Brundage and had to go to Carrizo Springs to do some shopping. She then decided to visit her sister who lived the other side of Catarina.

Williams said, "I heard that the Border Patrol was stopping traffic leaving Carrizo Springs going toward Brundage. Anything to that?"

"Oh no, they do sometimes but they're not stopping anybody today"

Williams oiled the cleaned cables, put them back on and the car cranked right up. She thanked him profusely, and left with the three children waving goodbye.

When Williams walked back to put his tools away, he noticed that Neptalí was sitting at the table in the RV sound asleep. The four days that he spent since he swam across the Rio Grande left him exhausted. Mr. Williams sat down on one of the park benches to figure out what he ought to do.

Neptalí reminded Williams of Ernesto, his farm foreman for the past 30 years. They both had the same frank way of talking. He thought that, given half a chance, he would make someone as good a hand as Ernesto had turned out to be.

Ernesto had come across the river to work when he was about the same age as Neptalí. He took great pride in his work and showed a great natural ability to operate farm machinery. After the harvest was over that year, he offered Ernesto a full time job and he worked for Williams ever since.

A couple of years later, when Mrs. Williams first started having health problems, Mr. Williams mentioned to Ernesto that it looked like he was going to have to hunt a woman to help his wife around the house.

Ernesto asked for some time off to visit his family in Mexico. When he returned a couple of weeks later, he brought Lupe back with him.

Mrs. Williams and Lupe got along just fine. Lupe treated her like she was her own mother. Later on that year Ernesto and Lupe were married. They moved into the old rundown tenement house that Mr. Williams used to store hay in.

He got them green cards when they became eligible and Mrs. Williams taught them English at night after work. They took the place of the family that the Williams never had. It was a happy day indeed when Ernesto and Lupe became U. S. citizens.

Today, the old tenant house was transformed into a beautiful country cottage with beautiful flower gardens in front and chickens and hogs in the back yard. Ernesto runs the farm as a sharecropper. His and Lupe's three children are all attending the University of Texas at Brownsville.

Remembering his experience with Ernesto, Williams made a decision. When Neptalí woke up, he told him. "Neptalí, your situation is a lot more complicated than I thought. I'll tell you what I'm going to do. I'll take you across Highway 85 to Interstate 35 and help you get the money."

"I really appreciate this, Mr. Williams," Neptalí answered. "I can't tell you how grateful I am. I hope that someday I may be able to return your kindness"

So they drove to Carrizo Springs, turned right on Highway 85 right past the Border Patrol station. When they came to the Nueces River, Williams parked on the shoulder real close to the river bank. "Old buddy," he said, "these last four days that you spent walking through the hot country side left you smelling kind of rancid. I'll get you some soap out of the RV. This looks like a good place to take a bath."

Williams gave Neptalí a bar of soap, a pair of socks, a pair of under shorts and a short sleeve shirt. He was wearing two pair of pants. Walking through the brush frayed the outside pair, which he discarded at the river bank. The inside pair looked pretty decent. He bathed in the river and washed his socks and t-shirt. When he got back to the RV, he asked for some baking soda, which he put in his armpits for deodorant.

Before they got to Interstate 35, Neptalí asked Williams to stop by the side of the road. He looked through the contents of his *mochila,* took out a tube of toothpaste and set the *mochila* down in the roadside ditch. He said that he didn't want anything that would identify him as having crossed from Mexico.

Williams asked: "Aren't you at least going to bring your toothbrush?"

"No, it's a Mexican toothbrush. But the toothpaste is Colgate Total, the same over here as in Mexico. I'll get a new toothbrush."

Then he gave Williams four Mexican coins, all his financial resources, 1 peso, 2 coins of 50 centavos, and one of 20 centavos. Total value less than 25 cents. He did not want anybody to see him with Mexican coins.

Williams turned north on Interstate 35 and took the business route to Pearsall and an H.E.B. store with a large parking lot. Western Union was inside. Neptalí called his brother collect in Florida but got no answer. Then he called his cousin Cecilia collect in Minnesota. She promised to send $100 to Mr. Williams.

Two hours later, the money hadn't arrived so he called Cecilia again. She explained that she didn't have the whole $100 and had called her sister in law in Arizona who was sending her enough to make up the difference. She advised him that when he got the money to buy a bus ticket to Immokalee, Florida where Santiago lived.

The money finally arrived. Williams drove down to the bus station. It was Sunday and the station was closed. A sign on the door said that the next bus headed north was due at 5:00 o'clock and the station would open shortly before that time.

At a public phone booth Neptalí called Santiago again. He answered on the first ring. He told him to take the money and rent a motel room for two days. He would leave to come pick him up as soon as Neptalí could call him back with the name and address of the motel.

Williams rented the room in his name because no one can rent a room in Texas without identification. Neptalí paid the bill and Williams breathed a sigh of relief. He left to continue his long delayed trip to Big Bend National Park.

An exhausted Santiago arrived in the afternoon of the second day. He decided to spend the night.

The next morning they were ready for travel to Florida. Santiago looked at the map and decided to cut across country to avoid the rush hour traffic through San Antonio. They left Pearsall on Highway 140 and joined Highway 85 at Charlotte.

Meanwhile, two Hispanic males robbed a convenience store in Charlotte and were last seen headed east on Highway 85 toward Jourdanton. The police, sheriff and highway patrol quickly set up roadblocks at Jourdanton. Santiago and Neptalí were caught in the trap and taken to the county jail. Santiago's social security card turned out to be a forgery and Neptalí had no identification. Normally, the sheriff would have released them after the robbery suspects were caught because there were no funds in his budget to handle illegal immigration cases. It so happened that a Border Patrol agent was in the courthouse that day on some other business. The sheriff asked the agent what he should do with them.

The agent said: "I'll be glad to take them off your hands. I will take them down to Brownsville and let a judge decide what to do with them.

Much later, Santiago and Neptalí appeared before a federal judge in Brownsville, who deported them back to Honduras.

Perhaps the immigration laws should be changed, Williams thought as he drove to Big Bend. Under the present law, people like Santiago, Neptalí and Cecilia could never get visas, and these workers were the people in most demand.

He always figured there should be a guest worker program. He could never have been successful as a truck farmer without the legions of "Wetbacks" who swam across the Rio Grande every year to harvest his crops. Men, women and children camped on the irrigation ditch banks under tarpaulins. They drank the water from the ditches and bathed in them. They traveled from farm to farm in old school buses. When the harvest was over they returned to Mexico to do it all over again the next year.

The Trip Home
By Marianna Nelson

On U.S. 77, a motor home with a Michigan license plate headed north in the desolate section between Raymondville and the Border Patrol checkpoint in Sarita. Only an isolated ranch here and there broke the monotonous landscape, along with occasional clumps of trees and soaring hawks looking for prey.

Inside the motor home, snores came from Kevin sound asleep on the couch. The family's lumbering brown lab, Caramel, filled the space between Kevin's brother Randy who is driving and their mother Elaine dozing in the front passenger seat. A few days earlier, Randy and Kevin were headed south on this same highway. Their father, Eddy Baker, was very ill, and the family reunion in Michigan had to be moved to an earlier date. They all knew if they waited any longer, it might be too late. So, Randy and Kevin dropped their lives—just like that—and drove to the Valley to bring Eddy and Elaine back to Michigan.

As fate would have it, Eddy died the day before his sons arrived. Now, instead of a very sick man, they were bringing home their father's dead body. Their dad—always careful with money—had wanted it that way. "If I die before I get to Michigan, it'll cost nothing to drive my corpse home," he had told them. "Eh gads! Think how much you'd have to pay to ship a heavy casket with my body inside."

Randy remembered Eddy saying he looked forward to being with the family, especially five-year-old Josh, his favorite great-grandson, but he had doubts about the journey to Michigan. "I don't know if I can live through that long trip, even if I'm lying down the whole way." Eddy was so concerned that he prayed to God: "Dear Lord, if there's an easier way for me to get home, please let it happen."

"Well," Randy mumbled, "God sure answered Dad's prayer." With that difficult period behind them, Randy's fingers nervously tapped the steering wheel as he worried about the next problem—the Border Patrol checkpoint. There shouldn't be any difficulties, right? Still, federal agents and trained dogs are stationed there to search suspicious vehicles—after all, that's their job. If they question me, I just might tell a white lie about that box in the bedroom. It wouldn't hurt anyone and it might prevent a delay."

Eddy Baker's embalmed body lay in a casket, concealed in a big carton in the motor home bedroom. He had really wanted a plain pine box. Why spend money on a fancy casket that's just going to lie underground? But Mickey wasn't comfortable about his grandfather's final resting place so they bought a casket made of ash, fancier than the pine box Eddy had wanted.

Eddy's newly released spirit floated around the motor home, marveling how much easier it is to be dead and free than to be old and attached to an oxygen machine 24/7. Back in his little park model in the Valley where he and Elaine spent winters, he had to be careful not to stumble on the oxygen hose or trip over Caramel. One time the dog plunked down on Eddy's tube and made it fall out of his nose. Then he lost his balance and his shorts fell to his ankles. A friend of Elaine's had witnessed the whole scene—Elaine pushing Caramel away, then steadying him and pulling up his pants while he put the tube back in his nose. Worst of all, he wore Depends.

Thank goodness, my spirit no longer worries about losing dignity over wearing Depends. As for my dead body, it's of no use to anyone, expect perhaps the mortician who was paid to embalm it; slip my favorite Kiwanis golf shirt over me, and fold my hands across my chest real peaceful like.

Near the end of his life when Eddy was unable to leave the house, he was especially grateful for visitors. A few weeks before he died, three of the grandkids came to the Valley for their Gramper's 83rd birthday. Eddy even had enough energy, briefly, to compete in a fierce game of cribbage—just like the old days. He had taught all the kids and grandkids to play, some as young as six. He always took great pride in winning, but this time, he did not try as hard. Let the grandkids win a little. Give them some encouragement, something to remember and talk about later.

Eddy often talked to God. "Dear Lord," he would pray, "you've given me much to be thankful for—children, grandchildren, great-grandchildren, many friends, a satisfying career, and wonderful winters in the Valley. Thank you for my good wife who takes care of me and bakes delicious bread. Now, dear God, please guide me through my final days on earth."

Randy slowed his approach to the Border Patrol station. He stopped behind a line of vehicles waiting to be questioned. Some were given an okay to move on, while others were being searched in a holding area...like that slick-looking tour bus from Mexico with two officers that emerged from the bus carrying pieces of luggage to be inspected.

The sudden stop startled Elaine. As her eyes opened, they focused on a sign that read, "K9 on duty - restrain your pets!" She attached a leash to Caramel's collar and pulled it tight. The dog whined and punctuated her whine with a bark. A second "woof" came from the search dog outside.

After at least 10 minutes, it was Randy's turn to move forward. An officer stood at attention, waiting. A second guard held on to a taut leash attached to a big search dog, alert and ready to check and sniff the motor home.

Randy opened his window. The guard looked in and asked, "Are you all American citizens?" They nod.

"How many in the vehicle?"

"Three."

"Pull over. I'm coming in."

The officer stomped up the motor home steps. Kevin came to attention on the couch while Randy and Elaine sat rigidly in their seats staring straight ahead. Elaine, still with a tight grip on Caramel's leash, is relieved that the Patrol dog is outside with the other guard. The officer walked through to the bedroom. He returned and asked, "What's in that big box?"

Randy looked the agent in the eye. "A gas grill. We're bringing it to Michigan for our family reunion."

The officer returned the look and said, "That's a mighty big grill you have there."

Randy, Kevin, and Elaine each took in a deep breath and held it until the agent grinned. "Nice rig you have," he said. "Okay, you can go."

After the agent left, Randy pulled away slowly. "Whew! We were lucky," he said. "Timing is everything. With all that luggage from the Del Norte tour bus needing to be searched, the agents must have had bigger fish to fry than us."

The family buried Eddy in the Baker family cemetery the week before the reunion. At the reunion, his spirit was still on earth checking on unfinished business, making sure everything was all right. As it hovered above the tallest beech tree, dusk settled over the family homestead, Beechhurst. In the west, the sky still glowed after a crimson sunset over the lake.

His spirit watched the Baker clan celebrate—from the youngest, little Josh, to the oldest, Elaine. Over the noise of "fifteen two, fifteen four..." cribbage being played and steaks sizzling on the grill, Randy said, "Boy, I sure was nervous coming through the Border Patrol checkpoint on the way home, but at least we brought Dad's body back the way he wanted. If we hadn't, Mom would have had to pay $5,000 to ship it and that would have made Dad turn over in his grave. I can just hear him grumbling that we didn't have any money sense."

The cribbage game finally ended and granddaughter Jennifer proudly announced, "I beat you, Grammaw." Elaine gave Jennifer a knowing look, remembering what Eddy always said, "The first game is the kids' game."

No one paid any attention to Caramel except Eddy's spirit hovering above the scene. He watched as Caramel ambled over to the grill and opened her big brown muzzle around the biggest, juiciest piece of meat there. Eddy was heartened to see that his favorite dog is up to her old tricks. His spirit fondly remembered what she did the day he passed from one world to the next. She lumbered up onto the bed and sniffed his face until the mortuary men came to take him away. When they carried him out the door and laid his body on a gurney, Caramel followed and licked the bottoms of his feet, kissing him goodbye.

"Thank you, Lord, for showing me an easier way to go home. Lying in a casket was certainly better than barely being alive, fearing every breath would be my last. Now I'm ready to go to my home in heaven with You. I don't want to be a wandering, restless spirit any longer."

A rush of wind that sounded like the long, contented sigh Eddy used to make when he won a cribbage game rustled the leaves in the mighty beech tree. A brief flash of light illuminated the night sky before it faded into the darkness.

"What's that noise, Mama?" little Josh asked. "It sounds like Gramper when he beat us at cribbage."

"It's just the leaves rustling in the wind, Josh. Gramper is in heaven."

"Yeah, I know," Josh said. "I just saw him waving good-bye to us on his way up there."

THE UNWANTED VISITOR
By Judy Stevens

Nobody wanted to see him back then. Certainly, nobody had invited him. But what did that stubborn blowhard care? He'd fixed his sights on us. He was that unwanted visitor who barges in and practically wrecks the place, then says "adios-goodbye" without so much as a "gracias-thank you." But what could we do? He was coming our way, and that was that. All we could do was hide what we didn't want him to take.

Luckily, my little family had few valuables to lose. True, we had a plot of land in the mid-Valley but our home was far from elegant—just a trailer to some. Our true valuables were a kid and a cat, some papers that told the world we existed, and ourselves—me and my husband, that is.

We got word a few days ahead of his arrival so we had time to get ready for him. I could tell everyone was nervous by the amount of jibber-jabber in the air. Back then, I was a waitress, so I heard more than the usual.

"Do you think he'll go north of us instead?" someone asked.

No one answered; even the know-it-alls were silent. No one in fact, knew where he was fixing to land. He and his whole kinfolk were like that: indecisive to the end. With a shudder, we remembered one of his ancestors, a real beaut. People still talked about her.

One thing for certain: the whole lot of them would scare the devil himself.

"They say he's comin' straight at us," someone said just before I left work.

My heart skipped a nervous beat. If that was true, I knew he would take all our stuff too.

The radio barked the news: "All those in mobile homes prepare to evacuate to fixed structures."

It was official: Hurricane Allen, the "unwanted visitor," had set his sights on us.

The phone rang. It was my mother-in-law. "We're going to my sister's," she said matter-of-factly, the catch in her voice betraying her anxiety. I felt a wave of relief: That house had survived Hurricane Beulah in 1967.

I've watched tornados form, been less than ten feet away from a tree struck by lightning, and I'm no stranger to earthquakes; but Hurricane Allen was a category all to himself—a Category Five, to be exact . Now he was in the Gulf of Mexico, bearing down on Brownsville with two hundred mile-per-hour winds.

We had to get out of our trailer.

The sight of a wall of clouds is common in areas prone to killer thunderstorms, but the leading edge of a hurricane is not just a wall; it is a fortress the color of which I cannot describe. Even the air takes on an ominous cast.

I glanced through our living-room window at my husband and daughter hard at work securing what they could in the yard just as an unearthly glow from the clear sky to the west cast them in sharp relief against the deep gray curtain of clouds to the east. I felt, despite the moist oppressive air, a chill down my spine: our once-secure haven had just become a deathtrap.

I suddenly realized that, no matter how traumatic earthquakes, tornados and lightning bolts were, they were no match for hurricanes— because hurricanes make you wait. Before a hurricane arrives, there's time to think, time to re-think—time to imagine. This "unwanted visitor" was giving us just enough time to make irreversible decisions about our life's accumulation of trash and treasure, but not enough time to really comprehend which was which. What was on the list of things we couldn't give up? Would the list be the same the next year? I stood there indecisive, wondering what to take and what to leave behind. What would I never miss? What would I miss terribly? In the end, I told myself that these were in fact, just things; what was important was completely intangible— our lives; our memories.

Oh, how I wanted it all to be a bad dream, and oh, how I wanted to wake up.

In the end we stored things that could not be replaced in plastic bags inside plastic garbage cans, knowing a tornado would spare none of it.

Then I dragged my old beat-up backpack from the closet and crammed it full of photos and birth certificates and memories and a change of clothing for each of us. I looked around at the bare walls, the furniture and lamps bunched away from windows and the objects normally high in cupboards now on the floor, like a ship ready to weather a storm at sea. I checked the taped and shuttered windows then glanced at the clock: It was six-o'clock in the evening. We sat down to eat a hasty dinner amidst the disorder of our kitchen and waited for the next advisory.

Now it was time to leave. We piled in the car and left for the aunt's home a couple of miles away. The house had weathered Beulah in 1967; it might just weather Allen in 1980. We had no choice but to leave our housecat behind in the trailer, for the aunt was allergic. We tried not to think too much about what might happen.

The aunt's house was homey and cozy, just the place to be in a crisis. We settled in amongst nervous hugs and hellos, grateful to be there instead of in one of the Valley's rapidly-filling and over-crowded shelters.

Early Saturday afternoon we lost all power, a diversion of sorts, for we were growing tired from waiting. Our "unwanted visitor" had stalled forty-four miles east of Padre Island. Had Allen been named "Alice," no doubt someone would have made a crack about "indecisive women."

The hours dragged on. Fifty miles inland, waiting for the deluge, we sat in our little "ark"—but instead of animals two by two, our ark contained youngsters bored with a capital "B." To battle boredom and pass the time, we turned to old-fashioned ways—card games, quiet conversation, shadow puppets on the wall; popped corn on the propane stove. Amazing how good popcorn tasted despite the knots in our stomachs. An odd sort of camping attitude prevailed, which the kids seemed to enjoy, despite the unspoken and oppressive anxiety we elders felt.

Our aunt, a former nurse, remarked that she'd known since Friday that Hurricane Allen would hit the Rio Grande Valley because the wire services were sending their reporters to Brownsville instead of north to Corpus Christi, and the Red Cross had mobilized for our area.

Radio communications came in intervals of five minutes in English and five minutes in Spanish in hopes of warning those in northern Mexico of the impending disaster. The border between our two countries with all its bridges and checkpoints remained open for anyone seeking shelter, and the local shelters rapidly filled to capacity. Now all anyone could do was wait.

At four o'clock a bulletin from the National Weather Service in Brownsville caught our attention and hushed the room:

"Brownsville...now appears the likely point of landfall for Hurricane Allen. No storm of this strength has struck this area in recorded history... Flooding will be a problem...even after winds die down...we will remain on duty throughout the night...Our computers have already failed... making composition of these messages slow...By Sunday morning the worst of the winds should be over...From now on we must just endure... May God help us."

The winds rose. We were in the second squall line with gusts of gale force.

The wind roared in gusts and waves, first dying down, then slamming into the north side of the house again and again. Later, when it reached hurricane force, it settled into a dismal roar.

Then our "unwanted visitor" stalled again—twenty miles off South Padre Island. People ventured out of shelters in Brownsville because the curious double eye wall structure caused almost no wind there, while we—thirty miles inland—were in the final squall line.

By six in the evening, we knew Allen would hit us sometime before three in the morning. We couldn't help remembering our joke that Allen would never come ashore Sunday because of the Texas Blue laws, which prohibited selling certain merchandise on the Sabbath.

By eleven, the kids had long since sprawled fast asleep, and the door facing the storm was finally braced well enough so that no one needed to man it despite the constant roar from the other side. We tried to catch some sleep, knowing that come daylight the area would resemble a water-soaked bombsite, since Allen's eye was going to pass right over our little trailer and our poor little housecat.

I fell asleep as the words, "imminent disaster," came from the radio in a voice of measured steadiness. I remember thinking drowsily, "Nice. I love it. Trailer all paid off; van and car all paid off; real NICE." I drifted off to the radio's static and the muffled roar of a wild beast trying to get through the front door.

We slept right through an historical event.

While we were sleeping, Allen's eye-wall came ashore on South Padre Island, crossing the Laguna Madre to Port Isabel, destroying an old fishing landmark, Purdy's Pier. Then, as if on a whim, our "unwanted visitor" veered north. His storm surge forced Gulf water across the narrow island into the shallow Laguna Madre and cut that narrow strip of land in sixty-eight places, obliterating the road north. Then—finally—Allen made landfall at 3 a.m. slightly south of Port Mansfield, about twenty-five miles from where our little rag-tag bunch of survivors slept.

I heard all this from that same steady voice on the radio, while I checked the windows on the south side, certain the winds would slam us after the eye-wall passed. Earlier, I woke with a start then realized what woke me was the silence. Now, as I stood there peeking out the window, all I heard was the sound of intermittent wimpy wind gusts. We were out of danger.

At that moment a curious wave of relief mingled with frustration hit me as I realized we lived through an entire terror-filled weekend with nothing to show for it when we went back to work tomorrow.

Then I felt a wave of shame as I realized South Padre Island and Port Mansfield must have received the destruction we missed. Not only were we lucky, we were blessed.

Still—we had yet to see our trailer.

The others were up. We shared the news and the relief with mixed reactions of annoyance and thanksgiving. Our "unwanted visitor" who had overstayed his welcome was finally leaving and we could pick up the pieces in—well—peace.

By mid-morning we began to resettle into our trailer disappointed at how our Sunday had been ruined. It was a bit surreal to see our trailer just as we had left it, only scrubbed clean. Closer inspection revealed the citrus blown off the trees, a little water damage where the wind tilted the trailer enough to let the rain under the roof, and a small uprooted tree. Down the street a large palm tree had fallen, partially blocking the road. Our drapes showed signs of our housecat's terror the night before. Now there she was curled up on our sofa, peacefully sleeping it off. By mid-afternoon, as I was mopping the floor around the refrigerator, Allen was downgraded to a tropical depression. My husband peeked into the kitchen and joked that it took a hurricane to force me to clean the cupboards and defrost the freezer. Some of us are geared for domesticity and some of us have learned to ignore comments like that.

Meanwhile, down on South Padre Island, where the eye of our "unwanted visitor" first made landfall, they began selling T-shirts we couldn't afford with the caption "I survived Allen—1980," to tourists who were not even there.

THE WANDERERS
By Hernán Moreno-Hinojosa

Pariahs among their contemporaries, this small band of wanderers, shunned and distrusted by other peoples, served *Del*(*) and no one else. Was it not one of their own who attempted to steal the nails that the heathens would use to crucify the Christ? The risk was great, the effort valiant, but alas, the boy managed to snatch only one of the four nails. And *Del* alone appreciated what the dark haired boy had attempted. The penalty for theft from the Roman Army—death by crucifixion, sewn within an animal hide, the boy's legs smashed to assure death by sundown. For a Gypsy boy the hide of a pig would surely be selected and he would be crucified with the Christ alongside Dismas and Gesmas, the two thieves. Instead of gratitude, the multitudes accused his people, expert blacksmiths, workers of base metals, artisans and prognosticators, of forging the very nails the pagan Romans had used.

1500 years later, these wandering people, true servants of *Del,* keepers of great secrets, again, would serve and none but *Del* would know. It was their lot in life, their destiny and but one short year before they came to this place that the Spaniards called Tejas, to the place known as el Valle del Rio Grande at the far reaches of the known world. An undeveloped land rich with native vegetation and vast growth of thorny trees that scratched, pricked and stuck the unwary traveler. This strange land they now found themselves in was a virtual forest of hostile trees and cactus with vicious stickers and snakes that rattled and struck out with venomous fangs. Their grandfather had brought the Beast to this strange land thirty years before.

Now the time had come to ensnare it forever in a casket from which there could be no escape. It was their service to *Del* and to Mankind before the region became glutted with immigrants from the civilized world.

Stefan, the unofficial leader, spoke to his brothers. "There will be a sacrifice. One of us will not return." Stefan, at thirty-five, was the second youngest man in the group; a thinker and a man of action hardened by the nomadic life of his people. Stefan knew that his young wife would comfort their four children and tell them that their father will soon return from his task in the thorn-tree forest(**). His wife Maria knew that they probably saw him for the last time, but she lied to her children nevertheless, and found comfort in the lies she told. Stefan and Renzo truly are siblings; the brotherhood they share with two other men is their relationship in the same clan and the task that they must now carry out. "No man lives forever, Stefan," Viviano the Valiant said. "I shall ensnare the Dark One within the casket." Viviano, tall and dark of hair and eyes, good with a knife and quick to fight—Viviano known as the Valiant.

"Viviano is not the only fearless one among us," Renzo, the young impetuous one with curly black hair and handsome looks, snapped with a cracking voice. "I shall wrestle the Beast and Stefan, and Ramon can lock the casket with the Beast and me within."

Viviano looked at Renzo with disdain; the boy tries so hard to be brave. If he lives to be his age, he might succeed. "And what would you have me do, Renzo, while you *dánz* with death and have your two other brothers slam the lid? I too am sworn to serve *Del*."

Renzo looked at Viviano with remorseful eyes. "I did not mean you should do nothing." He extended his right arm apologetically. "Viviano, the four of us can defeat the Beast. I have no woman, no children. I should be the one to die."

"I have had many women and many children, my years have grown numerous and my time to serve *Del* grows short." Viviano stared solemnly at his compatriots. The gift of second sight, precognition ran strong in his Gypsy veins. With a sigh of resignation Viviano added, "Perhaps it is not my destiny to return to the Old World." Only yesterday, Ramon and he had deposited the casket of the Dark One close to the cave, concealed in the thorny brush. It was then, so close to the lair of their sworn enemy that the vision struck him. "If it is *Del's* will," Viviano stated emphatically, "that I remain in Terra Nova…then so be it. I shall ensnare the Dark One within."

"I have a plan," Stefan interjected. "Perhaps we can all survive to serve *Del* another day." In his heart Stefan knew that only three of them would return. He yearned to see his wife and children one last time.

"What is the plan, Stefan?" Ramon spoke for the first time, his face cloaked in rags. Ramon the repulsive one; Ramon, the loner, whose face was destroyed by a rabid bear in the old country when he was but a boy. The elders knew how to stop the malady, which now infected the boy. Ramon was immersed naked into a cauldron of increasingly hot water, over and over again, until the sickness was purged. Many were the ones who did not survive the treatment. Ramon survived and had neither wife nor children, nor prospects for future wives. Still, he was a staunch believer in *Del* and a handy man to have in a fight.

"One of us must enter his lair before the Dark One returns." Stefan spoke softly, in conspiratorial tones. "Remove enough soil to line the bottom of the casket, then we shall seal the entrance." Stefan made eye contact with his brothers. "It is known that the Beast must repose in the soil that spawned it, the slime of Lilith(***), the mother of abominations."

Viviano asserted himself, his hands on his hips. "I shall enter the cave to bring the soil out in a bucket."

"I shall go with Viviano," Renzo insisted. "I will carry the torch that we may retrieve the soil quicker."

"How can we seal the cave, Stefan?" Ramon inquired.

"We must work quickly and pack the entrance with branches, mud, rocks and clay. Then we shall leave the casket nearby with the soil within for its bed."

Viviano smiled. "The plan may work, but how do we keep the beast from simply insinuating his way into the cave? The seal we build in haste will be far too weak to keep him out for long? The Beast will only lay to rest in the very soil that our grandfather deposited there to keep it from returning to the Old World."

"Mirrors," Stefan said. He smiled. "If *Del* so wills it, enough light shall burn through the cloud cover. Then we can concentrate our mirrors on the entrance. The Dark One hates the light and will have no recourse but to seek repose within the casket."

Viviano gripped his brother's shoulder. "Renzo and I shall enter the lair! We shall fetch the soil!"

"It is decided then," Stefan said. He faced each brother in turn. In the dim, early morning light four resolved men marched single file into the fog-shrouded thorn-bush armed with knives, mirrors, and their unshakable faith in *Del*. They know that there, in the bowels of the thorn tree forest, *Beng*(****) awaits, and the devil is still hungry

The cave entrance was small, barely larger in circumference than a meter. Inside, the cave was dark and dank and the ceiling much too low, barely more than a meter in height. Both men squatted and twisted through the winding tunnel. Deeper within, a strong stench of musk assailed the men.

"The lair of the Dark One!" Viviano screwed up his face in disgust.

"That smell!" Renzo wiped his nose with the sleeve of his baggy white shirt.

"The odors of the lives it has stolen…," Viviano said with a grim voice, "…men's lives and animal's, and more."

"More, Viviano? What could be more?"

"The stories I heard, Renzo, when I was growing up told that where the Beast wandered entire forests dried up and died. That is what I heard, anyway, when I was young."

Two buckets full of dirt sufficed to line the bottom of the casket. The casket was long and deep enough to accommodate a man, if he pulled his knees up. It was constructed of hard black wood found only on the Dark Continent. Artisans built it with a double-wall that accommodated thin sheets of hammered lead in between.

The four men worked with haste. Renzo and Viviano dragged buckets of mud from the banks of that river the Spaniards named el Rio Grande. Stefan and Ramon hacked at branches from the willows that grew near the river. The entire morning has been overcast, since the Dark One left its lair to prowl for life. Satiated with a stolen life force, the Beast must soon return to repose for another hundred years. In its dormant stage, it is like smoke, unapproachable, unmanageable and completely beyond reach.

They completed the barrier as the sun approached its zenith. The Dark One had not yet returned.

"Renzo and I shall hide among the boulders," Stefan said. "Ramon and Viviano, you two hide behind the trees by the riverbank. Be wary of the thorns! When the darkness that walks approaches, shine your mirrors on the barrier and do not be deceived by its appearance. Have your mirrors ready my brothers."

Ramon groaned, "I dislike mirrors, Stefan."

Stefan stared at Ramon. A rare attempt at humor on the repulsive one's part? Stefan acknowledged his attempt with a smile and said, "Have faith and believe in *Del*!"

Ramon nodded.

From their places of concealment, Renzo was the first to see the meandering shadow approach from the winding wooded trail. Excitedly, Renzo shook Stefan's shoulder and whispered, "Look!"

"Be silent Renzo, so that we do not become its next meal."

The cloud cover was too solid to let the mirrors collect light to shine at the entrance. The Dark One stopped contemplated the barrier that grew here since only this morning. He sensed the presence of several interlopers. The Dark One rushed Stefan and Renzo hiding in the boulders closest to his cave

Renzo leaped up on the boulder and challenged the creature, now a huge black snake. Renzo was stunned, mesmerized by the sight. It was as big around as a tree trunk and reared its ugly head, up, up, up level with Renzo's face.

"NO!" Viviano shouted. He rushed at the creature that changed instantly into a scorpion the size of a man.

Stefan had his back to the rocks, terrified of the huge hairy spider that moved slowly toward him and Renzo. Ramon saw a ravenous bear, foaming at the mouth. Only Viviano was able to react.

The scorpion backtracked facing Viviano and swept him with a multitude of flashing blue eyes. Claws scissored open and close, cracking loudly. Beads of cold sweat erupted on Viviano's forehead. With knife firmly in his right hand down by his hip, he walked slowly, steadily toward the big scorpion.

Quick as lightning, the deadly stinger plunged forward. Viviano lashed out with his blade and hacked the venomous stinger off at the base. The scorpion retreated. It stared at Viviano in disbelief. Viviano sneered; this was his greatest moment. He leaped on the scorpion's back and grabbed it below the snapping, scissoring claws in a powerful bear hug. The scorpion's tail jabbed impotently at Viviano's head, neck and back leaving wet smears of venom that did no more than burn his skin where it touched him.

The sun broke through the cloud cover. Ramon grabbed his mirror and steered the reflected light at the beast Viviano grappled with. Stefan and Renzo did likewise. Viviano lugged the big scorpion, weakened by the light, toward the casket and forced it within. He slammed shut the lid.

Renzo grabbed the big brass lock from his brother and rushed to Viviano, struggling to hold down the lid.

A locksmith had fashioned this lock without a key or keyhole. It cannot be unlocked once it is secured. Deftly, Renzo slipped the lock into the casket's hasp and staple, and snapped it shut. "It is done!" Renzo danced with joy. "We did it Viviano, we are triumphant—Viviano?"

Viviano knelt on the ground, his head low, his shoulders stooped... silent.

"Viviano?" Renzo reached for his brother's shoulder.

Viviano slowly raised his head. Renzo stared in mute surprise at the aged man that took Viviano's place. Viviano the Valiant, a strong and vital man of fifty now looked older than their grandfather.

"I regret to inform you my brothers..." Viviano's voice was flat and hoarse as he declared with acquiescence, "I shall not accompany you back." He stared at his brothers, hollow-eyed and weary. "My time has come. My service to *Del* is done. Bury me here, my brothers, and remember me always to our People."

Epilogue

And so the Wanderers returned to the Old World and the stories were told and ballads were sung of their lost brother Viviano—Viviano the Valiant, the Gypsy who defeated the Dark Lord.

Glossary:

*Del: Domari (E. European Gypsy language) for God, the Supreme Deity.

**Thorn-tree forest; these people use language familiar to them: Mesquite brush to them is a thorn-tree forest.

***Lilith: According to Jewish sources (omitted from the Old Testament) Lilith was Adam's first wife and the mother of all unseemly creatures known & unknown to Man as a result of her coupling with demons. The wanderers are Judah/Christian (Catholic) and so they know of Lilith.

****Beng: Domari for Devil.

THE WAR BRIDE
By Verne Wheelwright

During the Second World War, thousands of American troops were stationed overseas, particularly in Great Britain, or the United Kingdom. Even before the enormous buildup of troops prior to D-Day, the U.S. Army had a large Air Force based there to fly bombers and fighters over occupied Europe and Germany from the middle of 1942 through the end of the war. Together, the U.S. and British constructed or improved over 140 airbases in Britain. That effort led to joking descriptions of the island nation as "the world's largest aircraft carrier."

Most of the young Americans stationed on those bases were in their late teens and early twenties, away from their homes for the first time, in a country that shared their language. Naturally, they met British, Scottish and Irish girls, fell in love and married them. After the war, they brought their wives home to the U.S. where the newspapers, radio and movie-news greeted them as "War Brides."

Norma was a recent widow just beginning her recovery from a series of stringent treatments for terminal cancer. She and her husband had both moved to a local nursing home where they expected to die. When her husband died, Norma phoned her son and told him she did not want her life to end in a nursing home. Her son came that day and took Norma home to live with his family.

I met Norma on her first day outside the house. Spring in the Valley is warm, but that day, the temperature had dropped into the high seventies after the sun went down behind the palm trees. She had not been out of chemotherapy long, so she still avoided direct sunlight. She wore a robe, and I could see only a little bit of reddish hair on her head. She took careful, hesitant steps with a walker in the cul-de-sac in front of our home. I walked out to meet her, introduced myself, and we talked. My wife came out and joined us. The two women took to each other, instantly, and in a short time became good friends.

Norma suffered a moment of embarrassment when she realized how she was dressed. She pulled the robe a little closer around her and said, "I don't usually meet new neighbors in my bathrobe!" A warm, mischievous look sparkled in her eyes. This was a new experience, and the old rules didn't matter any more. Her life had been turned upside down and she was still righting it . Now she could make new rules. "But why not?" I thought that in that moment she stopped being a cancer victim and started being a survivor. In reality, the process probably took longer, but it was a moment I remember.

After all the years of raising and caring for her own family, Norma was now on the other side. She was the one being cared for. Her son, his wife and their three children, Norma's grandchildren, took her in, looked after her, and helped her with her recovery. The youngest grandchild, Katy, about ten, seemed very close to Norma. She spent a lot of time with her grandmother, especially that summer. They often came over together to visit my wife. Katy usually sat quietly and took in the conversation while Norma and my wife drank coffee and talked about nearly anything. My wife noticed how Katy watched for the signs and knew when her grandmother was tiring. She would touch her grandmother's hand gently and say, "Grandma, maybe we should go." Then Katy took her grandmother's arm and walked her home.

This quiet Katy bore no resemblance to the Katy I had watched playing basketball with her dad in the driveway. In one typical instance, she'd charged him with the ball, talking trash. She pivoted, bumped him, then scooted under his arm and up to the basket. Quick. Tough. Only ten, yet with Norma she was quiet, gentle and very protective.

By May, Norma walked without any assistance. Her red hair grew out and her health improved dramatically She had a quick, happy smile and a mischievous sense of humor. Soon she began driving again. We often saw Norma and Katy at the local HEB grocery.

During the next six months, Norma and I talked often there in the cul-de-sac. Not long after we met, I had told her that I was doing research, interviewing people over sixty. I asked if I could interview her.

"Of course!" She appeared delighted at the prospect. The conversations started immediately. In one of our conversations she teased, "I once knew a celebrity."

She left the thought hanging, so I asked.

"I joke about it, but it is true," she said. "Sean Connery delivered coal, milk and fish to our home in Edinburgh. He's a lot better looking now!" Then she added, "When my son was young I took him to a movie starring Sean Connery. Afterward, I explained that this man had once been a deliveryman in Scotland and was now a movie star because he had worked hard to change his life. I told my son he could be anything he wanted to be if he was willing to work hard for it."

Norma spoke with a charming accent that I won't attempt to imitate here. Our interviews took the form of long casual conversations. During one, she told me, "I was a War Bride." She said she had met her husband during the war. They married in Scotland when she was nearly twenty. Two years later, they had a daughter. Not long after, her husband completed his tour of duty, so the small family left Scotland and came to Harlingen.

She said it so simply, "…left Scotland." Yet she left everything she had known for more than twenty years.

Something nagged at me. I hesitated to say anything, but I had to. "I'm sorry, Norma, something isn't adding up for me. We're nearly the same age, but at the end of the War, I was only twelve."

I felt embarrassed about bringing this up…about questioning what she had told me. Her eyes twinkled and she laughed. I knew I had missed something important here, but I didn't see it coming.

"Wrong war!"

The phrase burst out of her with unconcealed glee. She had set me up! I laughed with her.

"During the Korean War, my husband was stationed at the old RAF air base near Edinburgh. It was like he was in charge of this whole run-down old air base, because he was the only one there! I learned later, he worked on a secret project, installing radio equipment in one of the abandoned buildings. It became a secret listening post.

"After work and on weekends, he'd hitch a ride, borrow a bike or walk into town. We met at a dance, fell in love, and married. He'd bring me candy and flowers, something no Scotsman would ever do!"

Even fifty years later and after the harsh effects of chemotherapy I could see why he was attracted to her. She was charming and intelligent, had an easy laugh and a gentle, teasing manner.

Norma did not talk a lot about family life in Scotland, but she remembered that other war—World War II with blackouts and air raid warnings and the very real fears of a German invasion.

"My parents had already decided that if the Germans invaded, none of our family would be taken alive."

What a terrifying bit of knowledge for a little girl only five or six years old. Even without an invasion, Norma's family endured a war related tragedy. Norma, especially, suffered, and the memory still troubled her.

Norma and her younger brother, Thomas, both of early school age, were walking along a road on their way home from school when a Polish military truck lost control and swerved into the two children. Norma tried to pull her brother out of the truck's path, but not in time. He died instantly. "I can still see him," she said, quietly. Her eyes glistened with tears. "My mother always blamed me. She brought it up again and again."

The war ended and the military pulled out. The town settled back into its own ways. "When the Korean War started, we didn't expect the airbase to reopen, and actually it didn't. Just one American airman came. And I married him!"

Again, the happy eyes and the easy laughter. "We talked for more than two years about going to Texas when his time came to be discharged, but the reality was almost overwhelming. In all of Texas and the United States, I only knew my husband and our daughter. I never thought about starting out with no friends and no family close by. But my husband had family in Mercedes, and they welcomed us to Texas, to our new home."

Once settled in the Valley, Norma and her husband worked hard and saved diligently, "...like thrifty Scots" she said, smiling mischievously. A serious look erased the smile. "When my husband died in the nursing home, I was in the hospital in some kind of coma...something brought on by the chemo. My son came to the hospital and even though I looked like I was asleep, he whispered into my ear to tell me that his father had died. The strange part is, I sat up in my bed as though I had been jolted with those electric paddles they use for heart patients, and told him we had a lot of things to do!

"I remember going to the wake and being upset that my husband didn't have a six-pence in his hand. The six-pence is Scottish tradition. It's symbolic, meaning, 'I will always be with you.' I must have made a fuss, because one of my son's friends gave me her lucky silver dollar that she always carried with her. I'll never forget that."

Norma was getting her strength back. Her hair grew out a much darker red, almost auburn, and she laughed more when we talked. She sold the family farm and bought a car, a small sports coupe. Bright red. She would back out of the driveway, wave if she saw me, then accelerate out of the cul-de-sac with enthusiasm; as though she couldn't wait to see what the world had waiting for her today. During that summer, I saw her and Katy and the little red car all over Harlingen. When Katy went back to school in the fall, Norma's friend from the next street traveled with her. We saw them at restaurants or events, and Norma was always happy and in a bit of a hurry. She seemed to thoroughly enjoy her new life. Yet, she still had time for our cul-de-sac conversations. Her articulate insights and perspectives on aging and nursing homes became solid contributions to my research.

I was in the yard, cutting old fronds from a palm tree when Norma hailed me, waving vigorously. "I'm going to Scotland!" She was exuberant!

"How soon?"

"Next month. I'll be gone two or three months. I'm staying with my mother in Scotland and I'll see all my family and friends that are still alive. Then we're going to the continent to see more friends that I haven't seen in years." She had not only returned to good health, she was radiant. Every facet of the planning and preparation for the trip excited her—even making the airline reservations. "This time I'm flying First Class! Very un-Scottish!"

During the weeks before she left, Norma's daughter flew in from California to spend some time with her mother; then, after a flurry of excited preparation, Norma was gone. The cul-de-sac was quiet.

Two months later Norma returned to Harlingen. She told me about the wonderful time she enjoyed in Scotland and Europe…the time spent with her aging mother, family and friends. She showed me photos of her mother and her hometown. She had thoroughly explored the places she left so long ago. She was still excited about the trip, but her manner seemed subdued.

Norma had seen a doctor while in Scotland. "At first it was stomach problems. Then, somehow I came down with pneumonia, so they put me in the hospital."

She stayed in the hospital in Scotland for several days and was still not very strong. She cut her trip short by nearly a month and came home to see her own doctor. Although something seemed unspoken, she recovered and told me she was flying out to California to see her daughter and grandchildren. The happy laughter was back.

She loved living with her grandchildren, but Norma felt she had stayed with her son's family long enough. Not wanting to be a burden, she started thinking about a home of her own. A few weeks later, she invited my wife and me to see the two-story condo she intended to buy. It was just a few blocks down the street—far enough to be independent but close enough that the grandchildren could visit easily. She gave us a full tour, and enthusiastically explained her plans for changing or updating each room and the back patio. The anticipation of furniture shopping excited her because she had nothing for the new condo. When she sold the farm, she sold everything. Now she relished the idea of starting fresh. Her own home. Her own things. Her own time.

She started with a blue awning. Rounded and just a little wider than the door, it set her home apart from all the others. The new awning gave her new home instant identity.

When we visited her several weeks later, she was settled and clearly content. Norma had caught up with her life now and didn't have to hurry any more. The twinkle was still in her eyes, the easy laughter that was almost musical, but with less urgency. She seemed very comfortable with her life.

Every evening, on our walk around the two-mile loop, we passed Norma's home. Occasionally we saw her out front, or she called to us from a window, but after a few months, we felt like we were seeing her less often. I saw Katy in the cul-de-sac one afternoon and asked about her grandmother. "She's been in and out of the hospital a few times lately. I think she's pretty sick."

We took flowers for her patio, but no one answered the bell, so we left them at the door, under the blue awning, with a note. A few days later, Norma called my wife and thanked her for the flowers. They had a long, easy visit. No rush now, just two friends catching up with each other. A few weeks later, we heard she had a full time nurse staying with her.

Occasionally, when we walked by in the evening we noticed the curtains part in her upstairs bedroom window above the awning, but only once did I actually see Norma in the window. She smiled and waved.

We were out of town when the funeral notice and obituary appeared in the Valley Morning Star.

Today, we think of Norma every time we pass her blue awning. No real sadness, just the remembrance of a friend that we still miss. The young woman who left her home in Scotland to start a new and different life in the Valley had become the Norma I met when she struggled with her recovery from chemo treatments. She had blossomed and lived a new and different life for two years.

Knowing her had enriched our lives.

THREE VULTURES SEEK FOOD
By Eugene Novogrodsky

Mid-day, and the eastern *Guanajuato* village shuts down
In the Sierra Oriental's direct sun ....
A bull paces, caged in the back of a racked farm truck,
His organs huge, and the owner takes a taco and beer break ....
Deserted streets, with lunch near, tortillas made,
Pick-ups parked; road builders dozing in shade ....
And up where the cacti-stuck dry slopes and peaks meet,
Beyond the dry river and dry streams, three black vultures
Glide, up and down, up and down, seeking death or
Exhausted life ....

THREE WHITE MAMMALS
By Janet R. Wilder

This is the third day in a row that a white animal has crossed my path on my way to the gym in the early hours of the morning.

The first was a white cat that I would have smashed if I hadn't stopped just in time. Recalling the icy look that cat threw over its snowy shoulder as it passed within inches of my front tires gives me the shivers.

Yesterday it was a medium-sized white dog. It, too, made direct eye contact with me as I slowed to let it pass in front of me.

Today, a smaller, white dog. More eye contact. Am I being haunted by ghost pets? Have I stumbled into a Stephen King parallel universe? Are these white beasts augers of something momentous about to occur? Whatever it is; I get the creepy feeling that something is not quite right.

I live where the locals call "out in the country." I'm right on the city limits line, but there aren't many homes here. Mostly farm land. It's quiet. The only disturbance is the low-flying yellow crop duster zooming in over the cotton crop up the road. One never sees anything interesting on the long stretch of straight Farm to Market road between my house and the expressway. I've seen plenty of birds, but who in The Valley hasn't? I've never seen any mammals and now I've seen three in a row and all of them white. Everyone knows bad things come in threes.

One white cat and two white dogs. What could it possibly portend? I frighten myself further by dragging up my limited knowledge of animal lore. Cats have been funerary attendants in many cultures. Think Egyptian. Dogs are guardians of the gates of the afterlife. Greeks, Celts, Native

Americans all have a dog connected with death, but none of them are specifically white.

I have obsessed about these animal encounters all day. It is late and I am tired. I will go to bed and try to sleep. If I don't wake up tomorrow morning, maybe there was something to those three white animals crossing my path three days in a row.

Where Are You, Home?
By Brenda Nettles Riojas

Where are you—
Buried in a past
Across a river with two names—
El Rio Grande,
El Rio Bravo,
A river that swallowed family?

Where are you—
Lost between two sides,
Between two languages?
In a mother, whose tongue I tried to hide?
In a father, whose skin I tried to emphasize?

Where are you—
At the edges of an ocean,
The Gulf that leads to other lands,
In the palm trees that need trimming,
In truths buried in sands?

Where are you—
In the mesquites I climbed as a child,
In the tree house made without nails,
Wood planks balanced on branches
Teased by *Kukulcan*?

Where are you—
In the echoes of Aztec and Mayan
Chants and sacrifices,
In winds from continents divided
That caress my thoughts and whisper
Their direction?
To which tribe do I belong?

Where are you—
In the cord once connected to offspring,
In the breasts that nursed them,
In the stars surrounding *Nuestra
Virgencita Morena*, our faith mother, our guide?

Where are you—
In a state once independent, once Mexican,
Down in the tip of the Rio Grande,
Atzlan, the lost region, home?

Why am I still searching
When Texas, they say,
Is home?

A GOOD ENDING
By Ruth E. Wagner

The sun has set.
Tall, white-haired, still handsome at ninety,
He stands by the door,
Gazing at the lunar eclipse.
He dines with wife and family
And teasingly flirts with a dark-haired neighbor.
At 9 p.m., he smiles,
And goes to bed.

At 2 a.m., a crash and knock in the dark.
"He's gone," she says.

We rush out to look for him.
"No," she cries. "He's gone."
We enter the guest room where he lies quiet.
She, of sixty years with him,
Leans over, kisses his forehead and says,
"Goodbye darling."

About The Authors:

Hugh Barlow is a stay at home father who has worked in a number of industries. He has been a tow truck driver, a gas pump jockey, a junk yard mechanic, an electrician, worked in the food service industry as a cook, and cut meat in a packing plant. Hugh has worked on road crews, and has owned his own business doing home and house trailer repairs. He is an avid Volkswagen collector with 4 air cooled VWs in his collection, loves reading and writing Science Fiction and fantasy, and repairs computers for fun. He has been published in his college paper, and had one poem published nationally. His desire for the future is to go back to college and continue his education.

Irene Salinas Caballero. has been writing poems, lyrics, rhymes, etc. for a very long time. *"Chicle Negro*—her first published work—is a poem that depicts a little piece of Valley culture as it relates to this region. "I thought it might stir some memories," she said. Irene lives in Mercedes but was raised in the small town of Sebastian, Texas. Her husband is Eduardo Caballero, M.D., and she is the mother of two, Karla Virginia Caballero, 22 and Omar Andres Caballero, 20.

Robin Cate has been writing poetry for more than thirty years. She finds the Rio Grande Valley a "gorgeous" subject for her verse. She devises small books of poetry (Pocket Books) that she sells for non-profits and gives to interested readers.

Don Clifford is a retired U.S. Air Force officer whose nonfiction articles appeared in various archaeological journals, UT/Brownsville historical studies, and Valley newspapers. His first published short story appeared in the September 2009 issue of the McAllen Monitor's *Festiva*, Writers Edition. In 1995, he served as editor of the Cameron County Historical Commission's *NEWSLETTER*, and won the Cotton Award from the Texas State Historical Commission for producing the best nonprofit newsletter in the State. In 1996 he co-edited *A Blast From The Past* for the Brownsville Historical Association; in 1998, he co-authored *A Kid's History of Brownsville*, and in 2008, he published his first novel, an action/adventure story titled *Ben Solomon: A Bastard Prince Denied A Throne*.

Edgar Clinton, Jr. is a native Texan born in Houston. He has spent his adult life in the Valley, and is involved in Internet and private publishing. He says *A Tejano Country Christmas* "…is the first time in a real book."

Beto Conde was born in 1947 and raised in San Benito, Texas. After he returned from military service during the Vietnam War era, he first started writing about his experiences in the war as a release of sorts for pent up emotions. "As I wrote more and more," he said, "I started writing about my growing up and living in the dual cultures of south Texas. I mostly write short stories and some poetry. I have no specific formal training in writing and write as a hobby and to retain memories and history of my life. My favorite books and authors are about life down at ground level." Beto is a co-founder of the Narcisco Martinez Cultural Arts Center Writer's Forum in San Benito, Texas.

Prenda E. Cook came to the valley from Odessa, TX in 1976. Her activities include teaching Survival Spanish and the international language, Esperanto. She has attended conventions in more than a dozen different countries where everyone communicated in the neutral language, Esperanto, which she promotes as the working language for the "European Congress" as well as the UN, saving probably a million dollars in translations. Each country could then have only "necessary and personal" material translated into its own language.

Julieta Corpus has been writing since the age of eleven. She graduated from UTPA with a Bachelor's Degree in Interdisciplinary Studies. She's been an elementary teacher for the past eleven years but has never stopped writing. She's been published by UTPA's *Gallery magazine*, <u>Tendiendo Puentes</u>, a poetic anthology, *Mesquite Review*, STCC's *Interstice* and <u>Tierra</u>

<u>Firme</u>, and in the September 2009 issue of the McAllen Monitor's *Festiva, Writer's Edition.* She also organizes poetry readings, and is an active member and participant of the Rio Grande Valley Poetry Festival and the San Benito Writer's Forum. Julieta blames her penchant for the dramatic in her poetry to a life-long addiction to Mexican soap operas.

Rudy H. Garcia lives in Laguna Vista, Tx., and is married to Rita C. Garcia. They have four daughters. Rudy's writing appears in *Telling Tongues,* Calaca press, Northwestern University; *poets of the east village* N.Y./ N.Y.; and *poetry pachanga*, Border Senses.

Irma N. Guadarrama is a Professor of Education at the University of Texas Pan American. She received her Ph.D. from the University of Texas at Austin in 1982 and since then has been a faculty member at several universities in Austin, Fort Worth, Denton, and Houston. Her specializations are language and culture in education and teacher education. "I've published academic books and articles, but not poetry," she said. "This is my first one." Her creative writing interest in poetry and music began at a very young age, and she is a proud member of the San Benito Writer's Forum.

Eunice Greenhaus was born and raised in New York City. She went to school in Massachusetts, lived in Connecticut, California and Texas, and finally settled in a San Benito trailer park where she teaches Mah Jongg, and writes her memoirs and poems, two of which appeared in *Tales Told At Midnight Along The Rio Grande.* As a member of the Writers Group at Fun N Sun, she wrote for and helped edit *Fun N Sun Then and Now*, a history of the RV resort, its residents and activities.

Marjorie (Marge) Johnson moved to Weslaco in 1957, where she authored publications for the Rio Grande Valley Partnership/Chamber of Commerce for more than 35 years. She published the *Valley Proud History Cookbook* in 1991 and *Historic Rio Grande Valley* in 2001. Since her retirement in 2004, she does publicity for the Weslaco Museum and other good causes.

Milo Kearney is a Professor Emeritus of history at the University of Texas at Brownsville. He and his wife Vivian now live in San Antonio, close to their daughter Kathleen and son-in-law Danny Anzak, with their boys Eli, Ben, and Jeremy, and to their son Sean and daughter-in-law Lisa, with their boys Ian and Collin. Milo has twenty published books—nine edited and eleven authored, including *Stories that Brownsville Told Its Children* and *Border Walls: A Musical About Redbeard of the Rio Grande*.

Jack C. King was born in 1936 in Raymondville, Texas and after some moving around, finished high school back in Raymondville. He pulled a three-year hitch in the Army, then worked eighteen months in heavy steel fabrication and 5 ½ years in gas pipeline construction. He started college at the age of 29 and earned an A.A. in architecture at San Antonio College, then a B.A. in humanities at U.T. Austin. He worked for the Texas Department of Health for ten years, taught high school English for two years and art classes for more than twenty years. Jack lives in Harlingen with his wife, Nina and daughter, Miranda, and have a son, Cody, in college.

Sarah Bishop Merrill, M.S, Ph.D., has authored two books and edited one published collection, the *Festschrift* for Helga Doblin,, and more than 40 articles and conference presentations. For more than 35 years, she has taught Ethics, World Religions, and Philosophy (emphasis on history, the rise of science, critical thinking and other logic). She has also reviewed manuscripts for publication, taught online, and authored online scenarios and interactive tutorials for major publishers. She was a founding member of the Association for Practical and Professional Ethics, and the Association for Moral Education, and has taught at every grade level, from Pre-K and day care through post-graduate courses. Her casebook on *Ethical Challenges in Construction Fields* is under contract with a major publisher.

Hernán Moreno-Hinojosa, a police officer retired from the Houston Metro Police Department, published his first major work, a true ghost story titled *Candelaria's Sorrow*, in 1994. "When I was sixteen I found Candelaria's lost grave at the old La Florida Ranch. Learning that the story of Candelaria was real and not an urban legend made me think, if the story of Candelaria is true, then what about all the other stories we have always heard from the old folk stories—of ghosts and apparitions? *La Llorona*, stories of *lechuzas*, headless horsemen and such—why are we so quick to dismiss them as superstition and folklore?" Since then, the University of Houston published his *The Ghostly Rider and Other Chilling Stories* in 2003; and the Virtual Bookworm in College Station published *The Night The Moon Came Down* in 2004. He considers the Valley his second home.

Marianna Nelson and her husband, Bruce, arrived in the Valley in 1998. They soon grew roots at Fun N Sun RV Resort. Two years later Marianna started the "Writers Group at Fun N Sun." As she listened to members read stories about their lives, she admired their strength and grace in dealing with life's punches. In her story, *The Trip Home*, Marianna writes about the greatest punch of all—the end of life. Her first major work appeared in the Byliners' *Tales Told At Midnight Along The Rio Grande.*

Eugene "Gene" Novogrodsky has lived in the Lower Rio Grande Valley in Brownsville for 21 years. He is a co-founder of the Narciso Martinez Cultural Arts Center Writers Forum in San Benito. He says, "He has rarely been published. He fears rejection!" Instead, he loves to read his work in the Writers Forum, Savory Perks and Valley International Poetry Festival events. What he enjoys the most is reading to several friends, or even strangers, in small groups . He is married to his friend and companion, Ruth E. Wagner, who is also a poet and craftsperson.

LeRoy Overstreet writes mostly about his unique adventures that began during the Great Depression and continue today. His stories include experiences on some of the vast cattle ranches of central Florida, rodeos, alligator hunting, inventions and many other subjects. One of the most successful of his published stories is about alligator hunting in Florida that was included in a coffee table book by Martha A. Strawn, who teaches art and photography at the University of North Carolina, Charlotte. Its title is *Alligators, Prehistoric Presence in the American Landscape.* The book includes 151 of Martha's most memorable photographs of and about alligators.

Brenda Nettles Riojas, a mother, writer, and creative spirit, grew up on the border of South Texas and Mexico. She is currently working on an MFA through the University of New Orleans. Her most recent collection of poetry is titled *La Primera Voz Que Oí.* Her poetry has been published in *di-verse-city* (Austin International Poetry Anthology), *Ribbons* (Quarterly Journal Published by the Tanka Society of America), *2008 Texas Poetry Calendar, Interstice and Ezra -- An Online Journal of Translation.* She is a member of the Narciso Martinez Cultural Arts Writer's Forum and a founder of the Rio Grande Valley International Poetry Festival. Brenda works for the Diocese of Brownsville as Diocesan Relations Director and is the editor of *The Valley Catholic* and hosts a weekly program, *Diocese Insight.*

Judy Stevens finds time to be a rock hound, potter, cartoonist, and eclectic collector. Originally, from Minnesota by way of Southern California, she came to the Valley in January 1997 with her husband and daughter. Nowadays, she delights in watching the grandkids grow and hanging out with grandpa. Two of her "ghost stories" appeared in *Tales Told At Midnight Along The Rio Grande*.

Nelly Venselaar was born in The Netherlands. As a young child, she pledged to see the world, which she did. She traveled with her husband and, later, children to England, Indonesia, Australia, U.S. and Canada. She taught for twenty years in Canada. After the death of her husband, she started to write her memoirs, which evolved into writing poetry and novels. *Musical Voyage* is her latest book.

Ruth W. Wagner, born by the bank of the Delaware River, moved to the bank of the Connecticut River and now lives by the bank of the Rio Grande River, is a nurse, teacher, gardener and artisan. She has also been a lobbyist, waitress, union organizer and a Red Cross disaster worker. She recently became a poet and storyteller. Ruth is married, has three adult children and several grandchildren.

Bidgie Weber was born and raised in the Rio Grande valley. "I have a deep abiding love for the area. I enjoy writing poems and stories about my childhood. Fiction is a new endeavor for me. I enjoy poetry and short stories. Like everyone else though, I would love to write that novel that is hovering at the edge of my mind. My first experience in this medium was writing commercials for KELT-FM radio. I hope to keep writing till my fingers are too stiff to hold a pen." Bidgie's first appearance in a Byliner publication was in *Tales Told At Midnight Along The Rio Grande*.

Verne Wheelwright, PhD. is an internationally recognized professional in the field of Foresight and Futures Studies. He is the author of *It's Your Future, Make it a Good One!* as well as *The Personal Futures Workbook*. He has published articles in a number of professional journals and other publications, and has addressed audiences in major cities across the U.S. and in several international cities about how to explore and plan for the future. His web site is **www.PersonalFutures.Net**. Verne wrote stories for an earlier Byliners' book, *Tales Told at Midnight Along the Rio Grande*. He and his wife Betty live in Harlingen.

Janet R. Wilder found The Valley as an RVer and after 9 years made the Rangerville area her permanent home. The former publisher of an RV newsletter and freelance Travel and RV consumer publication journalist, Janet now concentrates on writing fiction, which includes a ghost story in *Tales Told at Midnight Along the Rio Grande*. She serves the Byliners as editor of its newsletter.

Janice Workman—Texan since 1986, Yankee for life. Writing since I could put crayon to paper. Published in the recent *Tales Told at Midnight*.... Enjoy various hobbies and adventures that keep me in writing ideas. Live with my husband and dog pack, not so quietly, in Harlingen, Texas as I await discovery, fame and fortune.